# Trials and Tribulations

S.W. Campbell

Published by Shawn Campbell

Trials and Tribulations

ISBN: 979-8-9870287-6-6

To Jessi and Tyler, here's to good seafood, good beers, and better than great friends.

*Trials and Tribulations*

# Table of Contents

*Trials and Tribulations*

# Preface

With the sun having made another revolution around the Earth, here is another collection of short stories. What can I say? I've written a lot of the bastards. Written in 2015 and 2016, these twenty-six stories span a length of time wherein though the sheer volume of stories I wrote declined from the highs seen in 2014, my writing also became much more divvied up into many different buckets. While short stories continued to be a dominant portion of my writing endeavors, they were joined by attempts to publish my first novel, the start of what would become *Professor Errare*, and my first forays into writing family history. I had a job which often involved sitting at a desk for long periods of time doing next to nothing, and as a result I had plenty of time to explore a lot of different options.

It should come as probably no surprise that my main focus during this time period was getting *The Uncanny Valley* published. Completed in early 2015 after two years of effort, my first novel provided proof that in many ways the writing of a novel is the easy part, or at the very least, the part which is the most fun. Editing, suckering people into reading it and providing notes, and more editing gave way to countless letters to prospective literary agents, most of which went unanswered, with a select few declaring that the book was quite interesting, but that they had no idea how they might sell it to prospective publishers. It is the rare literary agent, either too young to know better or too old to care, which looks for anything unique. I spent more than a year trying to sell a book which people seemed to like, but nobody seemed to want, and in the end I had to accept surrender, self-publishing it in late 2016 because I figured books are written because they are meant to be read. Today only a couple hundred people have read it, a humbling experience, which I chalked up to travelling down the learning curve and starting again. If nothing else, I've always been a stubborn man, which is why after several false starts I began writing what would become my second novel *Papaya* in 2016.

Regarding my short stories during this period, I saw them as more of a means to an end, rather than anything of much value on their own. That is not to say I did not enjoy writing them, because I most certainly did, only that in my mind at the time they were part of a grand strategy of fattening up my resume in order to more easily get a novel published. Over the two year period of 2015 through 2016, I sent out some 512 story submissions, of which only four were accepted for publication. As with *The Uncanny Valley*, it was a humbling experience, though not one which dampened my want to keep writing, for in my mind continuing forward against such headwinds was just separating the wheat from the chaff, and if I kept working at it, one way or another, I would achieve the things I wanted to achieve, and even if I didn't, at the very least I was greatly enjoying the attempt.

As for the rest of it, *Professor Errare* and the books about family history, I won't bore you with a lot of detail. The family history books were the culmination of a hobby originally established in me by my grandmother, and *Professor Errare* began as a series of Facebook posts about how each president was a jackass, meant to help people feel better about the chaos of the 2016 presidential election, which as it turned out, would prove to be a historical pivot point, after which nothing was ever the same again. Both side projects continued on for years afterwards, perhaps sucking up time and energy I could've put into writing short stories and novels, but no less worthwhile to do in my mind given I derived enjoyment from each.

Well, that's probably enough talking about myself, given I doubt you are here to hear someone meander on about a past part of their life. No, I imagine you are here for the stories, which is how I prefer things to be. That being said, before we jump in, I feel that there are two areas where I need to add further context.

The first is with regards to the use of some pretty terrible slurs in a few of these stories. When I first wrote the stories containing said slurs, I felt that it was important to not shy away from such things. There are most definitely people who use such slurs and hold related views, and though there seems to be a want to pretend that they do not exist, I have never found a problem to be solved by hiding it away. Writing is a practice meant to capture worlds and in this world such things exist. Trying to understand someone is different than empathizing or condoning their actions and words. That being said, I also believe that it's important to explore such issues thoughtfully. Such things are wrong, and as such, should be represented as such when writing about them. There is a fine line to all things.

As for the second, I don't usually believe in explaining individual stories, unless asked to, but I think with regards to *The Closet* it is worth saying some things because stories of a personal nature involve people one loves and cares about. I had a good childhood overall. I got to grow up in the middle of nowhere in a setting relatively few people get to truly experience. I've never wanted to trade it for anything. I was a lucky kid. I had parents who loved me and cared so deeply that even when I was angry with them I never questioned it. If anything, I wish I could go back to my childhood and be better to them. I was not an easy child. I was a different child, or at least that's the way I felt, though others must have seen it somewhat too for I got picked on a lot as a kid. It's hard to explain, but I always felt like an outsider no matter where I went or who I met. I sometimes imagined a spaceship dropping out of the sky to take me to the world where I belonged.

Growing up is a confusing time, not just for yourself, but for your parents as well, especially when you feel different. I was not an easy kid. I was extremely finicky, picky, and had a violent temper. I was angry at being stuck on this world, and so I acted out against it. I latched onto odd things and ideas with an amazing amount of force for somebody my age, defending them against encroachment with a righteous fury that often came out in unhealthy ways. I know I worried my parents and scared them a lot too. I don't think they knew what to do with me, though they did everything in their power to help and understand me. As a kid, so many actions by your parents don't make sense at the time they're happening, only later revealing themselves as proof of how much somebody loves you. I don't know how my parents could've done any better with me. How could they be expected to understand something that I certainly didn't understand then, and even after forty-one years of living with myself still can't satisfactorily explain now.

I was a lucky kid. My parents loved me and cared for me. There are so many kids who don't get such things, and who knows what I might be if I didn't have such a foundation. I am who I am today because of them, and there's no way for me to repay such a gift. As for the rest, I guess eventually I learned to go native, accepting as best I can that I am where I'm supposed to be. Though I will admit that I often still look up at the stars wondering if a spaceship might be on its way.

Well, there you go, now I have gone and rambled on more than I really wanted and more than you probably needed me to do. I guess I should probably close, but of course with the usual last reminder. These stories, as with any writing, contain pieces of lots of different people, some of which you might recognize. However, fictional characters are amalgamations of many different people, and even if they are not, they only represent windows from a single point of view of a single point in time. In as such, don't get your bonnet in a twist. We are all after all just humans, all doing our best, even within the confines of a short story. Happy reading.

# Decent People

It was a lonely stretch of the Yellowhead Highway, fifty kilometers either way to any kind of civilization. The sun sat fat on the western horizon, mostly obscured by evergreen sentinels. The walls of the river canyon fell to the north side of the highway, blanketed by pines and firs broken by the occasional face of jagged rock. The black mass of the Skeena River slid past the south side. A moving barrier dividing the highway from the rise of the canyon on the opposite bank.

The car sat facing west. Its hood up and its blinkers on. The man leaned against the side of the car, one hand holding a cigarette and the other keeping to the pocket of his faded coat. The man reclined, smoked, and waited, listening to the sounds of the wind through the trees and the constant gurgle of the river, watching the lengthening stretch of his shadow. He shivered with every burst of wind. It was getting cold. A pile of cigarette butts lay scattered about his feet. The paint of the car was faded and the edges of the fenders were flecked with rust. It was an old car. The man would probably not be having his trouble if it had been a new car, but it was the car he had. No point musing about how things could be different.

A set of headlights crested the hill to the east. A new model pickup truck. Blue. Diesel engine. The gentle roar moved closer, slicing through the twilight air. The man's eyes watched the pickup approach from beneath heavy brows. The hand in his pocket tightened. The hand with the cigarette rose into the air. Stop. C'mon stop you mother fucker. The pickup seemed to slow. There you go. Help a poor bastard out.

The pickup didn't stop. It moved halfway across the yellow line and swept past. The man turned his head and covered his eyes to protect them from the buffeting wall of wind. He shivered. The red taillights moved on down the highway. Brake. Hit the brakes you asshole. Come back. The brake lights stayed dark. The man's hand in his pocket loosened. He spit on the ground and muttered a few choice curses under his breath. Eight cars in five hours. Not one had stopped. There just weren't any decent people anymore.

Down the highway a deer poked her head out of the undergrowth. An old dry doe. She took a couple of steps to the edge of the pavement, looked both ways, took another few steps, looked again, and then walked to the other side. The man watched her as she moved. The deer looked rough. Her coat was ragged. Too many ticks and fleas. Her ribs poked through. Poor old bitch. Probably missing half her teeth. Lose those and she was good as dead. Animals don't die from old age. They starve, get eaten, or shit themselves to death. Hell of a way to go. The deer moved out of sight down towards the river. If she was lucky a truck would hit her on the way back.

The man took the last hit from his cigarette and tossed it to the gravel at his feet. He crushed the ember with his worn out shoe. His finger probed at a hole in his jeans and then moved up. His hand rubbed his jaw, rough with stubble. He needed a shave, and his mustache needed a trim. Not important now. No reason to give much thought to problems you can't solve. The wind picked up a bit. Wisps of hair broke loose from their fellows and floated on the breeze.

Twenty years ago there had still been plenty of decent people around. If you saw a broken down car on the side of the road you stopped and offered to help. You're lucky I came along, not much traffic on this highway. Let me look at that engine for you. Any idea what it is? Do you need a lift into town? Hop on in. No problem at all. Hope somebody would do the same for me. It wasn't that way anymore. Nowadays decent people were far and few between. Maybe he'd head south. He had heard there were still decent people down south. People who didn't judge you by the way you looked or the car you drove.

The man spit again. It was getting late. The sun was below the horizon. The stars were starting to twinkle. It was going to be a beautiful night. Clear as hell out in the middle of nowhere. Probably be able to see the Milky Way. Damn cold though. Too damn cold to be sitting out hoping to get lucky.

The man lifted himself from the car and walked around to the back. He pulled keys out of his pants pocket and opened the trunk. Jug of water, pile of rags, jumper cables, jack, length of rope, duffel bag full of clothes, shovel. He took the short piece of heavy pipe from his coat pocket, placed it on the rags, and shut the trunk. The man walked to the front of the car and closed the hood. He opened the car door and climbed into the driver's seat. He reached behind him and pulled a pistol from the waistband of his pants, nestled against his back. The pistol went into the jockey box.

The man fumbled with his keys and started the car. It coughed and roared to life. The belts squealed. They'd need to be changed soon. The blinkers went off. The headlights went on. The car turned and headed east down the highway. Fifty kilometers to Terrace. He could stay at the Rainbow Inn there. It was cheap. Not nice, but cheap. Tomorrow was another day.

The man took a pack of cigarettes off the dash and lit another smoke. It was just so hard to find decent people anymore.

# Scio Girls

The motel phone on the table between the two queen beds rang, the little red light flashing in time. Paul looked up from the small table by the window, a 39 cent McDonald's cheeseburger in his hand. Bill glanced over from the bathroom where he was using a lint roller on his blue corduroy FFA jacket. The phone rang again. Bill gestured with the lint roller.

"You gonna get that?"

Paul sighed. Bill was 17, three years older, three years bigger. He put the cheeseburger down on the table next to the bag filled with its fellows. It was 39 cent Sunday. A high school kid could eat like a king on 39 cent Sunday. The phone rang for a third time. Bill shot Paul an angry impatient look. Paul sighed again, pushed his chair back, and walked over to the phone.

"Hello?"

It was a girl's voice. Paul could hear more prattling in the background.

"Hello, is Nate there?"

Paul unconsciously lowered the tone of his voice.

"No. Nate's not here."

A hand over the other receiver. Nervous tittering.

"This is room 143 isn't it?"

"Yeah. Nate's in this room. He just isn't here right now."

The hand over the receiver again. Laughing. Muffled encouraging whispers.

"Okay. Could you tell him to come down to room 265? The Scio girls want to see him."

"Okay. I'll let him know."

"Room 265."

"Yeah. I got it."

The phone on the other end hung up. Paul put his own receiver back in its cradle. Bill gave Paul a questioning look.

"Some girl for Nate."

Bill snorted and gave a little half smile. Paul sat back down at the table and went back to eating his cheeseburger. Bill hung up his FFA jacket, walked over, and took a cheeseburger out of the bag. There were thirty cheeseburgers in the bag. Whatever didn't get eaten tonight would go in the fridge. Cheeseburgers reheated in the microwave weren't that bad. Bill lay down on the bed, dropping crumbs on the comforter as he ate. The two sat silently, watching MTV. The sound of a key in the lock. The door opened. Nate came in with a waft of cold air and closed the door behind him. His coat was speckled with rain. Bill sat up.

"Did you get it?"

Nate smiled.

"Yeah, got some homeless guy to buy it for me. Just had to give him a few bucks."

"Lucky the bastard didn't just take it."

"You didn't have any better ideas."

Nate pulled up his shirt and pulled a pint of whiskey from his pants. Bill eyed the bottle.

"What kind did you get?"

"R and R."

Bill made a face. Paul looked out the window, pulling back the partially closed curtain to get a better look.

"Did Mr. Schultz see you?"

"No."

"Are you sure?"

Bill punched the side of Paul's leg.

"Christ. Schultz is either in his room chewing or out having beers with Mr. Spoon."

Bill flapped a limp wrist. Nate laughed. All the older kids were always insinuating that the two FFA teachers were lovers. Paul didn't think it was true, older kids were always saying things that weren't true, but you could never tell for sure. The thought of Mr. Spoon running his hands through Mr. Schultz's thinning hair, staring deeply into his eyes, was a little unsettling. Bill got up and walked towards the bathroom. He glanced back at Nate.

"There was a phone call for you?"

"Yeah, from who?"

"I don't know. Paul took it."

Nate turned towards Paul, who was still glancing nervously out the window.

"Who called?"

"Some girls from Scio. They said to tell you they were in room 265."

Nate whooped and pumped his arm. He walked over to his suitcase on the floor, leaving the bottle of whiskey next to the TV, and took out his shaving kit.

"Was one of them Heidi?"

"I don't know. They didn't say."

"God I hope Heidi is there. She owes me a blowjob."

Nate rubbed his hands along the top of an imaginary head at crotch level. He bucked his hips and stared at Paul, waiting for a reaction. Paul turned up the volume of the TV. Nate opened his shaving kit and took out a small bottle of cologne. He sprayed some on each wrist and smeared it behind each ear and down the sides of his neck. The room stank of sandalwood.

"Scio girls are easy."

The toilet flushed. Bill came out, buttoning his pants, and washed his hands.

"More like Scio girls are skanky."

Nate's smile never quit.

"Either way, I'm going to get my dick wet."

Bill rolled his eyes and sat down on the edge of the far bed next to his suitcase. He was two years older than Nate. Next year he would be going to college. He was a man of the world. Nate washed off his wrists in the sink and smoothed his curly hair with a wet hand. Smiling, he grabbed the whiskey bottle and headed for the door.

"Where do you think you're going?"

Nate turned back towards Bill.

"Room 265."

Bill gestured towards the pint bottle of R and R.

"I paid for part of that."

Bill and Nate stared at each other for a moment. Paul watched them both. Nate smiled, twisted the plastic cap, breaking the safety seal, and walked over. Bill reached into his suitcase and pulled a bottle of Coca-Cola bottle out of one of his cowboy boots. The bottle was two-thirds full with golden liquid. Nate gestured towards the Coke bottle.

"Where'd you get that?"

"Been sifting it off the top of my dad's bottles for the past month."

"What is it mostly?"

"Mostly Canadian Mist. Little Jim Beam in there too."

Nate made a face. Bill unscrewed the lid of the Coke bottle. He held it steady while Nate filled it to the top with the R and R. Paul watched the whiskey flow from one container to the other.

He licked his lips. The transfer finished, Nate headed back towards the door. Paul raised his hand, started, stammered, and started again.

"Hey.... Hey... I put..... I put some money in too. Some of that is mine."

Nate stopped with his hand on the doorknob. He turned to look at Paul, then at Bill, and then back at Paul.

"What would you do with it? It would just be wasted on a little shit like you."

"I'd drink it."

"Sure you will. Have you ever even had a drink before?"

"Yeah."

Nate snorted and started to pull open the door. Bill rubbed his hand across his stubbly chin. He needed a shave.

"He did put in two bucks."

Nate stopped. He stared at Bill. Bill added nothing. He just sat and watched the TV. Nate's eyes went to Paul, sitting with a nervous look on his face, to the door, and back to Bill. Nate snorted some snot back deeper into his sinuses and let go of the door handle. He walked over to the sink, took the paper top off of one of the water glasses, and poured it halfway full of whiskey. Paul watched every move. Bill coughed and stared at the TV. Nate added the tiniest fraction more, screwed the lid down tight, and put the bottle in his pants. Bill said nothing. Nate walked back to the door, paused to grab a cheeseburger out of the bag, and with a cold draft of air, was gone.

Bill and Paul sat in the room watching MTV, neither speaking. Outside the sun sank below the hills surrounding Roseburg. A light rain tapped against the window glass. After a while Bill glanced at the digital clock next to the phone, checked his watch, got up, and put on his coat. In one pocket he put the Coke bottle full of whiskey. In the other he put a can of Copenhagen, pausing to put a pinch in his lower lip. Onto his head went a Super Sonics ball cap. He headed towards the door.

Paul watched Bill and as he moved, leaning forward in his chair.

"Can I come?"

"No."

A quick burst of cold air. Bill was gone. Paul sat alone in the room. He changed the channel over to Comedy Central. An episode of South Park was on. Paul watched, chewing on his fingernails, spitting pieces on the floor and wiping the saliva off on his pants. The half glass of whiskey sat next to the sink. Paul got up and put the bag of cheeseburgers in the mini fridge. He walked over to the sink and looked at himself in the mirror. Skinny arms and knobby joints. Glasses. Zits. Braces. Paul took the glass off the counter, took a sip, made a face, and put the glass back. Scio girls are easy. Scio girls would do anything you wanted. Paul put on his coat and a Trail Blazers ball cap, put his wallet in his back pocket, double checked to make sure the room key was in his pocket, and headed out the door.

Paul's breath steamed in the evening air. Small raindrops lightly flicked the side of his face. He pulled the zipper of his jacket all the way up. Several cheese wagons of varying sizes sat in the parking lot. The pool sat unused under its tarp, covered for the winter. Paul turned and walked down the row of identical doors and past the lobby. The night manager, a fat bald man, sat behind the desk, reading the paper and chomping on an unlit cigar. Paul rounded the corner and walked to the other side of the motel. Another half filled parking lot. More cheese wagons. Two floors of identical doors, each with its adjacent window, some lit, some not.

Paul walked down to the street. It was a busy street. Two lanes both ways. A constant thrum of passing automobiles. Across the street was a strip mall. Safeway. Jo-Anne's Fabric. McDonalds. Liquor store. Paul walked down to the corner, beneath the motel sign, and hit the crosswalk button. Cozy Inn. HBO. Paul's eyes tracked across the second floor

doors. 263. 264. 265. The window was bright and
welcoming. Scio girls are easy. Scio girls will do the things you
like. Just go right on up. Knock on the door. Walk right in.
Say Nate had a phone call from his mom. Stay. Introduce
yourself. Say some jokes. Be relaxed. Let things happen. Paul
bit his lower lip and adjusted himself. The red hand turned into
a walking man. Paul crossed the street.

As Paul approached the Safeway door he waved his fingers
slightly. The automatic door opened. It was stupid. It didn't
matter. The store was warm. Too warm. Paul unzipped his
coat. He wandered through the aisles. Two girls stood in the
candy aisle, debating what to get. Paul stopped about eight feet
away and studied the colorful boxes and wrappers. He could see
them out of the corner of his eye. The brunette had her hair up in
a ponytail. She was tall and lean. The blonde was shorter and
rounder. Her hair was in a braid. Snickers. Butterfinger. Skor.
Kit-Kat. Gimme a Break. The girls were laughing about
something. Paul's eyes traveled up and down. Starting and
stopping. Witty. Think of something witty. The girls stopped
laughing. Paul turned his head. Both were staring at him. The
brunette had blue eyes. The blonde green. Paul could feel sweat
in his armpits. He leaned down, grabbed a carton of Whoppers,
and walked swiftly away down the aisle.

Paul stood in line at the checkout counter. He grabbed a
bottle of Pepsi out of the small display fridge. An old man and a
tired looking woman were in line in front of him. The checker
was young. Maybe college age. She was attractive. She had big
tits. Round tits. Beautiful tits. Every time she moved her tits
jiggled. The top few buttons of her shirt were undone. Every
time she leaned over the start of cleavage poked through. Paul
concentrated on the magazine rack. Guess Who's Anorexic?
Bat Boy Found in Omaha. Hurricane Mitch Headed for Central
America. Top Twenty Ways to Spice Up Your Sex Life. Eight
New Ways to Please Your Man. Swimsuit Issue. The checker

licked her lips.  Red lipstick.  Long supple fingers moving items across the scanner.  Jiggle jiggle.  Caressing hands.  A downward tug on his zipper.  Paul's jeans felt tighter.

"Hey."

Paul jerked his eyes upwards.  The checker was skewering him with a look of annoyance.  The old man and tired woman were gone.  The woman snapped her fingers.

"Pay attention.  You got people behind you."

Paul shuffled forward.  He wished his coat was longer.  Go down damn it.  Go down.  Jesus Christ.  The checker swept his items across the scanner with her beautiful hands.  Hands wrapping.  Hands tugging.  God damn it.  Think of something else.  The woman cleared her throat.  Paul looked up again.  The Pepsi and Whoppers sat in a plastic bag.  Paul dug into his wallet and handed the checker some money.  Her hand brushed against his for a moment.  She handed him his change.  His palms were sweaty.  Paul took his items, zipped up his coat, and headed towards the door at a swift trot.  He wrapped the plastic bag around his wrist and jammed his hands into his pants pockets, balling them into fists.  Damn it.  Everyone can see.  Everyone knows.  Go down damn it.

Paul waited at the street corner.  The red hand turned into a walking man.  Paul walked across the street.  Two cars sitting side by side.  Paul's profile illuminated by the prying beams of the headlights.  Should have moved the plastic bag to the other wrist.  It might have provided some cover.  No good.  Still there.  Fuck.  The light from the window of room 265 shined like a lighthouse.  Come on over.  Come on up.  Knock on the door.  Hi, my name is Paul.  I brought some mixer.  Oh that, yes, that's my boner.  You mind if he comes in too?  Soft bodies.  Beautiful tits.  Take it out.  Fondle it.  Put it in your mouth.  Scio girls.  Scio girls are skanky.  They'll do anybody.  Dumb.  Really fucking dumb.  Paul rounded the corner and headed for the safety of his room. In the lobby, the night manager had chewed through half his unlit cigar.

Paul laid down on the bed closest to the window and turned on the TV. Nothing much was on. It didn't matter. There was nothing much to do. The source of his embarrassment faded. He opened the bottle of Pepsi and took a couple sips. He opened the carton of Whoppers and popped several in his mouth, sucking on them, wearing away the chocolate to get to the malt ball center. He sucked on a few more. He filled his mouth with Whoppers and chewed through the whole mess of deliciousness. A new TV show came on. Then another. Bill and Nate stayed gone. Fuck those guys. What right did they have to tell him what he could do? Where he could go. The half glass of whiskey sat on the counter by the sink. Fuck those guys. Paul stood up and filled the glass to the top with Pepsi. He picked the glass up and looked at himself in the mirror. Fuck those guys. He chugged it all down. It tasted terrible.

Back to the bed. More Whoppers into his mouth. Another episode of South Park came on. He hadn't seen this one yet. It was a good one. Paul laughed out loud, the sound echoing off the ceiling. Someone pounded on the wall. Paul pounded back. The light rain outside turned into a downpour. A percussion beat against the car roofs in the parking lot. Paul turned down the TV. He got up to use the bathroom. The world was a little wobbly. He sat back down on the bed. The carton of Whoppers was empty. He felt a little sick, but not much.

Paul flipped through the channels. Some HBO documentary about strippers. Tits. Nice. What the fuck was he doing here? He should be out there, hanging out, having fun. Not sitting around like a jackass. Fuck Nate. Scio girls are easy. Scio girls will do things. Dirty things. His hands on tits. What do tits feel like? Making out. Put your tongue in her mouth. How much tongue should you put in her mouth? How long do you leave it there? Neck. Girls like that. On TV they always suck on their

neck. Don't leave a hickey. Girls don't like that. Jesus
Christ. Just get up. Just go over. Knock on the door. Tell Nate
that Schultz was looking for him. Go right in. They're drunk.
You're drunk. Everyone's relaxed. God knows what might
happen.

The motel room door opened. Bill stumbled in. His face
was red and his eyes were glassy.

"Hey Bill."

Bill grunted and flopped down face first on the other bed.
The door opened again. Nate came in, his face split by a wide
smile.

"God damn those Scio girls will do anything."

Bill raised his head from his pillow.

"Shut up needle dick."

"I mean anything."

"Shut up and go to bed."

Nate grabbed a pair of shorts out of his bag and headed
towards the bathroom. Bill looked over at Paul.

"Shut off that fucking TV. I want to go to bed."

Bill was slurring his words. Paul turned off the TV. Nate
came out of the bathroom in his shorts. Paul got a pair of shorts
and his shaving kit out of his suitcase. He changed in the
bathroom and then brushed his teeth at the sink. The world
while standing was still fairly off kilter. Nate was already in
bed. Paul turned off the lights and started to get into the other
side.

"What the fuck do you think you're doing?"

"Going to bed."

"What are you, gay?"

Paul stared at the dark silhouette, unsure what to do. Nate
stripped off the comforter and threw it on the floor between the
two beds. The blanket below had three big cigarette burns.

"Sleep on the floor."

"What about a pillow?"

Nate threw one of the four pillows on the bed onto the floor. "There you whiner. Now go to bed."

Paul wrapped himself in the blanket. His head lay just below the end table that held the phone. Nate started giggling to himself.

"God those Scio girls are dirty."

Nate leaned over the side of the bed and leered down at Paul.

"Dirty bitches. Just dirty dirty bitches. They love it. They fucking can't get enough of it. Hell Paul, I bet they'd even suck your dick if you asked."

Bill's head reared up.

"Either you shut the fuck up or I'm going to pound your face in. I'm trying to fucking sleep."

Nate's smirking face retreated. Bill's head fell back to his pillow. Soft breathing on either side. Paul lay wrapped in the comforter, staring up at the ceiling. Scio girls were dirty. They'd do anything. Even to him, Nate said, even to him. Handjobs. Blowjobs. God only knows. Things were on the rise. Paul took in a deep breath and let it out. Dirty girls. Dirty dirty girls. Scio girls were skanky. Maybe they were still awake. Go over there. Knock on the door. Say Nate had forgotten something. Scio girls are easy. No. It's dumb. Quit being so dumb. But maybe. Room 265. Maybe just call. Start talking. Maybe they'll say come on over. They're skanky girls. Isn't that what skanky girls do? They love it. They can't get enough of it. It hurts. God damn it hurts. Like a rock. Dumb. Just being dumb. But maybe. Just maybe.

Steady breathing on either side. Room 265. At worst just say you dialed the wrong number. Jesus. Just do something. Do something besides sit on your ass. They're asleep. They'll never know. Paul sat up slowly. Both Bill and Nate were facing the other way, sides rising and falling. Bill let out a slight snore. Paul's hands rose and clasped the telephone. He picked it up and lowered it to the floor. Good. Nice and steady. Paul laid back down and stared at the tan plastic in the darkness. He lifted the receiver and put it next to his ear. The dial tone was louder than normal. How do you dial another room? Shit. Was it 9? Did you hit 9 first? Maybe you didn't need to hit 9. Maybe you just put in the number. The receiver started emitting a loud rapid beep. Fuck. Nate popped up in his bed. Paul slammed the receiver back in place with an audible clang. Nate peered over the side of the bed.

"What the fuck are you doing?"

"I don't know."

"What's the phone doing down there?"

"I don't know. I was sleeping."

"Dude, did the phone fall on you?"

"My hand must have gotten wrapped up in the cord."

"Are you fucking serious?"

"Yeah."

Nate started laughing. Loud guffaws that ricocheted off the ceiling. Bill rose up.

"Shut the fuck up."

"Fucking Paul pulled the phone onto his head in his sleep."

Bill looked down at Paul and then back up to Nate. He reached down, grabbed the phone, and put it back on the end table.

"I don't give a shit. I'm tired as hell. Go back to fucking sleep."

Nate laid down and rolled over, still snickering.

"Idiot. What a fucking idiot."

# Strays

The father eats the same breakfast every morning. Oatmeal with milk and sugar, two eggs over-medium, toast, and a couple cups of coffee. The older boy, eleven years old, emulates his father, minus the coffee. The younger boy, age seven, eats a bowl of Kix with milk. The middle boy, age nine, eats the same, but dry. The mother leans against the kitchen counter in her robe, eating a piece of toast. The family consumes their respective meals in silence. Birds chirp outside, warming up their morning songs. The father finishes his breakfast, puts his dishes in the sink, and heads for the back bathroom. The older boy rushes to finish his breakfast. He only has fifteen minutes until it's time to go. The younger boy gets caught up in the competition, going full board with no destination in mind. The middle boy eats at his own pace. The younger and older boys put their dishes on the counter and then race towards the back of the house. The mother watches the middle boy eat.

"Are you sure you don't want to go?"

"Yeah."

The middle boy finishes his breakfast. He chugs his milk as fast as he can. He doesn't like the taste of milk in the morning. He can't get enough in the evening, but in the morning it's just disgusting. He can't leave the table until he drinks his milk. The chugging always makes his mother worried that he'll choke. He almost never does. The middle boy's dishes go on the counter. The mother turns on the sink and starts the washing. The father comes out of the back bathroom, quicker than average, the older boy isn't ready yet.

"C'mon, let's go."

The older boy runs from the back of the house, socks in hand, drying toothpaste at the corners of his mouth. The younger boy follows, still in his pajamas.

"I want to go too."

"Sorry, not today."

The younger boy pouts and retreats. The father and the older boy put on their boots by the back door. The mother dries her hands on the towel hanging off the fridge handle.

"You're just putting out salt this morning, right?"

"Yeah, might fix a little fence too if we have the time."

"Okay. See you at lunch."

"See you at lunch."

The father and older boy leave. Background noise. The diesel bark of the pickup starting. The grind of it getting put into gear. The roar of the engine as it heads down the road. The opportunity is truly gone. The mother looks down at the middle boy.

"What are you going to do today?"

The middle boy shrugs.

"I don't know."

The middle boy can see the disappointment in the mother's eyes. He knows that she wants him to go, but he doesn't want to.

"Be sure to brush your teeth."

"Okay."

The middle boy goes to the back of the house. He brushes his teeth. His mother would prefer if he combed his hair, but he doesn't. The younger boy is in the room they share, playing on the floor.

"Do you want to play Matchbox cars?"

"No."

The middle boy changes out of his pajamas into old faded jeans and a t-shirt with a hole in it where it had gotten caught on a strand of barbed wire. The younger boy watches him. The middle boy puts on a ball cap for the Charlotte Hornets and grabs a book off the dresser. The family lives nowhere close to Charlotte, but the hornet logo looked cool.

"Where you going?"

"I'm going to go read."

The younger brother watches the middle brother leave, then goes back to his cars. The parents' bedroom door is shut. The mother is changing. The middle boy goes to the back door and puts on his shoes. He goes outside. The weather is warm, but with a nice breeze. It's June, the valley shifting from the green of spring to the yellow of summer. Schools out. Summer break. Freedom. Liberty to do whatever he wants. The boy doesn't mind school, but he's glad that it's over. It's not the classes, rather the people, which fuel the misgivings. Playground cliques and schoolyard bullies.

The house sits between the rolling flat of the hay fields and the rocky hills of the pasture. Across the fields the pickup containing his father and older brother moves down the road, kicking up a great wave of dust in its wake. The middle boy watches it disappear from view, headed towards the mountains in the distance. The boy walks around the house and outside the yard. When he was younger, five or so, he wasn't allowed outside the yard. His mother had been worried about rattlesnakes. Now he can go wherever he pleases, as long as he's back for lunch.

The boy crosses the two boards spanning the ditch which flows from the spring house in the grove of cottonwoods to his right. A little bit upstream, underneath an apple tree, sits a mud dam, an unusual survivor to the catastrophic failure that most often ends the play that led to its creation. To the left the ditch flows past old narrow poplars, its banks crowded with cat tails which make great grenades when playing war. The boy walks up a beaten path cut in the tall grass. At the top of the path is the chicken house, the pen with the older brother's 4-H pigs, the corral above the house, and an old building made of ammo boxes.

All but the front of the building is made of wooden ammo boxes, surplus from World War II. Stacked and nailed by some long gone clever craftsman. The front of the building is slumped, an old man slouching in his chair. Wooden doors, gray with age, no longer fitting in their frames. A large door, big enough for a car, that will never again open, and a smaller normal sized door held shut by a large rock. The boy moves the rock and opens the half rotten door, it rattles on its loose hinges. Small shapes scatter and hide. The boy goes inside and closes the door behind him. It is dark in the building, at least darker than outside. Light flows in from windows on the far walls, most of the glass broken from their panes, between the seams of the loosely fitting doors, and through small cracks and holes in the roof above. Dust motes float in the light, magically defying gravity as they slowly prance through the air, shifted by every movement. The walls are rows of square shelves, each row offset from the one above and below. Junk lays across the ground. Rusted tools and pieces of long dead machinery, an old style wheel with rotting rubber, and an old oil pump with a glass head that bubbles when you turn the squeaking metal handle. A collapsing stack of dusty straw bales sit in one corner. Several large sacks of wheat and barley for the pigs lay propped near the door.

The boy kicks the grain sacks to make sure no mice are inside. Once he had forgotten to do it, and a mouse had run from his shoulder to his toes. Nothing. No skittering. The boy sits down on the ground, his legs crossed, his back leaning against the sacks, and begins to read. He patiently waits. The sound of the breeze and the birds is cut off by noise of the starting lawnmower. The buzz is distant, drifting with the breeze. The boy's pupils scan the words on the pages but watch the pile of straw bales out of the corner of his eye. Time ticks by, a steady constant beat. The trick is to watch without looking like you're watching.

The smooth black one is the first to make an appearance. She is the bravest. She had been the first with everything over the past week. The first to emerge, the first to approach, the first to sniff at an offered hand, the first to allow herself to be touched, and the first to be petted. Her dark head emerges from her hiding place in the loose straw around the bales. Her yellow eyes appraise him. She lets out a high pitched meow. The black kitten only hesitates for a moment. She approaches on soft footsteps, stops, mews again, and then approaches within arms length. The two lock eyes. The boy's arm moves at a glacial pace. Fingers stroke across a bony back. A small black head nuzzles the boy's hand and a purr of contentment emerges. The mower cuts off. The black kitten jerks away, but then lets itself be stroked again. The mower starts again.

The next is the gray one with the white muzzle. Her hair is long and bits of straw stick to it. She comes from behind one of the bales, leaping to the top, sitting and watching the stroking of her sister. She mews, looks at something behind him, and mews again. She doesn't approach. She just sits and watches. Taking it all in. The black kitten approaches the bale and the gray kitten jumps down on the black one's back. The two wrestle, silent, but for the moving of their forms, throwing up dust and straw. The black one gains the upper hand, it's bigger than the other. The gray one breaks free and runs towards the door. The black one cuts it off. They wrestle again before collapsing in a heavy breathing heap of black and gray. The boy laughs and both heads jerk around towards the sound.

The boy leans forward slowly. Neither kitten moves, but the gray one opens its mouth and hisses. The boy picks up a long piece of straw and pokes at the two kittens. Both bat at the straw with their paws. The gray one with claws out. The boy slowly pulls the straw back towards him. The black one follows, swiping at the offending length. The gray one hangs back, but creeps forward bit by bit, pausing and watching, moving forward, pausing again. The black one comes right up next to his leg. The boy reaches down with a finger and strokes the top of its head. The gray one watches, still unsure. The boy wiggles the piece of straw with his free hand. Moving it closer to the gray kitten and away. The gray kitten swipes again. One step back. Two steps forward. It grabs the straw between its paws and chews at it.

The boy's arm moves slower than ice melts. The gray kitten watches. Inch by inch the boy's fingers reach out. The gray kitten cowers close to the ground, but does not move away. The black kitten stays close to the boy, eyes on its sister. The boy holds his breath. His fingers brush along the gray fur. The kitten is shaking. This is the first time she has ever been touched. From the middle of her neck to the center of her back. The hand retreats. The gray kitten watches it go. Another stroke for the black kitten for being brave.

"There you go. There you go."

The boy's voice is soft, almost a coo. The black one stays put, but the gray one flinches and pulls away at the sound of the boy's voice. First the touch, then the voice. Making the unknown into the known. Making the scary into the common place. Everything is fine. This big monster is not a threat.

The kittens move off to play more. The boy goes back to his book. Out of the corner of his eye he can see one last kitten, a mackerel tabby head poking out between a bale and the wall, wedged into the hollow of one of the ammunition boxes. The boy doesn't know what sex the kitten is. It has never gotten close enough for him to see. It hides, rarely ever emerging. It takes a long time to tame a cat. They have to be used to you. They have to know you're not a threat. Some people put on leather gloves and a heavy sweatshirt. Some people grab them and hold them, clawing and biting, hissing and spitting, until they run out of energy, shaking with fear and frustration. It was better if you sat with them. Spent the time for them to get to know you. Be patient. Let them come to you on their own. The tabby was proving difficult.

It's a beautiful kitten. A striped pattern across its body. It's different from the others. Smaller. The runt of the litter. It does not run and play with its siblings. It's less outgoing. It lies just within sight, its big greenish yellow eyes taking everything in. Curious, but afraid. Nervous. Frightened. It is a big world out there, even bigger when one feels alone. There is something about the solitary figure which makes the boy want to pick it up and hold it. A need to pet and comfort the bony frame, to let it know that for every scary thing there are two or more good things in the world. He yearns to hear the purr of contentment from the tabby's throat.

The tabby sees the boy watching and draws back. The other two kittens, the black and the gray, walk past the boy and lounge in the triangle of sunlight which pushes its way past the closed door. The triangle moves across the dirt floor. The kittens awaken, shift themselves back into the sunlight, and fall asleep again. The tabby watches. The boy pretends not to watch the tabby. The tabby wants to join its siblings in the sunlight, but it doesn't want to get anywhere close to the large figure sitting in between. Stalemate. Indecision. Fear.

The tabby rises up. The boy forces himself to stare at the words on the page. The tabby takes a single step forward. The boy turns the page of his book. The tabby pulls back. Indecision again. The tabby mews plaintively. Its siblings ignore it. The tabby takes a few steps forward. It's now out in the open, the safe confines of its lair left behind. The boy puts his near hand down on his knee. The movement makes the tabby cringe, but it does not retreat. Another few steps forward. The boy keeps his breathing even and calm. The black kitten yawns big. The boy slowly rubs his index finger and thumb together. A small circular motion that catches the tabby's eye. Slow and hypnotic. Curiosity gradually overtaking fear. One step after another. A pause between each. The boy's nose itches, but he does not scratch. The kitten reaches forward to sniff. The feeling of a cold wet nose on the side of the boy's hand.

The door opens with a solid thwump as it swings back into the dirt. The kittens scatter, running for hiding places. The younger boy stands in the doorway, chest puffed with the importance of his task.

"Mom says it's time for lunch."

"Okay."

The middle boy closes his book and rises to his feet. The younger boy looks at the interior of the building.

"Have you been up here all morning?"

"Shut up."

The younger boy runs back down the path towards the house. The middle boy emerges into the sunlight, closes the door, and puts the rock back in its place. He walks down the path, takes off his shoes on the backstep, and goes into the house through the back door. The father, older boy, and younger boy are all sitting at the table. The father is reading the newspaper, the older boy the comics. The mother is standing at the stove, cooking Top Ramen.  She looks at the middle boy as he comes in.

"What have you been up to?"

"I was sitting up with the cats.  I touched the gray one today, and almost touched the tabby."

The mother smiles down and as he walks past pulls the middle boy into a side hug, holding him close as she stirs the Top Ramen.  For a moment the boy feels content, then he breaks away.

# My Favorite Christmas Memory

Okay, this might not be the most favorite, but of the ones I can remember at this moment, it is top of the list. Every year for Christmas my family would first open presents at our own house, and then go to my grandmother's in Fossil, a town of about 400 people, for a second round of presents/family get together/Christmas dinner. In essence, I pretty much got the excitement of two Christmases within a single day, which I have to say, was pretty damn awesome.

Now my grandmother loved holidays. In fact, loved is probably not a strong enough of word to describe my grandmother's feelings towards holidays. This was an all out affair. She always had a big Christmas tree, covered in an assortment of store bought and handmade ornaments, many dating back to when my mother was a child, an overabundance of tinsel, and numerous strands of old school glass Christmas lights, the kind that would burn the crap out of you if you touched them. The tree in the dark was really something to see. The rest of the house was just as decked out. Numerous

Santa's of all shapes and sizes, including several rubber variants
with poseable wire skeletons, a nativity scene made up of at least
five different sets, resulting in a decidedly over abundance of
livestock, but still only three wise men because more than that
would be ridiculous, and an entire light up Victorian village with
nearly as many people in it as the actual town of Fossil.
However, of all of this, the thing that most sticks in my mind
was the Christmas music.

Fossil is built along a creek surrounded by hills of varying
heights. My grandmother's house sat up on a hill overlooking
the town, the porch along the back of the house providing a
sweeping vista of the community below. My grandmother,
always one to take advantage of an opportunity, saw this lofty
perch as the perfect avenue to spread Christmas cheer throughout
the city.

This cheer came in the form of Bing Crosby, and a number
of other crooners, belting out their favorite Christmas songs via a
pair of surprisingly large speakers set on the porch. I am not
sure where my grandmother got these mammoth speakers, but
they were old, they were big, and they projected those songs
across the town, blanketing the houses below with an auditory
blizzard of Holly Jolly Christmas, Winter Wonderland, and
Rudolf the Red Nosed Reindeer. Each of us kids were allowed
to pick out a record from her staggering collection, and with our
own fingers place the needle on the spinning disc, unleashing the
fury of the yuletide season.

Now it should probably be mentioned that I have no idea
whether or not my grandmother ever got permission to spread
her holiday joy, or if it was just a matter of her exuberance for
the season being too great to be contained within the confines of
her own home. Regardless, I do know that not everyone was
pleased.

It sticks out quite clearly in my head. The family sitting
around in the post present opening daze. Parents and children

alike, examining their bounty and snacking from bowls of chocolates and popcorn strategically placed around the house. The phone rings. My grandmother goes into the kitchen to answer it. A loud muffled voice on the other end. The voice on the phone was loud, not so loud that you could understand a word of what was being said, but loud enough where one could get the jist that a great deal of the conversation was of words on the potty mouth end of the vocal spectrum. Throughout this tirade my grandmother kept a neutral face, making affirmative noises to prove that she was listening. When the caller wound himself down into silence, my grandmother gave him a moment to see if he had any more, replied, "why don't you like Christmas," and hung up the phone.

# Vikki Mulroney Is Missing

Detective Ken Hernandez sits at his desk and smokes his cigarette. The sign by the precinct door says no smoking, but no one ever pays it much attention. It's the damn night shift. No one wants to be there. The ones that are have better things to do than worry about the future dangers of secondhand smoke. Some little shit had come up and complained earlier. A traffic cop with peach fuzz on his lip. He hadn't even been able to look Hernandez in the eye when he spoke up. The little shit had turned tail and ran before Hernandez even got to his most choice curses. Undoubtedly he would file a complaint. That's what people did anymore, file complaints. Assuredly, Hernandez would have to answer to the captain in the morning. Fuck it. The cigarette felt good. It felt worth a little ass chewing.

Hernandez takes a drink of coffee from the chipped Number One Dad mug on his desk and grimaces. The coffee tastes like crap. Cheap shit. Store brand. Fuck it too. It's what they had. It was still better than nothing. Just barely. Fuck it. Hernandez looks at the open file folder on his desk. A picture sits on top of

the assorted papers.  Notes, statements, tips, bios, the works.
The girl in the picture is slightly heavyset.  Her brown hair is up
in a top knot ponytail.  Her ears are pierced.  Her eyes are blue.
It's hard to tell from the picture.  Her eyes scrunch when she
smiles.  She's wearing way too much eye makeup, at least in
Hernandez's opinion.  He inhales the last of the cigarette and
stamps it out in the ashtray next to his coffee cup.

Vikki Anne Mulroney.  Seventeen years old.  Born January
6, 1997.  Five feet five inches.  One-hundred-and-forty pounds.
Hair color, brown.  Eye color, blue.  Lives in butt fuck suburbia
with her mother, stepfather, and two half siblings.

A picture of the house is in the file.  A big four bedroom
cookie cutter affair.  An exact replica of the houses to either side
except for the slightly differing shade of tan paint on the exterior.
The girl in the picture reminds Hernandez of his own daughter.
They look nothing alike.  His daughter is two years younger.
Both girls have a mother, a father, and a stepfather.  The
resemblance is uncanny.  Hernandez closes the file and then
opens it again.  It's been a long two weeks.  Just a little
paperwork to finish up.  Just a little more paperwork, then he can
go home.  Maybe watch some Netflix, eat some dinner.
Probably just go straight to bed.  That sounded nice.

She's a nice girl.  Cheerleader.  Choir singer.  Volunteer
projects.  Okay grades.  Your all around all-American girl.
Never mind she hasn't done any of that shit for over a year.
Kids quit things all the time.  Hell, Hernandez's daughter quit
the track team just three months ago.  It didn't mean anything.
Just one more step in the constant shift of an organism going
through rapid metamorphosis into some kind of an adult.  She
isn't unattractive, and white to boot.  Lucky girl.

June 10th, 5:00 PM.  Vikki returns home.  Neighbors report
she's dropped off by a blue Volvo containing two African-
American men in their twenties.  All the neighbors who saw

anything note that the car seemed out of place, not from around there.

"What color was the car?"

"I'm not sure. Maybe blue or a bluish gray."

"Make and model?"

"I don't know, definitely some kind of Volvo."

"And the two men inside?"

"Yeah, something wasn't quite right about them. You just got a sense that they were up to no good. You know what I mean?"

"How so?"

"The driver could tell I was watching him. He drove out the opposite way that he came in."

"And you're sure they were Black?"

"Yeah, Black, definitely Black."

That little factoid had thrown the papers for a loop. Half had pretty much printed it in bold. The other half had avoided stating it all together. People are shitty like that. Everything has to be in extremes.

6:00 PM. Vikki's mom, Andrea Jaeger, gets home after a long day of work. Jaeger is her second husband's name. Her first husband's name is Mulroney. Jacob Mulroney. Neither Andrea or Vikki have heard from him since the girl was seven. He lives somewhere in Ohio. The family has dinner and goes for a walk around the neighborhood. They spend the evening watching television.

9:00 PM. Vikki goes to her bedroom. She's wearing workout clothes. Black spandex that go down just below the knee, gray tank top, white Nikes with lime green soles.

9:30 PM. Vikki sends a text to her boyfriend, Tyler Johnson. A picture of him is in the file too. Blonde, lanky, zitty. Just some kid.

*They were going to kill you and my family, and I loved you.*

Tyler doesn't text back.

9:34 PM. Vikki tries to call Tyler. He doesn't answer.

11:00 PM. Andrea goes upstairs to talk to Vikki. Vikki is gone. Her phone, wallet, ID, bank cards, makeup, anxiety medication, and glasses are all still in her room. Mrs. Jaeger freaks the hell out, as is to be expected. Frantic calls to friends and neighbors.

"Have you seen Vikki?"

"No."

"Okay. If you see or hear from her let me know."

June 11, 4:00 AM. Andrea Jaeger calls the police.

Hernandez leans back in his chair and listens to the squeak as he rocks. He glances up at the clock and notes the time. He leans forward, reaches into his desk, pulls out a pack of cigarettes, takes one out, lights it, and inhales. The cigarette pack goes back into the desk. Hernandez moves his fingers through the various photos of Vikki in the file. None of them show her wearing glasses.

4:30 AM. A patrol officer arrives at the Jaeger home. He takes down information in a little notebook and asks for a couple of pictures. The officer isn't worried. Kids sneak out at night all the time. They go down to the park, smoke cigarettes, drink beer, make out a little, maybe more. Pretty standard stuff. The family admits Vikki's broken curfew before. The officer tells the family to call again if Vikki doesn't show up by morning.

8:30 AM. Vikki is still not home. Donald Jaeger, the husband, calls the police. The case gets kicked farther up the line.

11:00 AM. The detective arrives at the Jaeger home to interview the family. Mr. and Mrs. Jaeger sit in a flowery coach in the living room. The detective sits on a dining room chair across the coffee table from them. Donald Jaeger is a big man, starting to go to fat, with thinning blonde hair. Andrea Jaeger is an older clone of her daughter except the eyes, Vikki must have her father's eyes. The detective wears a faded out of date suit and has a thick mustache, permanent frown, and tired eyes. The Jaegers are asked another round of questions. More answers are written in a little notebook.

"Did you and your daughter ever fight or argue?"

"No, we had a very good relationship."

"Has your daughter had any history of depression or other mental health issues?"

"No, she's always been a very happy and sweet girl."

A look is exchanged between husband and wife. Mrs. Jaeger speaks up.

"She hinted last year that she was having problems. She wouldn't give many details. We got her a counselor. It seemed to help."

"Has she ever run away before or threatened to run away?"

"No. She always seemed so happy."

"Okay. I would suggest looking through her things."

"We could never do that. Her privacy."

"Any little detail could help right now."

"How long until you find our daughter?"

"It's hard to say. About one in five runaways return after less than twenty-four hours. Seventy-five percent come back within a week. We'll put out calls to local shelters and neighboring precincts. On your end please try and call all her friends and family in the area. Anyone she might make contact with. Also, try to think of anything that seemed strange or out of place before she disappeared. Every detail can be important."

"What about an Amber Alert?"

"Ma'am, those are only for children we know are abducted or are known to be in imminent danger. If it gets overused people will start paying less attention to them."

"How do you know she hasn't been abducted?"

"We have no evidence to suggest it at this time."

"But....."

"Ma'am, less than one percent of missing children cases are abductions. Only a quarter of runaways leave their general area. We have her in the national database. Police across the country know to look for her."

"I just think….."

"Ma'am, please rest assured that we are doing everything possible to find your daughter. Please remember to make those calls, and that any information you can give us, no matter how small, will be helpful."

The detective leaves.

1:00 PM. The family calls the detective. They have new information. He drives back out to their house.

"Vikki had a second phone. We found it in the bottom of a drawer."

The phone is an older iPhone variant. No call records, but lots of texts. The texts are all encrypted. An app called Encrypt SMS. Both sender and receiver need the app. Access is protected by a password. The texts are erased if too many wrong guesses are made.

Hernandez stabs his second cigarette out in the ashtray and leans back again in his chair. His eyes move down the scratched metal drawers of his desk to an open box marked *Evidence* sitting on the floor. The box is nearly empty, just an old iPhone in a plastic bag and a spiral bound notebook with Wonder Woman on the front. Dead end leads. All the texts and contacts on the phone had been erased. The parents had fucked with it before they had called. The next few days had been fairly routine, or at least as routine as such things could be. The usual interviews. The usual calls to the usual places.

"Have you seen this girl?"

"No."

"Okay. Thanks. Let me know if you see or hear anything."

Interview with boyfriend. Tyler Johnson. Age seventeen. A bit of a whiny little shit. Less than helpful. He and Vikki had broken up the week before. She'd been swinging from being needy to pushing him away. She had called him immature. He just couldn't take it anymore. She was always bad mouthing her parents. Her mom loved her new kids more than her. Her mom didn't understand her. She wished she could be with her real dad. Pretty standard stuff. Nothing that Hernandez hadn't heard from his own daughter's mouth from time to time.

Interviews with friends at school. Even less helpful. All pretty tight lipped.

Interviews with teachers. Somewhat helpful. Vikki had seemed depressed, though nothing that raised up any big red flags.

Interview with therapist. Least helpful. Patient-doctor confidentiality.

Mrs. Jaeger calls every day at noon like clockwork.

"Have you heard anything about my daughter?"

"Have you found my daughter yet?"

"Why haven't you found my daughter?"

"You dirty son of a bitch. Find my daughter. You find her now."

Hernandez didn't hold it against her. He would probably be the same if it was his daughter. However, there was only so much that could be done. You can call the same people a hundred times, but it won't change anything, it just gets on their nerves. The majority are good people. They'll call back if anything comes back. Waiting is hard. Especially with something like this. No new leads. No new information. Other cases start coming in. Vancouver isn't a big city, but it certainly isn't a small one either.

June 19, 3:00 PM. The family calls the detective. They've found a notebook between Vikki's mattress and box spring. They think it might be her journal. The detective sends a patrol officer to their house to collect the new evidence.

Hernandez reaches down into the evidence box and pulls out a spiral notebook. He opens the Wonder Woman cover. Strips of paper are stuck between the spirals. A third of the pages are missing, ripped out. A single entry remains, dated May 24.

*If you're reading this I'm probably missing. I'm not missing because I hate you. When or if you find me, I'll be all used up or dead. Meth addict, heroine too, just so I can get through all the pain.*

Things kick into high gear again. A fresh round of phone calls. Nothing. No leads. Dead ends. Mrs. Jaeger is frantic. She starts calling every hour.

"Where is my daughter?"

"Ma'am, we're doing everything we can."

"Don't give me that shit you cock sucker. Why haven't you found her? What about an Amber Alert?"

"Ma'am, at this time we don't have enough evidence to suggest your daughter has been abducted."

Cold hard logic. Pointless against the power of emotion.

"Bullshit. There's no way she could be doing this on her own. My daughter's been abducted. You've read her journal. You saw her text. What's it going to take? Finding her corpse? Is that what you want? Is that what you fucking want?"

The calls from Mrs. Jaeger stop. An hour later the phone rings again. It's the chief of police, asking Hernandez to come up to his office.

"Where we at with this Mulroney case?"

"Classic runaway. Kid rebelling. Getting into trouble. Parents don't have a clue. Usual stuff."

"Any idea where she is?"

"No leads. We're jumping through all the usual hoops."

"The mother, she's going to be trouble on this. She's getting pretty frantic."

"I know, wouldn't you? She wants an Amber Alert."

"You don't think so."

"Nothing so far makes me think this is anything but a runaway. She's been gone a little longer than normal, but otherwise it's nothing we haven't seen before."

"Look Hernandez. We have to do something with this. If we don't, the mother will."

"Chief, I really don't think….."

"Shut it Hernandez. We can't afford to look like we're sitting around with our thumbs up our asses. I'm bringing in the Women's Coalition on this one."

"Sir, with all due respect…….."

"I don't need to hear it Hernandez."

"You know how those people get. It's going to be a media circus."

"That's not necessarily a bad thing. Hell, they put her face up on the news she'll probably turn up."

"Yeah, and needlessly freak out every parent for a couple hundred miles."

"I'm not suggesting Hernandez. I'm telling. I'm making the call first thing tomorrow. If we don't, the mother will, and if she does, we look like a bunch of jackasses."

"I think it's a mistake."

"Nobody is asking you. In the meantime, shake down some of the kids again. See if they know more than they're saying."

"We shake down those kids too much their parents are going to start to complain."

"Just do it Hernandez. When this shit storm breaks nothing but finding this damn girl is going to matter."

June 20, 10:00 AM. Second interview with Emily Evans, age seventeen, self-described BFF of Vikki. The interview takes place in Emily's house at the dining room table. Her parents wait in the living room, silent and listening to every word said in the other room. Emily is nervous and wary. The detective opens.

"Vikki has been gone awhile."

"I guess."

"Did you notice anything strange about Vikki over the past couple weeks?"

"Strange?"

"Abnormal behaviors, acting weird, that sort of thing."

"No, not really. She seemed a little frantic, but Vikki is always that way."

"Did she say anything strange to you?"

"No."

"Have you seen her with anybody you don't know? Somebody older?"

"No."

Silence. The detective stares at the girl. The girl tries to stare back but ends up looking at her hands.

"C'mon kid, your friend's been missing nine days. Anything you can tell us will help us find her."

Emily looks away towards the living room. She looks back at the detective, then back at her hands.

"It's not her fault, you know. She's got it pretty tough."

"How so?"

"Her mom can be a royal bitch. A couple of months ago I was over at her house. Her mom and her had a huge fight."

"A fight about what?"

"I don't know, dishes or something. Her mom kept comparing her to her dad, you know, her real dad, and then said she wished Vikki hadn't been born."

"I see. That sounds pretty screwed up."

"Yeah. Then there's the whole Tyler thing."

"Her boyfriend?"

"Ex. Tyler broke up with her. Called her a crazy bitch. He's such an immature little shit."

The detective leans back in his chair and drums his hand on the table. Emily stays silent, refusing to look up.

"Anything else?"

"No."

"Are you sure?"

"I don't want to get her in trouble."

"She might be in trouble right now. I don't want that. Do you want that?"

"Well....."

"What is it?"

"I know she's been experimenting with drugs."

"Drugs? What, like marijuana?"

"No. Look, she's been upset. Things have been shitty for her over the past year."

"What kind of drugs?"

"Meth, maybe something else, I don't know. I think she's only tried it a couple of times."

"Do you know where she got it?"

"No. She wanted me to go with her once or twice, but I wouldn't. She got pretty pissed."

"How long has she been experimenting?"

"I don't know. A while. We don't talk like we used to."

"Did Vikki run away?"

"I don't know."

"When was the last time you talked to her?"

The girl's eyes fill with tears.

"About three weeks ago. She was freaked out. She said she was in over her head. I just thought she was being melodramatic. She's always been so melodramatic."

The girl begins sobbing loudly. The parents come in from the living room. The interview ends.

Second interview with boyfriend. Tyler is again less than helpful. When quizzed about Vikki possibly using drugs he states that he doesn't know anything about it. Vikki was crazy. He hadn't had contact with her since he'd broken up with her at the end of the school year. She had sent some texts, half cursing him and half telling him she loved him, but he had ignored them all. They all sounded crazy. He'd known she was crazy, even before they started dating.

"So why did you date her?"

"Because she put out."

Second interviews with other school friends. Most parents deny permission. They don't want their kids to be any more traumatized than they already are. Once was enough. Bunch of bullshit. Teenagers always know more than they are willing to say. They live in a secret society of which the first rule is to never talk to outsiders. Outsiders judge. Outsiders don't understand.

Second interview. Hannah Holman, age sixteen. Admits that she and Vikki weren't really friends, but they knew each other. Vikki has a reputation. No facts, just high school rumors. Hannah had heard that Vikki had been giving blowjobs in the bathroom at the mall. Just pick out some random dude. What a slut.

"Did you ever see her do it?"

"No."

Just rumors. The secret world of teenagers.

Hernandez rises up from his chair and stretches his back. He picks up the Number One Dad mug from his desk and walks past the rows of empty cubicles and then across the hall to the break room. A beat cop named Jenkins sits at the table, reading a newspaper. The dirty coffee pot is half full. Hernandez pours himself a cup and turns around. Jenkins is staring up at him.

"You're here pretty late."

"Yeah, getting some work done."

"The Mulroney case?"

"Yeah."

The beat cop licks his lips.

"Hey, none of my business, but what exactly happened with that?'

"She's a minor."

Hernandez takes a drink of coffee and grimaces. Jenkins is staring at him, so he stares back.

"What do you want me to say?"

"Hey man, I got two daughters you know."

Hernandez starts walking towards the door.

"I have a daughter too."

Hernandez returns to his desk and sits back down. He picks up the papers off his desk, lights another cigarette, and goes back to work.

June 20, 2:00 PM. The detective is asked to sit in on a meeting between the chief of police, the family, and a representative from the Women's Coalition. Mrs. Jaeger seems agitated. Mr. Jaeger looks tired. The chief is sweating more than normal. The Women's Coalition representative, Ms. Ramsey, surveys the room with narrowed disdainful eyes. She has the posture of an alpha. This is her meeting and she knows it. She already has it all planned out. First, contact the local media. Radio, newspapers, and television. Plaster the world with Vikki's image. Get the Jaegers on camera. Pull some heart strings. Make people care. People have to care. Second, follow up with a social media blitz. Set up a special Facebook page. Give people a way to show their support. Give them something to join. Make them feel like they're a part of something. Do the police have a tip line set up? The chief nods yes. Good. It's already been nine days. They don't have much time. Ms. Ramsey leans forward. She clasps her hands and points with her index fingers.

"I don't want to alarm anyone, but in my opinion Vikki is the victim of sex traffickers."

Mrs. Jaeger starts crying. Mr. Jaeger tries to comfort her. The detective looks at the chief. The chief wipes his brow with his hand.

"There is little evidence at this time to suggest Vikki was abducted."

"No? Sweet innocent girl just disappears one night from her house? Leaves everything behind? Does that sound like a runaway to you?"

The detective rubs the back of his neck.

"It may be that there's more to Vikki than meets the eye."

Mrs. Jaeger raises her head from her husband's shoulder. She stares with hatred at the detective.

"What are you saying?"

The chief gives the detective a warning look. The detective ignores it.

"I'm saying that interviews with some of her classmates suggest that Vikki is a lot like many kids her age, angsty and rebellious. Some of her classmates indicated that she was becoming increasingly involved in experimenting with drugs and high risk sexual activity."

Mr. Jaeger leans forward.

"What do you mean...."

His wife interrupts him.

"How dare you. How dare you imply such things about my daughter. What proof do you have? The fucking high school rumor mill?"

"Ma'am, with all due respect, the parents are often the last to know when their children become involved in such things. Especially in cases where the child feels a sense of hostility towards their...."

"My daughter and I have a wonderful relationship. She knows that she can tell me anything. For you to even suggest otherwise......"

The chief lets out a long rush of air.

"My apologies Mrs. Jaeger. Detective Hernandez is just doing his job and following up on any leads that might help him find your daughter. That is what we all want. To get your daughter home safe and sound."

Mrs. Jaeger shakes with anger and then bursts back into tears. Mr. Jaeger wraps her in his arms and stares at the chief.

"Thank you sir. I know you're doing your best. This has been a very stressful time for our family."

The chief nods. The detective starts to open his mouth, but the chief shoots him a look to shut up. Ms. Ramsey leans forward.

"Irregardless, we shouldn't mention these types of things to the press. We can't give people any reason not to care about Vikki. She is the victim."

The detective nods his head.

"Agreed. But I think it would be grossly irresponsible to start labeling this as an abduction by sex traffickers."

"Are you saying that it's not a possibility?"

"No. I'm just saying that so far we have no proof that anything like that has happened. If we start throwing around words like abduction and sex trafficker, the only thing it's going to do is freak people out."

"We have no proof that she wasn't abducted."

"What right do you have to scare the shit out of people?"

"If we mention sex trafficking and abduction we'll get more press. More press means more people looking for Vikki. More people emotionally involved."

"More people convinced their kids are in danger."

"Maybe they are."

The chief loudly clears his throat.

"Enough. Hernandez is right. We're not inciting a panic. We're not going to speculate on what happened without any evidence. We stick to the facts. Is that clear Ms. Ramsey?"

Ms. Ramsey stares the chief in the eye, trying to force him to break. The chief dead eyes her. Ms. Ramsey gives in.

"Yes. It's understood."

6:00 PM. Press conference. The chief stands behind a podium surrounded by microphones, framed by camera flashes.

51

Ms. Ramsey stands to one side and the Jaeger's stand to the other. The detective watches on the television in the police office break room. The chief lays out the facts of the case. Everything they know, minus any mention of drugs or sex. All-American girl missing. Possible runaway. The police need the public's help to find her. The chief steps back. Ms. Ramsey prods the weeping parents to the podium. Mrs. Jaeger speaks through her tears. All they want is their daughter home safe and sound. Ms. Ramsey pulls them back. She steps up to the podium. Ms. Ramsey gives details on everything that is being done by the Women's Coalition. How people can help. How they can show their support. She gives the number people can call with tips. Her speech takes three minutes. In three minutes she mentions the words sex traffickers four times and the word abduction three times. The chief's face turns bright red. He steps forward to take questions. The first reporter fans the flames.

"Is this case being treated as a possible abduction by sex traffickers?"

The chief's hands clench the sides of the podium. His neck bulges.

"At this time we are investigating all possibilities."

The detective turns off the television. He pounds his fists on the table. Fucking bitch. Fucking wily bitch. The calls start coming in almost immediately. Most are concerned parents looking for more details. Do they need to be afraid? What should they be watching out for? If this wonderful All-American girl can get abducted, why not their daughter? The rest are a mix of pranks and tips. Almost all are bullshit. The officers manning the phones write them all down. All have to be checked. All have to be looked into.

June 21, 7:00 AM. The story hits the national news. Phone calls start coming in from across the country. Ms. Ramsey appears again on the television. She's been named representative of the family. A reporter asks the question.

"Is this more than a case of a child running away from home?"

"We have not heard from Vikki in more than ten days, which is one of the reasons we know that she just didn't run away, but that she was lured away. Until the investigation shows otherwise, that's what the family's believing and that's what our organization's belief is as well. She walked out of the safety and comfort of her own home without telling her mother where she was going. A runaway would have taken a bunch of stuff with her. Ultimately a runaway wouldn't be ignoring this kind of media coverage. They would've called and said stop the media."

8:00 PM. Candlelight vigil for Vikki at Newton Park. Hundreds of people stand around with lit candles. The detective is there, standing slightly to the side, watching the hot wax of his candle drop onto the paper guard above his hand. Some people start singing hymns. The detective was ordered to attend by the chief. It's best to keep up appearances. Things are getting out of hand. The chief doesn't have control of the situation. Appearances have become important, even when they're a waste of time. After half an hour the detective goes back to the station

Hernandez rubs his eyes with the back of his hand. He has to pee. He gets up from the desk and shuffles towards the bathroom. His legs are stiff. Too much sitting. Fuck. What time is it? Probably after midnight. Dull yellow piss sits in the urinal. Somebody forgot to flush. The whole place stinks to high heaven. Hernandez flushes the urinal, does his business, and flushes it again. He glances at the sink. Fuck it. He heads back to his desk without washing his hands. Hundreds of calls. Lots of new tips. Lots of panicky voices. Even his ex-wife had called to ask about it. Was their daughter safe? Should she be concerned? No new leads. The chief had fed the reporters what facts he could. Ms. Ramsey had kept the flames stoked as high as possible. Missing person posters went up on every power and light pole in town. She even managed to get the Jaegers on one of the big national news shows. Nothing.

June 23, 9:00 AM. Phone tip from Linda, last name not given. Officer Kent Vitrolli initially takes the call, but then gets the detective. Vitrolli find the detective drinking coffee in the break room. Vitrolli tells the detective that he had a tip he thought might be a good one. The detective goes out to the desk and takes the phone.

"Hello?"

"Yes, hello?"

"This is Detective Hernandez. You told Officer Vitrolli that you might have some information regarding Vikki Mulroney?"

"Yes, um, that is. We didn't know who she was. We just figured it out today."

"Excuse me?"

"She came to our running group yesterday. We all met up at a bar out in Beaverton. They were selling her drinks at the bar so we assumed that she was twenty-one, so we gave her some beer. You know, we didn't know."

"What bar in Beaverton?"

"The Stingray."

"Was she with anyone?"

"Yeah, she was with a woman in her forties. I've seen her before, the woman that is, but I don't know her. I talked to her a while, Vikki that is, she told me her name was Daisy."

"When was the last time you saw her?"

"Probably around nine or so. We finished up and had some beers at a nearby park. I can't remember the name. She seemed young, you know, just how she acted, but they let her in the bar, and you know how girls in their early twenties are."

"What do you mean?"

"You know. Flirty. Bouncy. I don't know. She latched pretty heavy on to one of the guys. Made him pretty uncomfortable. Some of the things she said, you know, just made you feel like she was trying to seem older and more experienced than she actually was."

"I see, and you are sure this was Vikki?"

"Yeah, I mean, she told us her name was Daisy. We didn't figure it out until this morning when somebody put some of the pictures up of the run. Definitely her though."

"Can we get those pictures?"

"Oh yeah, definitely."

"How was her demeanor? Did she seem frightened?"

"No. Not really. You know. She seemed nervous. All those new people and all, but she didn't seem scared. She said she was staying out at Forest Grove. Staying at some swinger house or something like that. I don't know. It seemed a little weird."

"Do you know where she was going?"

"No, not really. Back to Forest Grove I guess. I don't know. I went home and didn't give it much thought until today."

9:15 AM. The pictures arrive via email. It's definitely Vikki. The first solid lead. She's wearing running clothes. The same black spandex and Nike shoes she disappeared in, but a different top. This one is bright green. Vikki is smiling in all of the pictures. She doesn't look scared. She doesn't look nervous. She looks happy. Phone calls to the police departments in Beaverton and Forest Grove. They promise to keep their eyes out. Good news. She's still in the area. Phone call to the chief. The chief calls the family to let them know.

6:00 PM. Phone tip from Jennifer Statz. Officer Kent Vitrolli initially takes the call and then hands it off to the detective after ascertaining its likely validity.

"Hello?"

"Yes. Is this the detective in charge of the missing girl case?"

"Yes."

"My name is Jennifer Statz. I live down here in Milwaukie. You know, south of Portland."

"I'm aware where Milwaukie is."

"I saw that girl you're looking for?"

"Vikki?"

"That's what she called herself at first, but then she said she wanted to be called Daisy. I don't know, she seemed kind of freaked out, always nervous."

"Where did you see her?"

"I met her at a house party down in Oak Grove."

"Was she there with anyone?"

"Not really. She said she had come with some people, but they left her or something. She didn't say much. Looked kind of out of place. I don't know. Young for the crowd. Talked to her a bit, that's when she introduced herself. When things were breaking up she didn't seem to have any place to go so I offered to let her crash on my couch."

"How long ago was this?"

"Oh, last Thursday."

"And when was the last time you saw her?"

"She left early Saturday morning. Had a backpack with her with some clothes. It looked pretty new. Like I said, she was pretty drunk Thursday night. Pretty chatty. Said some weird shit. I let her use my computer for a while Saturday morning. Seemed harmless enough. She erased the history."

"I see. Why didn't you contact us earlier."

"Didn't know everyone was looking for her. Don't have a TV, just watch Netflix and Hulu."

"You said she said some strange things?"

"Yeah, the whole name switch thing seemed pretty weird. Then she said something along the lines that she was in a bad situation and needed to get out. I don't know. Couldn't get much out of her. All Friday all she would say was that some people were probably looking for her and that she was being forced to do things she didn't want to do. I couldn't get her to say anything else about it. I was just trying to help her. I didn't know what to do. She said she was nineteen. If I'd known I would have called the police right away."

"It's okay ma'am. It's okay. Around what time Saturday was the last time you saw her?"

"I don't know. She was gone when I woke up. It was around ten. I don't know."

Hernandez lifts the cigarette pack from the desk and shakes it open. Just one more cigarette. Damn. Hernandez puts it in his mouth and lights it. He stares at the empty pack and drums his fingers on the desk. The Ramsey woman had been out of control, pretty much inciting a panic, but it had been effective. Two good leads in a single day. Two good leads they wouldn't otherwise have had. Proof that Vikki was still out there. What the hell had she been doing? Did it really matter? His job was to find her. As long as he found her the rest didn't matter. Officer Vitrolli was a clever shit. He was the one who knew how to search social media. He was the one that found her MeetMe.com profile. A website to meet people. Her profile listed her as nineteen. So what? What teenage girl didn't pretend to be older than she really was?

June 24, 9:00 AM. Phone tip from Connor Dukowski. Self-described as college kid home for summer break.

"My friend suggested I call you. I saw Vikki last Saturday."

"Where did you see her?"

"Down at Barton Park. She was just hanging out. We got to talking. She seemed pretty cool so I asked if she wanted to go floating with me. We spent most of the day on the Clackamas."

"Are you sure it was her?"

"Definitely. She told me her name was Daisy. She told me she was nineteen."

"When was the last time you saw her?"

"Around four or so. She said she had to be going, she was supposed to meet some people out in Forest Grove. I gave her my number."

"Did she give you a phone number?"

"No. She said her phone was broken. Look, she told me she was nineteen."

"Yes, you said that already. How was her demeanor?"

"Huh?"

"Was she nervous? Scared? Frightened?"

"No, nothing like that. I'd say she was pretty bubbly. Very talkative. She smiled a lot. She was an amazing person. I hope she's okay."

"Okay. Let us know immediately if she ever calls you."

1:00 PM. Connor Dukowski calls the tip line again.

"Hey, she just called me and asked if I would like to hang out. She said she was back in the area."

"What did you tell her?"

"I told her I was busy."

"Did her number come up on your phone?"

"Yes."

"Where are you now?"

"Down at Clackamas Town Center."

"Okay. You know where the Costco is?"

"Yeah."

"Wait there. We'll meet you in the parking lot."

1:30 PM. The detective and Officer Vitrolli take an unmarked car to Clackamas Town Center. They meet Mr. Dukowski in the Costco parking lot. The kid looks scared. The detective tells Mr. Dukowski to call the number on his phone and to arrange a meeting at the bookstore in the mall. Mr. Dukowski dials. The phone rings. Someone picks up. It's not Vikki. He asks for Daisy. The someone passes the phone. Vikki answers. The arrangements are made.

2:15 PM. Mr. Dukowski sits at a table in the bookstore's coffee shop. He looks nervous. He tries to hide it. He can't. The detective watches from the Fantasy section, pretending to read a book with a dragon on the cover. A girl walks into the store. She waves at Mr. Dukowski and Mr. Dukowski waves back. The girl is about five and a half feet tall, a little on the chubby side, with blonde hair up in a ponytail. Her hair looks recently dyed. She's wearing a flower print yellow sundress and has on just a little too much eye makeup. Vikki Mulroney is smiling. She gives Mr. Dukowski a hug. Officer Vitrolli steps into the bookstore doorway. The detective puts down his book and approaches, at which point Ms. Mulroney notices him and Officer Vitrolli for the first time. The detective steps forward and introduces himself, at which time Ms. Mulroney stops smiling and her shoulders slump. She stares at the detective's shoes. She agrees to go with the detective without a fight.

The detective and Officer Vitrolli transport Ms. Mulroney back to Vancouver in the backseat of their unmarked police car. Officer Vitrolli drives while the detective attempts to interview Ms. Mulroney. She declines to answer any questions.

"Everyone has been awfully worried about you."

The girl ignores the detective.

"Would you like to tell us anything about where you've been?"

The girl says nothing.

"Okay."

The rest of the car ride is silent.

Hernandez stamps his half smoked cigarette out in the ashtray. He looks at the picture in the file again. A young woman wearing just a little too much eye makeup smiling at the camera. She hadn't smiled like that since they'd brought her in. Hernandez gnaws on his lower lip. He reaches forward and closes the file folder. He sticks a post-it to the outside of the file and writes a quick note. He puts it to the side in a basket marked

*Outgoing.* It didn't matter anymore. He had done his job. It was Juvenile Services problem now. Twelve more files sit on his desk. Hernandez rubs his face with his hands. It's late. They would have to wait. Hernandez pulls his phone out of his pocket. He scrolls through his contacts. His daughter smiles at him from the picture on his desk. He punches in a text.

*Have a good night. I love you.*

Hernandez stares down at his phone. He puts it on the desk and waits. Five minutes pass. Ten. Fifteen. Nothing. Silence.

# Late Bloomer

The Bengals were losing to the Rams 10 to 27. The fourth was just getting started. There was still a chance. Donna sauntered by, her wide hips rolling with every step. Larry raised his hand and she turned.

"Need something hon?"

Her voice was a high nasal.

"Another Coors."

Donna snorted and sneered.

"Wouldn't you rather have something good?"

"It's good enough. You couldn't get it here when I was younger."

"Yeah?"

"Yeah, something about it not being pasteurized. Couldn't get it anywhere east of the Mississippi or on the west coast."

Donna raised her eyebrows politely, as if she actually gave a damn about the influx of new information, as though she actually found it interesting. Her tongue worked its way across her teeth, searching for any remains of the chicken wings she had eaten earlier. Seeing that Larry was done, she turned and pulled a can of Coors from the fridge. The opening of the can and the turn back were one fluid motion. Larry watched, momentarily distracted from the game. Her t-shirt hugged tight to her frame. Muffin top and heavy breasts. A face still young and fresh. Big women always had pretty faces. The rest went to hell, but the face always stayed the same, protected by the plumpness, a monument to the glory that had once exuded from a temple of feminine form. Larry didn't judge. At forty his hairline was in retreat, what he had left was going gray, and his once flat belly was slowly pushing its way over his belt. Donna looked good. Age was like alcohol, it could make a three an eight.

The Lookout wasn't packed. Mostly just the usuals, plus a small group of young men and women in running clothes in the corner, sweating, making noise, and enjoying life. It made Larry feel old. Once he could have run ten miles, back in his Navy days, anymore he doubted his knee would even let him go one. The Bengals got a first down. The bar broke out into an assortment of cheers and jeers. Ribbing by old friends. Larry picked the can of Coors up off the bar. It tasted good. It tasted like being twenty-one. A road trip. The clink of glass bottles. Twelve cases in the trunk. The taste of cinnamon gum on her breath when they kissed. The crowd erupted again. Another first down.

The bar door opened, the usuals turned to look. A big man entered, accompanied by a gust of cold air. The door swung back closed. The big man unzipped his coat and paused to get his bearings. The guy was over six foot. He carried himself well, but with some extra pudge, only a few years into the long slide of getting fat. He had a baby face, which his goatee did little to hide. The man's eyes tracked across the bar and fell on the stool next to Larry. Larry quickly turned away, but it was too late. He could hear the heavy footfalls. Donna was smirking.

The big man hung his coat up underneath the bar and lifted his bulk up onto the stool. He smelled strongly of cologne. Larry did his best to concentrate on the game. Donna strode over and laid a cardboard coaster in front of the man.

"ID?"

The man was obviously over twenty-one. Probably in his mid-thirties. Larry didn't know if Donna was trying to be nice, or trying to be a bitch. It was hard to tell with her. The man pulled out his wallet and handed over his ID. Donna glanced at it and handed it back.

"What you have?"

The man sucked air in through his teeth. He looked up and down the bar, eyeing the drinks in the other patron's hands. He gestured towards Larry.

"What's he having?"

Donna eyed the man, considering smart ass answers. In the end, he wasn't worth the trouble.

"Coors."

"I'll have one of those."

Donna spun and pulled open the fridge. The big man gestured towards Larry again.

"Make it two please, one for me and one for my friend."

Larry tried to wave the offer away.

"I've already got one."

Donna spun back, popping the two cans open. She laid them on the bar. The man smiled.

"Thank you."

Donna nodded. Someone raised their hand down the bar. Donna moved down to serve them. The man watched her ass the whole way. Larry kept his eyes glued on the television. The man spun in his stool and stuck out his hand.

"Chuck."

Larry half-turned his head from the screen. He took the hand in his. Chuck had sausage fingers.

"Larry."

Chuck kept a hold of Larry's hand. Larry turned his head to fully face him. Chuck was still smiling, but his eyes kept dropping towards the two cans of Coors on the bar. Larry sighed.

"I already have a beer."

Chuck clapped Larry on the back with his free hand. The pat was light, but Larry could feel the strength in the other man's arm.

"No worries."

Chuck let go of Larry's hand. The Bengals started their third drive of the quarter. The two men watched in silence. Larry slowly drained his beer. Chuck's never left his lips. The can sounded hollow when he set it back down. The big man reached over, picked up the second, and raised it to his mouth. A wide receiver in the open. A long arching pass into the waiting hands of the man in orange. A broken tackle. Room to run. Touchdown. Larry raised his arms high, as though he was one of the refs on the field.

"Hell yeah."

Chuck smiled and pounded on the bar, rattling the plastic container holding olives, lemons, and limes. He tipped back the second beer and put another empty back down on the bar. He raised his hand to get Donna's attention, but his eyes were on Larry.

"Would you like me to get you one?"

Larry lifted his can and gave it a shake. Probably about a fifth left. He did some quick calculations in his head. If he had another, that would make seven, one more than he usually had. If he had seven he'd be on the edge of not being able to drive, but then again, there were probably fewer cops out on a Sunday night. Besides, a free beer was a free beer. Even if it was from a jackass.

"Okay."

Donna came over, Chuck made his order, and the two beers appeared on the bar. Again Chuck's eyes followed Donna's ass as she moved away. Larry turned his attention back to the game, 17 to 27. Chuck nudged Larry with his elbow. Larry turned to face him. Parts of the bar cheered. Larry's head snapped back. The Bengal defense had intercepted the ball. Chuck nudged Larry again. Larry turned angrily back to the annoying idiot.

"What?"

"Hey, by any chance would you know where I could get some weed?"

"Excuse me?"

"Would you happen to know where I could get some weed? I kind of want to get high tonight."

Chuck was smiling. Larry took a drink of his beer, buying time to collect his thoughts. Angry outbursts flowed through his head, but not out of his mouth. It was best to be diplomatic with the big ones.

"I'm not really into that kind of stuff."

Chuck's smile widened, showing off a set of straight white choppers.

"Me neither till last week. A friend gave me some. I'd never had it before. It was crazy. I could feel it going through me. One body part at a time. Just awesome. That's all I can say. Just awesome."

More hoots and clapping hands. Larry tore his gaze back towards the flickering screen above the bar. Bengals first down. The chains moved farther down the field. Chuck raised his hand and ordered another beer from Donna. He sucked it halfway down and lowered it. His eyes studied the can with interest.

"This is pretty good beer."

Larry gave the big man one eye.

"Coors is pretty good beer."

"I never even touched alcohol until three months ago."

Larry turned and fully faced the big man. In the dim bar light something twinkled in Chuck's goatee. Larry couldn't be sure, but he could almost swear it was a couple scattered pieces of glitter.

"Excuse me?"

"I never drank alcohol until three months ago."

"No liquor?"

"Nope."

"Not even a beer?"

"Nope."

"Jesus."

Another burst of noise. Larry half-turned his head. Another touchdown. 24-27. Only a minute left. Chuck drummed his hands on the bar and blew a raspberry.

"Yep, not a drop. I used to be Mormon. I never had any idea all this was out here. Never even dreamed."

Larry tried to concentrate on the television. The Bengals were lining up for an onside kick. Chuck kept nudging Larry with his elbow. Larry tried to ignore it, but the big bear was persistent. Larry swung his head around, trying to keep the anger out of his voice.

"What?"

"I said if I knew what the real world was like I would have left a lot sooner."

Cheers and hisses. Larry swung back towards the TV. The Bengals had recovered the onside kick. Chuck raised his hand again.

"You want another beer Larry?"

Larry gripped the bar with both hands, the knuckles turning white. Dirty son of a bitch.

"I have to use the bathroom."

The bathroom was back by the bar door. Larry got up and worked his way to it. Inside he pulled out his pecker and pissed in the urinal, reading the graffiti on the wall. Nothing clever.

Just garbage.  He put his pecker away and walked over to the sink.  His features bright red in the cracked mirror.  He washed his hands and splashed some water in his face.  Jesus Christ.  There were few enough enjoyable moments in his life.  Why wouldn't that big fucker just shut up.  Larry took in a big breath and let it out.  He did it again, and then one more time to be sure.  Larry pushed open the bathroom door.  The Bengals were within field goal range.  They could tie the game.  Chuck was leaning over the bar, talking to Donna.  She was toying with her hair.  Larry could hear the big man's voice over the murmur of other conversations."

"Tomorrow I have a date with a stripper.  We're going to a pottery class."

The Bengals' kicker was walking out onto the field.  Donna smiled at Chuck.  Larry turned and walked out into the cold.  Fuck it.

# I'm Bored, Let's Make Everyone Really Uncomfortable

Let's talk about abortions. Don't worry. I'm not going to share my opinion, and I really don't want to hear yours. I guess what I actually want to talk about is the abortion debate. Sorry about that. Probably should have started this in a better way. Oh well.

Few other topics seem to raise as big of an emotional response as abortions. In fact, it's one of the big no-go places for any conversation. Though in all fairness, most medical procedures, controversial or not, are probably not the best subject for dinner or drinks. For instance, few people are against colonoscopies, but that doesn't mean you should bring it up at Thanksgiving. Regardless, few other topics have the power to put you in either one camp or the other as much as abortion. Your opinions can isolate you from friends, family, the respect of colleagues, and huge portions of the dating pool. So why is that?

Like any classic story about the battle between good and evil there are two sides of the issue, and like any great story these two sides can be mostly boiled down into two binary generalities.

On one side you have the Anti crowd. We must stop abortions. Babies are people too. For god sakes you're killing babies. What kind of monster goes around killing babies? Have you seen babies? They're super adorable. Only a monster would ever want to harm one.

On the other side you have the Pro crowd. Abortions are a-okay. This is a women's health issue. What right do you have to tell a woman what to do with her body? I mean c'mon, what do you think this is, the Dark Ages? Hell no. This is America.

So you see, obvious polar opposites. Wait....no.....actually they're not. Wait a minute. What exactly is this debate even about again? These two sides are not polar opposites. Believing in one does not necessitate opposing the other. Being anti-abortion doesn't mean you have to think women have no rights to their bodies. Being pro-abortion doesn't mean you can't believe in the sanctity of human life. One side is talking about babies and the other is talking about women. They are not talking about the same thing. So what the hell?

These opposing messages, that are not opposite of each other, are part of what make the abortion debate so interesting, and heated. You literally have two sides talking past each other about two very different things. Women's rights and baby rights. If you're talking about two different things, you can't have a debate. The actual argument isn't about either one specifically, it's about which one has more precedence over the other. So is this a debate about women's rights versus baby rights? Not exactly. You see, there is one niggling problem that is at the root of all this. When exactly does a baby become a baby?

Let's look at the extremes. On one end pretty much everybody can agree that a baby is a baby once it is born. A baby outside the womb is definitely an individual which has the right to exist. On the other end pretty much everybody agrees that a baby is not a baby before the sperm and egg combine. Surveys show 99 percent of women of reproductive age in the U.S. have at some point used contraception, and men, well most men have the habit of practicing a lot for the big game. Granted, there are people on either extreme, super religious fundamentalists who have a very strict doctrine of not enjoying life, and those crazy folks who keep throwing their kids off of bridges for some reason, but at least in this country, both are a very miniscule minority.

So, we know that we definitely do not have a baby before conception, and that we definitely do have one at birth. What about the nine months in between? At what point does a baby cease being part of its mother, and become an individual? At what point does the baby's right to exist eclipse the mother's right to choose?

This is obviously a job for science. That's the only way to solve this. So......wait.....god damn it.......science can't help with this one. Nobody is debating the science. Both sides agree on how the process works. Nobody is arguing about when the maybe baby gets its fingerprints, heartbeat, etc. The order of operations is well understood and set in stone. What isn't set in stone is when a baby becomes a baby. At what point does it cross the imaginary line? At what point is the moral choice obvious? It's not a matter of science. It's a matter of interpretation and belief.

So, what's the right answer? When is a baby a baby? There is no right answer. It's no different than the arbitrary point in time we've chosen for getting your driver's license, the age of consent, voting, drinking alcohol, and retiring. Such questions are not answered by science, but rather by the general consensus of society. That's why the debate over abortions will never end and why it is so emotionally charged. It's based upon what each individual feels is right.

So, what was the point of all this? The point is to stop demonizing people who do not agree with you. The point is to stop assuming that people with a different opinion could have only arrived at that opinion because they are stupider. The point is that we need to stop with the nonsense that those who are anti-abortion are definitively against women's rights and that those who are pro-abortion don't value human life. This is only clouding the real issue. Debate is good, debate is healthy, but let's skip over all the bullshit and debate the actual question at hand. When is a baby a baby?

Welp, that's enough heavy stuff today. Have a good one.

# Snowball

"It's going to snow tomorrow."

The statement comes from the far end of the dining room table. Two seniors conversing in even matter of fact tones. The cacophony of the evening meal ceases in a wave moving down the long tables. Conversations at their midpoints fade into silence. A normal Tuesday evening dinner elevated in rank by the promise of the first snow.

"Are you sure?"

A double row of faces, forty-two in total, lean forward to listen.

"Weather report said 95 percent chance."

"That's not a definite."

"It's going to snow tomorrow."

The questioning senior smiles and the other grins back. Both go back to eating. The smile spreads its way down the dining room tables. The other seniors nod their heads and go back to their dinners. The juniors and sophomores beat the table with excitement, rattling plates and cups.

"It's going to snow tomorrow."

"First snow of the year."

"About damn time."

"Fuck yes."

One of the members on kitchen duty sticks their head out of the hole for the dirty dishes.

"What's going on?"

"It's going to snow tomorrow."

The head retreats back into the kitchen. Muffled voices followed by a war whoop above the sound of the pounding fists and shaking dinnerware. The freshmen look confused. Their eyes dart from the upperclassmen to their peers. The glances are filled with words unsaid. What is going on? Do you know what is going on? What's the big deal? What's going to happen? No answers come for the unspoken queries. One freshman, his curiosity overpowering, turns to the sophomore next to him.

"What's the big deal?"

The sophomore opens his mouth to answer, but a senior snaps it closed.

"Keep your trap shut. They get to know when it's time. Don't fuck this up."

The sophomore blushes. The dining room quiets down. Forks shovel food into hungry mouths. Conversations start again from where they had been cut off. The freshmen watch the upperclassmen, trying to weed out clues. The upperclassmen ignore the freshmen, but keep glancing out the windows, willing the white powder to fall. The meal ends. The dishes are stacked next to the hole and swiftly disappear within, accompanied by the sounds of spraying water and the heavy hum of the dishwasher. The freshmen are hustled off to the library to study. The upperclassmen split and go their separate ways. Some to their rooms. Bullshitting, studying, and video games. Some out the door. Bars, house parties, and get-togethers. The last load of dishes is finished and put away. The floors are swept and mopped. The main part of the house falls into silence.

At the library the freshmen speak in hushed voices. Trying to use their collective minds to put together all the pieces.

"What could all the fuss be about?"

"What is going to happen?"

"It has to have something to do with the snow?"

"My older brother once told me that...."

The watching senior leans over the shoulder of the speaker and puts a heavy hand on the table.

"We're here to study. So how about you shut up and get to it."

Hours pass. The furtive whispers are not enough. The mystery remains intact. The freshmen leave the library and walk back to the house on New Greek. It's cold out. Their breath puffs from between chapped lips. Cheeks and noses turn rosy. A nearly full moon shines from the sky above. No new knowledge has been retained. All thoughts are on what is going to happen tomorrow.

Back into the warmth of the house. It's growing late. Some stay up to chat with the upperclassmen still awake. Questions are only met by silence and knowing grins. One by one they break away and head to bed. No rules say that they have to, but why stay up to just be alone, besides, it's a school night. Lines form at the bathroom sinks. Scrub, spit, and rinse. Doors close. Lights go off. Young minds, confused but still excited, lay on pillows purchased by proud parents. Young eyes stare up at walls covered in posters of favorite movies, favorite tits, and snappy slogans about the imbibing of brews. Something is going to happen tomorrow. Something different is going to take place.

The front door of the house opens and closes. The drunks begin to return from their nightly endeavors. They pee on toilet seats and spit on the floors. They come into the rooms, turn on the lights, and laugh as their roommates shield their eyes. They stumble as they get ready for bed. The lights go out and another set of heads hit their pillows. Some pass out as soon as they go down. Others sit and stare up at the same walls, as excited as the freshmen. The drunks are always a good source of information. A few of the freshmen dare to ask the question digging through all their minds.

"What is going to happen tomorrow?"

Most get the same denial of anything or the brusque silencing of words which have been the theme since the announcement at dinner. However, a few, a lucky few, have roommates at just the right state. Just the right combination of excitement and lowered inhibitions. Just the right mind to whisper slurred responses.

"It's going to be one hell of a time."

"But what is it?"

"Something awesome."

"But what?"

"Snowballs. Tomorrow night we're going to snowball the dormies."

"What?"

"First snow of the year. Gets crazy man. Fucking crazy."

"Why?"

"Tradition. Keep it quiet. Don't tell anybody I told you."

Drunken roommates slip into unconsciousness. The lucky few freshman digest the revelation, find it lacking, and slip off to sleep as well. The snow falls while the world sleeps. Large gobs of solid water sink through the air and land silently on frozen ground. First just a bit, then more. Seven inches more. Giant clusters of flakes which cover the world and turn it white.

The earliest risers are the lucky ones. They get to see the virgin world before it is touched. The pristine which never lasts for long. Bodies rise from their beds. Showers turn on. Breakfasts are eaten. Huddled forms in heavy coats, baseball caps, and sneakers head out to class, plodding through the drifts. The passage of cars has reduced the snow on the roads to gray slush and ice. Many of the campus sidewalks are bare, warmed by the heat tunnels underneath. A solitary set of footprints cut their way across the Admin lawn. A single person going against the grain of common sense. One joker forms a snowball and is admonished by his fellow walkers.

"Don't you know that it's against the rules?"

"What's against the rules?"

"Throwing snowballs."

"What the fuck?"

The joker throws the snowball at the tree branches. Snow falls on the people walking just ahead. They look back, but all those behind look innocent. The joker doesn't make another one. Attention shifts to one of the lucky freshmen. He whispers to his fellows the secrets he learned the night before. The answer to what is going to happen. He has become a powerful person amongst his peers. He knows something that they don't. He tries to keep the secret, but he can't. With every person he tells his power is diluted. Spread out. In the showers, in the bathrooms, at breakfast, and on the way to class. The knowledge jumps, until by lunch all know what is going to happen. The seniors talk as well. Making plans. Preparing.

The members gather back at the house for lunch. Frozen bodies pound snow off their shoes in the entryway and snort back thawing snot. Everybody knows. Nobody talks about it. The illusion of ignorance is not broken. Cars come down the steep hill along New Greek and forget about the stop sign at the bottom. Eyes watch out the windows as brakes are slammed and cars skid into the intersection. One, two, three, and four. The third one is the best. The third one goes clear across and into the lawn of the Alumni building. The gathered men hoot and cheer. One of the seniors stands and raises his voice, demanding everyone's attention.

"Be ready to go at 9:30 tonight."

Nobody asks any questions. Lunch comes to an end. Everybody heads back to class. The freshmen pester the upperclassmen with queries for more details. The upperclassmen hold the line.

"It's going to be one hell of a time."

"Last year was awesome."

"Just be downstairs and ready at 9:30. You don't want to miss it."

"Be sure your throwing arm is stretched out."

Little details collect, gather, and disseminate. Bit by bit everyone becomes knowledgeable of what is going to take place. Dinner time comes. The dining room tables are filled. Electricity jumps from body to body, growing stronger with every leap. Freshmen and upperclassmen alike fidget in their seats. Eyes keep glancing up at the clock on the wall. Still three hours to go. The meal is finished, the plates are stacked and washed, each person finds a way to distract themselves. Eight o'clock. The first signs of movement. Groups head out to cars in the parking lot to share ice cold beers. Groups huddle in rooms, behind closed doors, passing liquor bottles around tight circles. The seniors stay silent, but the juniors and the sophomores start to speak.

"You should have seen last year. Hundreds of snowballs flying through the air."

"Blocked all the doors with snowballs so big it took four guys to push them."

"Broke a couple of windows."

"Cops showed up."

"Fucking crazy man. Fucking crazy."

"Isn't it illegal? Somebody said throwing snowballs on campus is against the rules?"

The bottle passes around once again.

"Drink up boys, drink up. It's going to be one hell of a night."

The little hand points at the nine, the big hand hits the three. They start to gather in the living room. The dome lights of cars brighten and fall dark as doors open and close. Bottles are tucked away back into their hiding places. Room doors are unlocked and the occupants spill forth. Men in dark clothing lounge on chairs and couches. A freshman comes downstairs in a bright red coat. A senior pulls him aside.

"What do you think you're doing? Dark clothes dumb ass. Dark clothes. In case you have to hide."

The freshman goes back upstairs. The seniors move down the hallways, checking all the rooms. Making sure everyone is coming. One sophomore is too drunk to stand. They leave him where he is. The clock hits 9:30. Forty-five men start to move en masse. Out the door and onto the sidewalk. Across campus, doors open. New Greek and Old Greek. Figures of all sizes in dark clothing. Houses empty. They gather in front of the Administration building. Mostly men, but a few smatterings of women here and there. Twelve tribes, together, but grouped by allegiance. A few spread out, greeting foreigners that they know. A few flasks are passed around. Hands rub together. Feet stamp in place. A few snowmen built earlier that day are knocked down and smashed. The crowd grows larger. A police car moves slowly down the street. The crowd watches it pass by through the trees. The hum of conversation fades. It's probably time to get moving.

A tribe breaks ranks and starts to move. The others follow. They move at a fast walk down through campus. Nobody wants to be behind. Everyone wants to be up front. The front is where the action is. The front is the place to be. The lines between groups fade and they mix and merge. The tribes melt into each other and become one. Another police car moves down the street. The mob breaks into a fast walk. A mass of drunken humanity moving with purpose, to reach the dorms on the other end of campus, the route chosen by whoever is in the lead.

Down the curving street from the Admin building, down alongside the Commons. A spotlight from the right. A police car slowly moving down the street past Morrill Hall. Another spotlight from the front. Another police car moving towards them from the cluster of the Engineering buildings. The fast walk turns into a jog. The crowd turns left and makes its way down a flight of stairs. Feet move rapidly down the steps, skidding on ice, but too afraid of the mass above to slow down. At the bottom of the stairs the crowd turns right. The area between the buildings is wide. The lights of the dorms shine across the street on the northern end, just past the AgiSci and Natural Resource buildings. Wallace, McConnell, Upham, Gault, and Theophilus, the Tower of Power. All open for the taking.

The jog breaks into a run. A few voices rise and cheer, but fall silent. Red and blue lights move down the street. A cop car comes into view and stops. The mob turns left again, and splinters as it filters between the buildings, reforming on the other side on Rayburn Street. The crowd condenses, turns right, and starts to move again. The lights of the dorms shine bright in the distance. Steam rises above the crowd. Hands clench tightly. Hearts beat rapidly. No one says a thing. Only the sound of moving feet, rustling clothing, and heavy breathing. Almost there.

The cop car pulls forward and turns up Rayburn. The mob slows and comes to a halt, red and blue flashes illuminating desperate faces. More flashing lights from behind. A second cop car comes and closes off the rear. Nowhere to go. The crowd stands, unsure what to do. The door of the cop car in front opens. The silhouette of a large fat man rises up. The screech of a bullhorn being turned on.

"Please return to your domiciles. You are performing an illegal activity."

The crowd boos and a few curse. The bullhorn is unaffected.

"Those who do not return to their domiciles will be cited."

Desperate eyes look in all directions. Searching for a solution to the problem. Figures in dark hoodies stamp from foot to foot. The ones in front move back and forth, caged dogs, but none take another step forward. The rear of the mob start to break away and make their way back between the buildings. Several have already slipped away. The police car behind starts to move closer in low gear. Its spotlight lances forth and sweeps across the crowd.

A figure steps forward. Young, probably no more than a sophomore. He takes five steps forward. The crowd watches. Waiting. The figure turns back, takes another step, and turns back again. His eyes search across the mass behind him, locking eyes with as many people as possible.

"Well fucking c'mon, there's too many of us to arrest us all!"

The figure turns and runs forward. The silhouette of the fat policeman lowers the bullhorn. One second. Two seconds. The dam breaks. The mob rushes down the street. The police car behind hits its siren. The officer in front dives back into his car and shuts the door. The crowd streams past the cop car, a few slowing just enough to pelt it with snowballs. Down Rayburn. Across Sixth Street. In amongst the dorms. The mob floods around the brick buildings.

The crowd yells. The crowd screams. The crowd howls upward into the night. Hundreds of snowballs fly through the air. A few ground level windows are open to let in cool air. Manic arms rip out screens and push the windows open all the way. Snowballs follow. Occupants cower and hide themselves from the assault. The crash of breaking glass. Six men push a giant snowball against one of the doors. More glass breaks. The screen pops off two windows on the third floor of Gault. Super soakers spray downward across the crowd. Dark figures retreat back out of range. A barrage of snowballs answers the assault. Curses from both sides. A mass of dormies flings open one of the doors of Wallace. They quickly gather ammo and try to mount a counter attack. They're driven back. They try to shut the door behind them, but several members of the mob are pulling on the handle. Back and forth the door swings, snowballs flying into the crack. A mighty heave by the dormies. The latch catches. Another window shatters.

Sirens and flashing lights. Three cops cars come in from the left, and three from the right. Three minutes. It's only been three minutes since battle was joined. The mob throws snowballs at the approaching cop cars. Two cruisers move down Rayburn. Two more appear in the dorm parking lots. A policeman jumps out and tackles a running figure. The prone form is pushed into the snow by the officer's knee and the boy's arms are forced behind his back. A snowball hits the cop's side, but is ignored. The mob breaks and scatters. Running figures move in all directions, running as fast as they can. More cops jump out. More members of the crowd are tackled. The sound of breaking glass again. In amongst the buildings. Into the shadows. A few hold back long enough to throw one last salvo at the police cars, then break up and retreat. Flashing red and blue lights illuminate nothing. The mob is gone.

Back across campus. Small knots and individuals. Everyone taking their own route. They filter back into the house. Wet, cold, high on adrenaline. Into the living room. Into the hot showers.

"Did you see that? That was fucking crazy?"

"It was like the window just exploded."

"Those cops didn't know what to do?"

"I got one, right in the side of the head."

"Were any of the one's grabbed ours?"

"You should have seen that dormies face."

"Holy shit."

"Awesome. Fucking awesome."

A cop car moves down the street outside. The walls of the house flash red and blue for a moment, then it is gone. The seniors and the lucky juniors head off to the bars. The rest sit and revel in their victory. The adrenaline fades. One by one they slip off to bed. The house falls dark and quiet. At 2:30 in the morning the drunks come back from the bar. They throw newspapers on the floor and run the lawnmower up and down the hallways. By 3:00 the house falls silent again. Fat snowflakes fall from the sky.

# The Closet

The boy lays in his bed in the dark and listens to the animals in the closet. He can hear them talking to one another in low voices, the words inaudible, but the feeling permeating the darkened room. It is lonely in the closet. It is frightening to be alone. They don't understand why they have to be there. Why they must coldly roost on dusty shelves while others lay warm, encased under warm blankets pulled tight up to their chins. They are trapped, and they are unhappy. It is unfair, but there is nothing to be done.

Moonlight, etched by the shadowy branches of the locust trees, floats in through the windows, illuminating a world of indistinct gray shadows. Toy shelf, dresser, bunk bed, and bean bag chairs. All there, but not quite all the way. The boy sits silent and listens. He rolls towards the wall. Away from the view of the slightly ajar accordion of the closet door. Towards the lumps of Pound Puppy and Puppet who lay beside him.

Pound Puppy is the older of the two. Tan hide and stubby ears, sad plastic eyes glinting in the darkness, the sewn threads of a repaired blowout on his right hindquarters, and a neck wrung by the crook of an elbow until no more stuffing remains. They had all received Pound Puppies, once upon a time, but only this one still enjoys the light of day, resting on his place next to the pillow. Puppet is the younger. An orange crochet body with a hole to allow in a hand, brown floppy ears, big bright red mouth, and two blue jewels for eyes. A gift from an old nurse to a little boy, then eight, who had lain in a hospital bed, saying nothing, watching the world, understanding too much, but feeling too worn out to care.

The boy clutches the pair to his chest. The ten dollar bill hidden inside Puppet crinkles beneath the pressure of his skinny arm. The boy is eleven. He is too old for such things. He knows this, but he can't seem to put them away. He is unable to banish them to the closet with the rest. They would be unhappy in the closet. It would not be right for them to be all alone. They are friends, confidantes, and companions. They stay quiet and they are always there. They never question and they never judge. From them he has nothing to hide. No thoughts are bad. No thoughts are good. They are just thoughts. Floating in an emptiness, bounced by echoes across the vastness of his mind. Free of the whispers of parents unaware that anyone is listening, not knowing how far one's name can carry in the dark.

When he was ten they had taken Blankie, soft white fabric which had been there from the start. The fringe ripped away and a small hole near one corner. Once held close against a frightened body, suddenly cleaved away and gone, taken while he was away at school. The parents had sat him down. They had explained how he was getting older. How it was time to give up such things. To them it had all seemed so reasonable. No question it was the right thing to do. The boy had thrown a fit. A tantrum that seemed to have no end. His brothers had watched from the periphery as his screams had shook the windows. He yelled until he could yell no more, took a rest, and then got back up to yell again. His parents did not break. The worst of the storm passed and the boy went to bed, his eyes full of tears. For a time he searched whenever he had a chance. All the closets, under his parents' bed, the brown chest in the living room, the attic, the crawlspace, the cellar amongst the Christmas lights. Nothing. The parents were too good at hiding. Blankie was gone, and that was that. Pound Puppy and Puppet took his place. A fight for another day.

On the lower bunk the boy's little brother farts in his sleep, rolls over, and farts again. The little brother is always farting in his sleep. A few times he has farted so bad that he has woken himself up, bursting into the world with a startled yelp of indignation that someone would dare to break his slumber. The little brother never hears the voices. The little brother is a good sleeper. He passes out the moment he's in bed, and he rises with the morning sun. He doesn't know about the world of the night, because he is never there to observe it. Not the rustle of the locust trees, the howl of the coyote, or the gurgle of the toilet. Not the mice skittering in the walls, the settling creak of the joists, or the shift of the logs in the wood stove. The sounds in the deep of night that nobody hears. The sounds that come out after even the whispered worries of the parents fall silent into guttural snores.

The boy does not sleep. His brain will not let him. It whirls in unending thoughts, stories, ideas, and worries. A mechanism of perpetual motion, never stopping until without warning it does, dropping him dead until jostling hands wake him to face the morning sun. He lays in his bed and waits for the sudden shift to the next day. He lays in his bed, quiet, listening to the world of the darkest part of night. They all have voices.

The toys argue amongst each other on the shelves, debating who will be the ones to be next played with. Sometimes the verbal turns to physical, and a favorite toy is shoved somewhere out of sight by other jealous playthings. In the drawers the clothing rustles. The shirts on top, looking forward to soon being worn, the shirts on the bottom, bemoaning the weight of their more comfortable brethren, knowing they will never see the light of day. The boy is finicky about his clothing, and many shirts lie near the bottom, never worn. It is worse for those who were once near the top. Those who now have unsightly holes or stretched out necks. They remember what it had once been like. They remember a better world. But it is the animals in the closet that tug at his heartstrings. It is the animals for whom he feels. They do not want to be played with. They do not ask to be worn. They just want to feel close to something. To feel connected. To feel loved.

In the morning the bus will come and the boy will be taken to school. He will ride the forty-five minutes with his nose buried in his book. He will sit in class and listen. He will go out to recess to play. Sometimes with others, but more often than not alone. Each month he can feel the divide growing. Each year the chasm widens more. When he was younger he had just been one of many. Another set of bright eyes amongst the crowd. Now he doesn't belong. An outsider looking in. A voyeur on the world. When he was eight he was woken in the middle of the night and taken to the hospital. He stayed there for a week. When he returned he did so with a body made of sticks. Perhaps that was the reason why. In his head, the boy always imagines his body was once more like all the rest, less thin, less weak. No, it is probably just in his head. Things have always been this way. Even when he was small he had known it would just be a matter of time. There was something about him different. He was not like all the rest. He did not belong.

The boy shifts in his bed again. The ten dollar bill crinkles in Puppet's head. All the voices go silent for a moment, then start up once again. The boy's voice is still hoarse with screamed denials. An unending litany of refused acknowledgment. Life is not fair, but why should he be the one who must always take notice? The parents once said that they did not want to spoil him. They had spoiled him when he was little and it had led to bad things. The boy has no memory of such a world. No thoughts to remind him of such a paradise. Did the parents say it often, or did they only say it once? Either way it is lodged deeply in his head. The idea that he is being punished for a world he can't remember. A world where he did not want. A world where things were fair. A world of which he was a part. A world where he was doing more than just looking in. A world where someone understood. Where others heard the voices. Where there were no worried whispers. Where nothing was alone. Gone. All gone without even a memory. Just a feeling that something is wrong. The sense that things will never get better, that they will only get worse. Why shouldn't he reach out and take whatever he needed? Who has the right to judge someone doomed to isolation?

The sad plastic eyes of Pound Puppy stare up at the boy. The blue jewel eyes of Puppet do not twinkle. With them the boy has no secrets. No defenses. They can see into his soul. He knows what they are thinking. Even the wanderer must have morals. Just because the chasm is widening, it doesn't mean he should try to escalate its speed. No wrong can ever make the world feel right.

The boy rises up and the voices cease. The boy pulls the ten dollar bill from Puppet's head and holds it tightly in his hand. He slips down the bunk bed ladder, doing his best to not make a sound. Little brother farts again, smacks his lips, and rolls over. Across the carpet. The bedroom door sticks, it must be yanked to be opened. Sit silent and wait to see if anyone heard. Even in the muted light, the boy can see the scars on the door's finish. Evidence of past battles with the world slipping by. The hallway is dark. No windows. Just the tiny orange flicker from the gap between the wood stove's gate in the distant living room. The dark shadow of the bathroom.  The closed door of the room of the older brother, and the slightly ajar door of the parents.

The boy creeps next to the ajar door and stops to listen. Heavy breathing.  A high nasal snore.  Familiar sounds.  The constant background hum of the deep night.  The boy pushes open the door.  Moonlight splashes across the hall.  Rustling in the bed.  Freeze.  Nothing.  Stay low.  Creep forward below their view.  Stick up one bony hand.  Feel the leather sitting on the cold lacquered wood.  Bring it back down.  Open it.  Put in the ten dollar bill.  Return the wallet to its place.  Creep back out. Slowly.  Put the door back into its original position.  Sit and listen.  Almost done.  Crawl back into his room.  Shut the door. Push it past where it sticks.  Sit and listen.

The voices are going once again.  The boy can hear the muffled sounds of the animals in the closet.  Sad sounds.  Quiet sounds.  Hopeless sounds.  The shadows of the locust trees shift with the rustle of the wind.  The boy thinks about going back. He thinks about retrieving the ten dollar bill.  He stays put.  He listens.  Poor bastards.  Poor lonely bastards.  Stuck.  Alone. The boy stands and opens the metal folding closet door.  The hinges squeal.  The voices stop.  The boy takes them in armloads and puts them up on the top bunk.  Bee and pink elephant from the claw machine, big koala bear, little brother's pound puppy and stuffed cat, the clown puppet, sleepy alligator, older brother's ragged teddy bear, pink panther stiff with his wire bones, little velvet mouse, and all the rest.  The boy climbs up and lays amongst them.  Everything is quiet.  Everything is good.  He can feel their happiness.  He can feel the joy coming off of them.  Pound Puppy's plastic eyes don't seem so sad.

# Tipping The Scales

The peak. A shudder. Synapses pop and go dark. He rolls onto his back, the mattress springs squeaking underneath him. They lay, breathing heavy. She pulls herself over him, her feet hit the ground, she stands. He watches her walk out. Her backside framed in the doorway. Black hair cut short. Her ass slightly jiggling with every step. A bit of cellulite on her thighs. He would have never noticed if she hadn't brought it up all the time. Fishing for assurances. Her small dog watches from the couch. Panting. Exiled from the bed for the duration. Fleeing from the quaking shake of the rattling frame. She rounds the corner. Footsteps. The bathroom door closes. The fan turns on.

He lays on the bed. Bare to the world. His engorged member pointing defiantly at the ceiling, calling for another round. His head swims through a sea of draining endorphins, caught in the whirlpool that drains his ecstasy and pulls him down. The sound of cars passing outside the open window. Sweat drying on skin. Blurry vision through dry contacts. He's careful not to wipe his eyes with his right hand. Only the left. Systems check. Restart initiated. Higher brain functions restarting. The sound of the shower turning on. What the hell is he doing?

She's a nice girl. A sweet girl. Maybe too sweet. A Polly Anna trapped in the cruel grip of the modern world. The sun will come out tomorrow. If you're a good person, good things will come your way. Silly platitudes, once believed in, but long since dispelled by the hard knocks of life's heavy fists.

The sex was good. There was no denying that. Animalistic fury combined with the willingness to push things towards the limit. Magic fingers unlock doors. Keep your fingernails trimmed. Reckless abandon. The bed frame was new. A testament to the tempest unleashed by biological factors beyond their control. The former had not been up to the challenge. It had gone to the junk bin, replaced by a stouter model. She had asked him to help her get rid of the old one. He had refused. She had asked him to help her go get the new one. He had refused. She had asked him to help put together the new one. He had refused. Each refusal a hammer blow to the decency he was raised to maintain. Sacrificed on the need to keep his distance. To not give false signals that were not there.

The little dog jumps off the couch, trots over, and jumps up on the bed. His fingers trace their way behind its ears, stroking the soft fur. She is in love with him, but she refuses to admit it. Minus the direct verbal, all the signs are there. The attention. The acts. The hinting statements. He can see it in her eyes. The longing. The need. The hope. It is painful to watch. A painful knot in his chest which pulls the sinew of his entire body tight. She will never say a word. As long as she never asks, he can never answer. As long as he never answers, the possibility can always exist. He often tries to convey the reality of the situation, and she always nods her head and agrees, but it is still there. That look in her eye. She is a terrible liar.

The dresser is half open, a gray camisole hanging out. A row of profile silhouettes in identical frames hang on the wall. People from another time. Top hats and bonnets. Lace curtains dapple the sunlight on his chest. It isn't that she wouldn't make a good girlfriend. She probably would. She is kind, thoughtful, and intelligent. Not a bad bone in her body, if one did not include his. A man could probably not ask for a better mate. She is resilient. The horrors of the world are met with a smile. She stands by him in the darkness, and helps lift him when he is down. But it is different from the others. No feeling. No push. No blaring trumpets with the declaration of this might be the one. She would be good for him, of that there is no doubt. A logical choice. A safe alternative to braving the winter storms of emotional uncertainty.

The dog licks his hand, demanding more attention. He stares up at the ceiling. Unmoving. His brain a tumultuous tempest of released chemicals and electrical impulses. It would be a lie, but would that be so bad? He is fond of her, but would that be enough? In thirty years would he look on her with compassion or with resentment? Glad for the reality he'd be in, or spiteful over the world that could have been? She is a nice woman. She deserves to get what she wants out of life. He cares for her, of that there is no denying. Maybe that is enough. Her feelings are a certainty, and he is getting no younger. Could he really throw such a clear picture of possible bliss into the fire? Sacrifice it in the hope of finding something that likely exists only in his head? What the hell is he supposed to do?

The little dog, unnoticed, licks his member. Near the tip. He violently rolls away with horrified disgust. The dog jumps back a foot, it looks frightened near the bottom of the bed. The two stare at each other. He looks away and looks again. The dog cowers, aware that it has done something wrong, but unsure how it fits within the relative scale. Their eyes lock. Neither can look away, though both want to. He pushes the dog off the bed.

It runs back to the couch. The shower turns off. He gets out of the bed and puts on his pants. The dog licks its chops. It's decided. He needs to get out of this relationship.

# The Best Movie Review Ever

Last Sunday afternoon I attended the first birthday of my friends' son. It's always a surreal experience to be a bachelor at a child's birthday party. I don't mean it in a bad way. I greatly enjoyed myself and am glad that my friends invited me, but that doesn't change the strangeness of the situation. The party had all the usual attendees. The birthday baby, parents, grandparents, friends with children, friends soon to have children, and me, the token bachelor. It's a bit like visiting another country. The time is pleasant, but the customs seem strange, and part of you is glad to get back to the normalcy of your own native land. I am thankful that my hosts provided me a of couple beers to help my easing into their world. I had thought of bringing my own, but decided against it given my relative position compared to the other guests. When traveling abroad it's best not to play into the stereotypes of the natives. I did enjoy a delicious Mexican Coke just prior to the party, but this was consumed in the privacy of my car, parked down the street to save the more choice spots for those with children either inside or outside their bodies.

Such events have the nasty habit of reminding me of my relative position in the world compared to the version of present day me pictured ten years ago. Part of me would like to immigrate to the strange country inhabited by my friends, but the application process is rather complicated, and I've always been loath to fill out the necessary paperwork. With these types of thoughts swashing about in my noggin, going home to sit alone afterwards did not seem the best course of action, so I compromised and decided to go to a movie. Many people flatly reject the idea of going to the cinema on their own, but I find it to be a rather relaxing use of my time. It allows me to become fully immersed in the story, releasing emotions as I see fit without judgment. Plus it guarantees that nobody else puts their filthy hands in my popcorn bucket.

Adjourning to the Eastport Plaza Cinema on 82nd, I nestled myself into the cushions of a theater seat, wisely avoiding the one with the still wet stain, foregoing my usual theater accoutrement since I had already thoroughly stuffed myself with hors d'oeuvres and cake at the aforementioned birthday party. Perhaps Sunday evening is not the most popular time for art flicks, but as the movie time approached I noticed that I was apparently going to be the only person in the theater. It should be of no surprise that this left me feeling a little creeped out. However, not so creeped out that I felt the need to leave. I had paid ten dollars for my ticket, and damn it, wasting money is a cardinal sin. Halfway through the previews, a couple around my own age came in. The woman said hello and waved at me, a greeting that seemed strange, but which I returned automatically in kind. Accepting that I was at least somewhat normal, or as normal as a man alone in a movie theater could be, they came in and took seats one row back and one seat to my right. A situation that proved creepier than just me being in the theater by myself.

He was a bigger man, fat over bulk, with a beard down to his sternum, baggy pants, and a wallet on a chain. She was a remarkably average woman, built like a rectangle, oversized sweater, frizzy hair, and eyes wide open, stuck in a permanent look of bemused surprise. She had difficulty modulating the volume of her voice. When she asked her partner whether or not he had silenced his phone, it was with such amplification that I assumed she was asking me. A mistake I realized when I answered with the affirmative. Blushing and stumbling over an apology, I decided to keep my head forward for the rest of the movie. They were a talkative couple, as in she talked and he listened. Throughout the movie she whispered to him just below my level of hearing. At times he would grunt, but it was possible that such sounds were unassociated with her constant hushed mumbling, which for me sounded like the chirping of a bird suffering from laryngitis.

About halfway through the film their communication must have taken a turn for the worst, for she got up and sat on the stairs even with my row. Now most people would have thought this behavior to be a little strange, but otherwise would have likely just written it off as the peculiarities of the human condition and just ignored it. My brain is wired a little different. The first thought that came to my mind was that these two were probably some kind of movie theater serial killers, traveling from town to town, going to movies with low attendance, and satiating their never ending blood lust with thrill kills of lonely bachelors who don't have the good sense to just go home and browse Netflix. The only question for me was which one of the two would make the first move. Would it be the man, coming from behind, choking me with his wallet chain, or would it be the woman, jumping at me like a crazed wolverine, plunging a nail file into the side of my neck?

Nervous, I put my hand into my pocket to clutch my keys, the only weapon I had. I kept my eyes shifting from one to the other, coiled like a spring in wait for any type of movement. Part of me felt a little silly, and even a little embarrassed. If they weren't serial killers, my hand jammed deep into my pocket, my fingers constantly caressing my keys, probably gave the impression that I was some kind of theater pervert. On the other hand, if they were murderous butchers of the cinema, my keys were my only chance of survival. I really doubted my ability to take gazelle like leaps over the chair rows to escape. It was a no win situation.

We sat that way, in stalemate, for a good thirty minutes. A teenage couple came in at one point, sitting far below, looking to score a free flick after the one they had paid for had finished, but feeling the blackness of death that permeated the theater, they wisely chose to leave after only about five minutes. Soon after, the woman got up. I tensed. My hand pulled out of my pocket, my car key projecting like a claw between my middle and index fingers. She walked down the stairs and out the door. Just me and the big guy then. She enjoyed the thought, but didn't like seeing the deed. We sat in silence. The man coughed. C'mon fatso. Let's dance. The woman came back into the theater. She motioned with her hand. Impatient. The man lifted his bulk from his chair and let out a wheeze. Through the corner of my eye I could see his wallet chain glitter in the light of the big screen. He stepped behind me. He cleared his throat. He moved past and down the stairs. The couple left the theater. I put my keys back in my pocket. The cleaning lady came in, but seeing me, gave out a dejected sigh and left. The movie ended. I went home.

*The Lady In The Van.* Four stars out of five.

# Passing Of The Old Guard

Norm hid the paper bag containing the fifth of vodka under his overcoat. The old shrew at the nurse's station of the ICU watched him as he walked past, her flabby hide bathed in the light of her lamp, made all the brighter by all the other lights being turned down for the night. Her eyes narrowed and Norm could feel them penetrate through the layers of cloth and paper to the bottle hidden below. Norm's heart raced. Memories bubbled to the surface. Two identical rail thin boys sneaking off behind an old one room schoolhouse. The more vocal twin pulling the cork from the bottle with his crooked teeth. The quiet twin watching nervously, knowing it was all just going to lead to a paddling, or worse. He just had to get past the desk. Once his back was turned there would be no trouble at all.

"Back so soon Mr. Roberts?"

"Yes, yes, just went out for a smoke."

Norm didn't slow his pace. His old work boots echoed across the tile. He turned the corner and headed down the hallway towards his brother's room. Norm breathed a sigh of relief and barreled right into a man in scrubs coming out of a supply closet. Both men tumbled to the floor and the bag came free, coming into view out from beneath the coat, still clutched in Norm's liver spotted hand. Norm started coughing, covering his mouth with his free hand. The nurse scrambled to get back to his feet, and then offered a hand to pull Norm back up.

"Oh my, Mr. Roberts, I'm so sorry. Are you....."

The lisping voice cut short. The nurse's eyes tracked downward to the paper bag in Norm's hand. The nurse glanced back up at Norm, and then back down at the bag. The nurse's thumb and index finger nervously flattened the thin blonde mustache on his upper lip. Norm ran his free hand through his thin gray hair, flopping it back over his part, dampening the lights dim reflection from his shiny dome. Both men sucked air deeply.

"Are you okay Mr. Roberts?"

"Yes. Yes. I'm just fine."

"I'm terribly sorry about running into you."

"Not a worry. Not a worry at all. Don't give it a second thought."

"Are you sure you're not hurt?"

"Yep. Not a scratch."

"I'm just so very sorry."

"Don't worry about it. Happens to the best of us."

Norm shifted the bag to his other hand. The nurse's eyes followed it, then snapped back upward to Norm's face. The nurse gave a little smile.

"We all thought that you had headed out for the night. You were gone for quite a while."

"No, just needed to step out a bit for a smoke."

"Of course."

"How's my brother doing?"

The nurse's face grew more somber.

"Pretty much the same unfortunately. He's stable, but we don't know for how long."

Norm grunted in response.

"Dr. White, that specialist I told you about earlier, he's going to stick his head in before he heads home tonight. He should be able to tell you more than me."

"Dr. Phelps didn't seem to think much could be done."

"Yes, but it's always good to get a second opinion from someone more specialized."

Norm grunted again.

"Well, I better get back to my rounds. Have a good night Mr. Roberts."

The nurse started to move down the hall, then turned back.

"Mr. Roberts, is it alright if I ask you something?"

"What is it?"

"It's just sir, it's just that everyone on the floor's been talking."

"Yeah, what about?"

"I know I shouldn't be asking, but so many rumors have been swirling about."

Norm stared at the nurse, waiting. The nurse flattened his mustache again and glanced back down at the bottle.

"Well, um, it's about those scars on his leg. The one's on his right thigh. He wouldn't tell any of the doctors how he got them."

"Yeah. What of it?"

"Well, I know it's really nobody's business or anything, but it's just that, a bunch of us were curious, that's all."

Norm stared at the nurse for a moment. The nurse stared back, then let his eyes fall down to the bag in Norm's hand again. The two stood in stalemate. Norm let out a sigh.

"He jumped out of a plane over Normandy. His chute didn't open. Dropped six hundred feet like a stone. Right through the roof of some Frenchies barn. Landed right in a big stack of loose hay. Would've been a real bit of luck if the stupid farmer hadn't left his pitchfork there. Didn't slow him down much though. He potted a couple Germans that were using the farmhouse for the night. Shot one when he came out to take a piss, and then three others when they came out to investigate. The shots attracted in the rest of his squad. The barn made a nice strong point until the boys from the beaches showed up. Even when it was an option, he wouldn't let them move him away from the front. His buddies finally knocked him out and took him to the rear when his leg started to stink."

The nurse's eyes were wide in his head.

"Really?"

"Yep. They figured out later that the German with his dick in his hand was some high mucky muck Colonel. General Eisenhower himself gave my brother the Silver Star."

"Wow."

"Anything else?"

"No. Thank you sir. Have a good night sir."

The nurse moved down the hall and Norm continued on his way to his brother's room. The lights were still on, and the television, hung high up on the wall, flashed with picture and sound. Three people were in the room, all watching the television. A skeleton lay in the bed, IV's in his arms and an oxygen hose in his nose. A skeleton with Norm's face. A woman sat next to the bed, the television picture reflected off her Coke bottle glasses, hair dyed a shade of brown it never was, holding one skeletal hand in hers. A man in his mid-forties sat in a chair by the window. The man had the look of his mother. All three looked at Norm as he walked into the room.

"How you feeling Gibb?"

"I'd rather be hunting." The skeleton started to laugh, but the sharp bark was broken by a racking cough that shook Gibb's bony frame. Norm could hear the gurgle in Gibb's lungs. It made Norm feel sick to his stomach, but also strangely made him crave a cigarette. Gibb lay back. Gibb's wife Sue leaned over and dabbed at the spittle on Gibb's chin with an old handkerchief. The man sitting by the window, Gibb's son Tommy, ignored the entire spectacle.

"You look pretty out of sorts Uncle Norm. Everything all right?"

Norm didn't take his eyes off his brother. He wanted to, but couldn't. The two had looked identical since birth. People had always been confusing them. Even up until recently they had been mirror images of each other, aged by similar lifestyles. Hard work. Hard play. Hard life. Looking at the wasted form of his brother made Norm feel uncomfortable. Gibb had always been the stronger.

"Yeah Tommy, I'm fine. Just ran into the nurse when he was coming out of the supply closet. Knocked me on my ass."

Gibb snorted, but was careful not to laugh.

"Which one? The old bitch or the fagot?"

"Jesus Christ Dad."

Gibb ignored his son's outburst.

"Bet the little fucker was probably in their sucking some other fagot's dick."

"You can't talk like that Dad. It's not appropriate."

"Fuck Tommy. It's a hell of a time to tell me what the hells appropriate. You're not the one that has to let some fagot take your temperature every hour."

Tommy's disgusted face looked around the room for support. Norm's face remained impassive. Sue's eyes never left the TV. Tommy cursed quietly under his breath and stared out the window at the lights of the city. Gibb chuckled, a hoarse grating sound deep in his throat.

"Fuck Norm, do you know who that fag nurse reminds me of?"

"Who?"

"Henry Johnson."

"Yeah?"

"Yep. Good old Horse Fucking Henry."

"I guess he kind of does."

"Of course that nurse is probably a bit smarter than old Henry."

"How so?"

"I guarantee none of his boyfriends kick near as hard as a horse."

Gibb started chuckling again. Norm allowed himself a smile. Norm pulled the bottle of vodka out of its sack.

"Drink Gibb?"

"Fuck yes. I thought you'd never ask."

Sue's eyes fell away from the TV.

"Are you sure you should be drinking in your condition?"

Gibb's features softened and he gave his wife's hand a weak squeeze.

"Not like it can do much harm now sugar bear. I might as well squeeze out what little enjoyment I can while I'm still able."

"The doctors said……"

"The doctors said I got the liver of a sixteen year old Quaker. It's my lungs that are fucked up."

"But the doctors…."

Gibb waved his hand to shush her and gestured towards the wheeled table sitting over his legs.

"Norm, just put it in that water bottle with the straw in it. See sugar bear, nobody's going to even notice the difference, so just relax."

Sue didn't look happy, but she did what she always did, let out a little huff, and stopped paying attention. Her eyes traveled across her husband, then her son, and then back to the TV. Norm cracked the vodka, filled the water bottle two-thirds full, and then gave it to Gibb who let go of his wife so he could grip it with both hands. Norm smiled at the sight of his brother, sucking at the straw like a little kid, then took a few slugs himself straight from the fifth. He thought about offering Tommy some, but remembered that he was back on the wagon. Guys in AA rarely appreciated being offered a pull. The room lapsed into silence except for the low volume of the TV, the beeping of the machines, and the hiss of Gibb's air hose, doubled by his sucking on the straw. Gibb laid his head back and gave out a pleasurable sigh.

"Damn that's good Norm. Only thing that could make it better right now is if I could get my hands on a cigarette."

"Don't think we'll be able to swing it."

"No, you're probably right about that one Norm. This has just been a hell of a month. Just a real bitch of a time."

Norm didn't answer. He took another pull off the fifth and let his gaze drift back upwards to the TV. The nurse walked by once, glancing in, but didn't stop. When Gibb's water bottle ran dry, Norm refilled it. It didn't take long for the fifth to be empty. Gibb chuckled.

"Fuck Norm. Guess you should have gotten the half gallon."

"Yeah. I guess so."

"Heh. Remember that time we were hunting up off the John Day a couple years ago?"

"Yeah. Up with Tommy and the boys."

"How many bottles did we bring on that trip?"

"I don't know. Probably two cases."

"Yeah, but we only had one because that little pissant friend of Tommy's dropped the other. What was his name Tommy?"

Tommy turned his head a bit towards his father, but kept his focus on the TV.

"Frankie Cafferty."

"That's the one. The little shit who couldn't shoot to save his life. Damn that got to be a dry trip once we got through the case we had left."

Tommy turned his attention away from the TV and allowed himself a smile at his father and uncle.

"You two assholes kept pestering me like two little kids. You kept telling me we needed to load back up and head into town."

"Well, a man has to have priorities."

"It wasn't even noon."

"You can thank Frankie for that."

"We had plenty of beer."

"If I wanted to drink piss I'd call that fag nurse in here."

Gibb chuckled, Tommy laughed, and even Norm let out a few appreciative grunts. Tommy leaned over and shook his father's knee through his blanket.

"My favorite was that time up by Enterprise."

Gibbs's chuckle broke into a few stabs at laughter. Sue looked at him, her face full of concern. Tommy didn't seem to notice.

"You ate that gas station corn dog the night before."

"Oh god, what a mistake that was."

"There I am, sitting on top of that ridge, looking across the canyon at you taking a shit right out in the open. Just moaning and groaning to beat hell. The elk we were waiting for broke from the trees, and there you were, stumbling around, trying not to shit on your pants or shoes, blazing away with your rifle."

"I got one though. By god I got one of the fuckers."

"Yeah, you got a cow, and all we had were bull tags."

"Meat is meat. I can't believe you made us leave it. I ruined a perfectly good pair of pants and didn't get a damn thing in return."

"Don't look at me. Frankie was the one who didn't want to put a poached elk in his pickup for the drive back."

Norm's voice was louder than expected. The way it always was when he'd been drinking.

"He did have a nice pickup. Had the full package. Electric windows and everything."

Gibb winked at his brother.

"Yeah, those electric windows did him a lot of good, didn't they?"

Tommy let out a laugh like a string of firecrackers.

"That time the cattle truck came around the corner?"

"Poor fucker couldn't get them rolled up in time. Just saw all that squirting shit coming right at him. The window slowly inching its way up. God, I can still see his face."

Gibb opened his eyes as wide as he could and let his mouth hang halfway down. Tommy and Norm broke into gales of laughter. Norm slapped his leg appreciatively.

"Those cows must of had a pretty rich diet."

Gibb and Tommy stared at Norm for a second, then broke out in peals of laughter. Gibb started coughing. He couldn't seem to stop. His body bent double and shook with each explosion. Sue scrambled to get the handkerchief over his mouth. The fit subsided. Gibb leaned back, breathing hard. Norm felt the strange combination of revulsion and craving for a cigarette again. The handkerchief was covered in blood. Everybody sat quiet. Norm put the vodka bottle and bag in the garbage. Everyone went back to watching the television. The nurse walked by again, glancing in as he went. After a while a big man in a white coat came in carrying a clipboard. Norm moved over by Tommy to get out of the way.

"Hello Mr. Roberts, I'm Doctor White."

The man stuck out a hand the color of milk chocolate. Everyone stared at the hand, but did nothing. Gibb's face twisted into itself like he'd just drank sour milk. The seconds felt like minutes. Norm reached forward across the bed and took the doctor's hand. Looking him in the eye he gave it a few firm pumps. Tommy, embarrassed, reached forward and shook the doctor's hand as well. Sue kept staring at the TV. Tommy, without thinking about it, wiped his hand on his pants. The doctor let out a sigh. Norm cleared his throat.

"I'll be back in a bit. I need to go have a smoke."

Norm walked out of the room. Careful to keep his footsteps straight. Half a fifth wasn't much, but he hadn't been drinking a lot since Gibb went into the hospital. It didn't feel right to drink alone. Down the hall, past the two nurses gossiping at the nurse's station, down the elevator, through the lobby, and out the big glass sliding doors. A yellow sign next to the door said no smoking within twenty feet. Norm lit up next to the door. Gibb would've wanted it that way. A light rain was falling. Norm shivered and pulled his coat tighter. His first cigarette turned to ash. He lit a second off the first. Halfway through the second cigarette an obviously agitated Tommy came out the sliding glass door.

"The doctor still with Gibb?"

"Beats the hell out of me. I had to get the hell out of there."

"What happened?"

"Dad called the doctor a negro. Shit. Old racist bastard. I've never been so embarrassed in my life."

Norm took out his pack of cigarettes and shook it towards Tommy. Tommy took one and then leaned in close to light it off of Norm's. He inhaled and started coughing. Norm tried to remember the last time he'd seen Tommy smoke.

"Your brother and sister not coming?"

Tommy snorted then spit.

"Fuck no. I'm the only one who will put up with the old bastard. Neither one of them really wants anything to do with him."

"It would be good for Sue."

"I know. I tried calling them, but neither one would call me back."

Norm lit a third cigarette off his second, and stared out into the night. The rain drops started to grow bigger. Tommy coughed again. He wasn't smoking his cigarette any more, just holding it.

"Can't really blame them. I can't believe some of the things the old fucker says. Shit, remember what he said to that groomsman at Martha's wedding. She hasn't talked to him since. Petey might of come, but you know how his wife is. Doesn't want him around their kids. What the fuck is wrong with him?"

"He's just always been that way."

"I know you two grew up in a different time, but fuck, there's a certain point, you know, a certain point you should at least know when to keep your opinions to yourself."

"Gibb has never been much good at that. He's always been a talker. Hell, even when we were kids he learned to talk a whole six months before I did."

"I don't know Uncle Norm. Just the look on that doctor's face."

"Yep."

"What an old bastard."

"That old bastard kept a roof over your head. Worked his ass off to get all three of you through college. Made sure none of you ever really wanted for anything. Never beat any of you or Sue, though god knows our father beat the shit out of us. None of my business, but it seems like it's best to keep it all in perspective. Both the good and the bad."

Tommy didn't say anything, just held his cigarette. Norm dropped his cigarette butt on the sidewalk and smashed it with his work boot.

"Won't matter much soon anyways. I'm going to head back inside. You coming?"

Tommy stared out into the night. The rain drops started to fall faster.

"Nah, I need a moment. I'll be up in a bit."

Norm walked back inside, went back across the lobby, and up the elevator. On the floor of the ICU the old shrew at the nurse's station gave him a dirty look. Norm ignored her. He rounded the corner and walked down the hall to his brother's room. The light was still on. Gibb was watching TV, Sue holding his bony hand. Gibb looked over at his brother, his eyes were sunken in and his head looked like a skull. Gibb turned to Sue, patted her on the arm, and smiled.

"Sugar bear, why don't you go downstairs and get me a Coke out of the machine."

Sue looked at her husband and smiled back. She gripped his hand tighter for a moment, not wanting to let go, then got up and shuffled out of the room. Norm and Gibb watched her go. The two sat in silence for a bit, listening to the beeping of the machines and the hiss of the air hose.

"What did the doctor say?"

"Nothing worth repeating. Besides, wouldn't let the black bastard touch me."

"He might have been able to help."

"Bullshit. I know the score. I've already made up my mind. I'm going to go tonight."

"If that's what you want."

"It is. Don't see much point sticking around. Sure as hell can't go hunting and it's been awhile since I've been able to do any fucking. Those damn pills don't do much for me anymore. Can't smoke and drinking can't be far behind. Not much fun left in life."

"Yeah."

"I want you to promise me something?"

"What's that?"

"I want you to watch out for Sue for me."

"What about the kids?"

"Fuck them, they're all grown. Just watch out for Sue."

"Okay."

"Now I mean just watch out for her. I'm not talking about what I used to rib you about. Get your own damn sugar."

Norm just grunted. It had been a long running joke of Gibb's. Norm had never married. Gibb had always joked that if Norm was ever hard up enough he could just sleep with Sue. The two were twins after all, she probably wouldn't be able to tell the difference. Sometimes Gibb had said it in front of his wife. He had always liked to make Norm turn beat red.

"It's a hell of a thing Norm. A hell of a thing. I never thought I'd be the one to go first. Must have been all my damn talking. Wore my fucking lungs out quicker than you did."

"Must be."

Norm looked down at his brother. Gibb had never seemed so small, so insignificant.

"I'm just so tired Norm. Just so very tired."

Gibb's eyes began to flutter. His ragged breathing slowed and started to become more regular. The bony hands convulsed, tightened around the blanket, and then let loose. The skin on his hands looked like paper. Large black bruises covered the left hand where Sue had been holding on. Gibb smiled up at his brother, for a second lost in some happier moment, and then his face turned serious once again.

"Promise me Norm. Promise me you'll look after Sue. Lots of niggers around here."

"Okay."

Norm stood quiet by the bed. Gibb fell into peaceful slumber, and never woke again.

# Tuesday

The eagle dove from the cliff edge. Its majestic body fell past the sharp drop of the basalt cliffs and then floated above the steady decline of the pale hillside, splashed yellow by the cheat grass waving in the wind, dotted with isolated patches of green marking the remaining bunchgrass. The eagle rode just above the tops of the junipers, gliding on outstretched wings. The wings began to flap, carrying the eagle higher. The hot sun above, slowly baking the world below, reflected off the hills. The eagle rode the thermals high into the sky. The world spread out below it. The bend of the river, surrounded by the pale green of the willows. The scattered buildings of the town. The black snake of the highway. Up into the sky. Up amongst the clouds. The brown and speckled form shrank into the blue. Shrinking to an indistinct dot, before disappearing entirely from view.

Three men sat and watched as the eagle made its ascent. They leaned against white painted cinder blocks below boarded up windows trimmed with gray and yellow, hiding in the slim pool of shade which slowly made its way around the wreck.

Isaac, the one furthest on the right, belched and scratched his prodigious belly through his heavily stained t-shirt. Once it was black, now just a grimy darkened gray. He tapped Joe, the man next to him, on the shoulder and Joe passed over the plastic half gallon jug with HRD blazoned on the label. Isaac kicked back his head and took a swallow of the clear liquid, grimacing at the taste. He handed the jug back to Joe and wiped the sweat from his forehead with the back of his arm.

"Hot today."

Frank, the man on the left, grunted, but kept his hat pulled low and his eyes shut.

"Hot every day."

"Yeah, but it seems hotter today than yesterday."

Joe took a pull and held the jug in his hands. His eyes traced across the empty cement block which once held pumps. Thin light poles which no longer lit. A tall sign devoid of markings, the plastic once in the metal frames all smashed and gone.

"I don't know. It seems about the same to me."

Frank grunted again and shifted his bulk, pulling his feet closer to get his worn leather boots out of the sun. Joe handed him the jug. Frank took a snort without opening his eyes and handed it back.

"Don't see how it really matters none. When it gets this hot, it's just hot. Nothing more to say."

Joe nodded and took a drink. Isaac ran a hand through his greasy salt and pepper hair and scratched his shoulder, next to the ragged line where the sleeves had been torn off the day before. Joe passed the jug. Isaac tipped it back, held the fiery liquid in his mouth, and then swallowed.

"Might rain tomorrow."

Frank grunted.

"Doubt it. Too damn hot to rain."

"If it rained it might get cooler."

Frank grunted again. Isaac looked out over the highway at the willows shielding the river from view.

"Maybe we could go down by the river. Might be cooler by the river."

The other two men stayed silent. Isaac studied the label on the jug. The letters black, red, and gold on the white background. His eyes ran across the concrete, ragged with cracks and scattered colonies of dandelions. A broken white cap lay next to Frank's feet. The plastic flow regulator from the jug lay out in the sunshine, next to a line of ants moving back and forth from one crack to another.

"I said, maybe we should go down by the river."

A car flashed by on the black strip of the highway. A big white pickup with duals. Joe and Isaac watched it whip past. Frank kept his eyes closed.

"Lots of traffic for a weekday."

Frank took the jug and downed a pull.

"Getting to be that time of the year."

A big yellow cat slinked along the edge of the concrete pad, pausing every few steps to stop and listen. Joe rubbed the scattered stubble on his face. The cat crouched for a moment, its tail flicking right and left, and then leaped. A small brown bird flew out from beneath a sagebrush, just out of reach. The cat looked at the three men in the shade, sat on its haunches, and began to clean its paws. Joe picked up an empty beer bottle and hucked it out into the sun. The brown glass glinted and then shattered on the concrete two feet from the cat. The cat leaped up and ran deeper into the grass. Frank opened his eyes for a moment and grunted.

"What the fuck you doing that for?"

"It's just a damn cat."

"Cut that shit out. If they start finding glass out here it's just going to be trouble."

"Calm down."

Frank closed his eyes again. Joe took the half gallon and swallowed a slug. He coughed a few times and spit. Isaac watched the cat moving through the grass.

"That cat oughta go down by the river. Probably a lot more critters for him to hunt down by the river."

Isaac took the jug and had a drink. Another car rolled by. This one an SUV with kayaks on the roof rack. A small child stared at the three men as it rolled past. Isaac lowered the jug and averted his gaze. Joe stared back, his eyes black, the whites turned yellow. The cat came back out of the weeds and sat mewing at the edge of the concrete. Joe hucked another beer bottle, which fell about five feet short. The cat ran back into the weeds, but kept mewing out of sight.

"Wish that fucking cat would shut up."

Isaac handed Joe the half gallon.

"Just leave it alone."

Joe took a pull from the jug, his Adam's apple bobbing several times. A skinny youth came up out of the willows by the river. He wore cutoffs and a once white shirt with its pearl snaps half unbuttoned. A fishing pole rested on his shoulder. The young man stopped at the black asphalt edge of the highway. His head moved left and right. He crossed, his flipflops flapping. The thin form moved across the concrete, leaving wet footprints in his wake, and stopped at the edge of the shade. Quick brown eyes, darting across the landscape and the three old bears. He licked his chapped lips and waited. Granules of salt stood out on his forehead. The three bears stared past him, only moving to pass the half gallon or to scratch their heavy bellies. The young man licked his chapped lips again.

"How are you guys today?"

Joe's eyes tracked across the weeds at the edge of the concrete, looking for the mewing yellow form. He let his jaundiced view come to rest on the pile of skin and bones.

"Hot today."

The young man shifted his weight to his other foot and moved his pole to his other shoulder.

"Yeah, I guess so."

Joe took the jug from Isaac and let his attention drift. Isaac eyed the rapidly drying footprints behind the youth.

"Catch anything?"

The nervous eyes of the young man flitted over towards Isaac.

"A couple of squaw fish. Cut them up for bait. Got a few good bites, but couldn't get anything to set."

Isaac nodded. The young man stood quiet, shifting his weight back to his original leg and moving the pole back to his starting shoulder. His eyes followed the half gallon as it moved to Frank, tipped upwards, and then moved back towards Joe. Isaac and Joe watched the young man's eyes. The young man licked his lips again.

"This heat sure makes a man thirsty."

Joe smiled in a friendly manner.

"Yep."

The young man rubbed the sweat off his free hand onto the front of his cutoffs.

"Mind if I have a drink?"

Joe gave a chuckle and leaned forward, holding out the jug. The young man took a step forward. Frank's eyes flashed open and he lunged, pushing Joe's arm back down. His other arm shot out, his index finger pointing back towards the river.

"You get the fuck out of here!"

The young man took a step back. Joe started laughing.

"Fuck, ain't no harm."

Frank gestured with his arm again.

"Get the fuck out of here. Go back to fishing or something else worthwhile!"

The young man's shoulders rose up. His free hand tightened into a fist, his knuckles turning white.

"Christ. All I did was ask for a drink. No need to get all crazy about it."

Frank snatched up an empty beer bottle and hucked it at the youth. The brown glass shattered next to the young man's feet in their flip flops. The young man jumped and backed away. Joe started laughing so hard that he broke into a coughing fit. Isaac watched in silence. Frank reached for another empty beer bottle.

"I said get the fuck out of here! I catch you around here again I'll beat your sorry ass!"

The bottle flew and landed with a crash. The young man ran down the highway, back towards the town. Frank lifted a third empty bottle, but then put it back on the ground. He took the half gallon from Joe and tipped it back. The jug sounded several good glugs. Joe kept laughing.

"Fuck man, what about the broken glass?"

Frank let the jug drop.

"Shut up."

Joe took the jug and passed it over to Isaac.

"You seemed awful worked up about it before."

Frank lowered his hat again, shut his eyes, and wiggled his body to get comfortable again.

"I said shut up about it."

Joe kept chuckling. Isaac took a drink and studied the willows across the highway. Another car came past, a little four door sedan. The sound of the passing car covered up the steady flow of the river for a moment. Isaac cleared his throat and spit.

"We should go fishing. It would be a nice day for it. I bet it's nice and cool down by the river."

Joe took the jug and took a drink. Frank breathed slow and steady. Joe took another drink for Frank. Isaac watched the clear liquid in the jug move down Joe's throat. Isaac twisted a finger in his ear and cleared his throat again.

"What do you say Joe? Why don't we wander up to your house to get some poles?"

Joe set the jug down on the concrete and spit out into the sun.

"You want to get the damn poles knock yourself out. I'm not going back there. The old lady is on a tear."

"What's got her all worked up?"

"The usual. That damn brother of hers been talking up his job again. Showing off his new pickup, having us over for dinner, all that shit. Peckerhead offered to hook me up with a job. The old lady wants me to take him up on it."

"That doesn't sound so bad. What would you do? Work behind a desk or something?"

Joe rubbed his forehead with the back of his arm and spit again.

"Oh yeah, wouldn't that be a sight. All dressed up and playing nice. Might as well just be sucking their dicks out back. End up with the same taste in your mouth. No, I'd be a fucking janitor. Cleaning toilets. Little shit had the balls to tell me we all have to start somewhere. I'm ten years older than that peckerhead. Almost knocked his block off. Now the wife won't shut up about it. Keeps going on about all the crap we could have. Fuck, the checks are coming in, don't know what more she wants. Might as well just start working on the side of the road for handouts. An ass fucking's an ass fucking. Fucking bitch."

Frank snorted and released a short chuckle.

"Why don't you just give her a good slap?"

Isaac glared at Frank. Joe grunted.

"Fuck, anymore the bitch is about as big as me. Can't say for sure she wouldn't be able to clean my clock."

Frank chuckled again. He reached over, grabbed the jug, and took a drink. A light wind blew across the willows, bending their branches for a brief moment. Isaac wiped the sweat from his eyes.

"God I bet it would be nice down by the river."

The other two men said nothing, lost in their own thoughts. The big yellow cat came out of the weeds again and slinked down the edge of the concrete towards the highway. Isaac's eyes followed the bony animal, watching the movement of tight muscles beneath mangy fur. The cat stopped at the edge of the black asphalt and sniffed at the hot surface. Isaac smiled.

"Looks like that cats got the right idea. Betcha he'll have better luck hunting down by the river."

The small head moved to the left and then to the right. The cat started its way across. A pickup came around the corner and started to blare its horn. The cat moved forward and then back, unsure which way to jump. The pickup swerved and the big tires squealed. Isaac turned his head away. The pickup sped on, the sound of laughter emanating from its open windows. The cat lay on the highway, its back half flattened against the asphalt. Isaac stared at the bloodied mound of yellow fur. Tears filled his eyes and flowed down his cheeks. Joe looked over and shook his head.

"What the fuck is wrong with you?"

"Nothing. None of your business."

"Fuck. Are you crying over that damn cat?"

The tears were really flowing now. An unstoppable torrent making their way down Isaac's chubby cheeks.

"Just leave it alone."

"It's just a fucking cat."

Frank opened his eyes and glanced over. The edge of his right side was lit by the sun.

"Shades moved."

The three men got up, moved seven feet farther down the wall, and sat back down. Joe brought the half gallon. He took a drink and passed it over to Isaac. Isaac wiped his eyes with the back of his hand, snorted, and spit a large loogie into the sunlight. He stared at the jug for a moment, studying the slosh of the clear liquid inside. He looked up at the dead cat, already attracting flies. A crow cawed from the willows and flapped over to the edge of the highway. Isaac breathed in deep, exhaled, and breathed in deep again. A light hot breeze rustled the weeds at the edge of the concrete. A drop flowed down the side of the half gallon, joining the sweat on Isaac's fingers. He took a drink and passed the jug back to Joe who took a drink and passed it on to Frank. Isaac blew a snot rocket out of each nostril.

"I bet he would of had a real nice time down by the river."

Frank opened one eye to look at the dead cat, and then closed it again.

"Yeah, I imagine so."

The hot sun climbed higher into the sky.

# Skills

The old Peterbilt crested the last hill and started the long drop into Roseburg. It had been a long haul. Nearly twelve hours to Burns and back hauling a load of backgrounders to fatten up for the summer. The drive hadn't been bad, a little heavy rain by Diamond Lake, but nothing that Dave hadn't encountered before. The sun sat low in the sky in the windshield, blocked by the lowered visor. The jake brake growled as the truck wound its way back and forth. Dave watched the empty cattle trailer through the rearview mirrors at each corner, keeping it on his side of the yellow line. Waves of shit poured from the aluminum walls of the trailer onto the highway with each turn. The steers had been loose today. There was no doubt about that.

The truck reached the flats and Dave opened her up, letting her scoot. The dashed yellow lines whipped past the driver side window. Dave's stomach growled. He hadn't had much lunch. Just a bag of corn chips and a bottle of pop. He had thought about stopping in Bend, but it had only been two so he had decided to press his way on through. It was best to keep going when you got into the groove, once your brain went into automatic and the miles started to whip past. The radio provided a comforting background hum. Songs that all sounded the same, ads for local businesses, and newscasters talking about celebrity gossip and the boys over in Iraq. Dave never really listened to any of it, but it was noticeable if it wasn't there.

Dave stifled a heavy yawn. He'd been up since four that morning. Far too long to be sitting in an old truck. His ass hurt, his back hurt, and his shoulders felt sore. He knew he probably shouldn't complain. Mr. Carrington paid him well. Dave was a hard worker and dependable. When Mr. Carrington needed a job done, he knew he could count on Dave to do it. That was more than could be said of the other assholes working for the old man. Most couldn't be trusted with a four wheeler, let alone a truck full of steers. They just worked to live. Dave took pride in the things he did. He tried to do everything to the best of his ability. Mr. Carrington knew it, and treated Dave accordingly. Dave had skills.

It wasn't as though he had much choice. He doubted Dana would put up with much shit if he let himself go. From the start she had made it obvious that it wouldn't take much for her to pack her crap up, take the kids, and go. Dave had been a little rough when they first married. The type that liked to have a few too many drinks and carry on a bit. It had never seemed that bad to Dave. He had never missed a day of work or done anything too stupid. He had never been like the other idiots working for Mr. Carrington, or the folks around town that Dana had termed as losers. Regardless of his opinion, it hadn't taken Dana long to smooth him up. By god, he was a family man now, and he had better damn well start acting like it if he wanted her to stick around. Dave had given in. He had never paid Dana and the kids much mind, she was always squawking about this or that, but like the radio, he was sure he'd miss it if it wasn't there.

Dave's belly gurgled again. It would be another half hour to the house up by Sutherlin. He might as well stop in Roseburg for dinner. There wasn't much reason to hurry his way home. Dana wouldn't be there. It was Thursday. Dana always spent Thursday nights down at the Seven Feathers with her mother, playing the nickel slots. The kids would be with her father, watching old movies that would most likely give them nightmares. Dana yelled at her old man every time about it, but it didn't seem to faze him. He had been at it a lot longer than Dave. There wouldn't be much to eat at the house. Maybe some hot dogs left defrosting in the sink if he was lucky. Eating in town seemed a much better option. If he went some place cheap Dana wouldn't be able to complain too much about the cost. She was always going on about the budget.

The red and green sign of Abby's Pizza rolled towards him. Dave hit the blinker, turned the wheel, and pulled into the big gravel parking lot. The clock glowed five o'clock. The roar of the engine died. Dave kicked open the door and felt cool evening air wash over him, followed by the stench of the trailer. He hung his legs over the side and shook them for a moment, enjoying the feeling of them loose and free, and then jumped to the ground below. Flies had already started to gather around the trailer. Dave's boots and the lower half of his pants were caked in dry cow shit. Dave kicked the bottom of each boot against the truck tire and scraped them on the hubcap, wiping off any bits still stuck in the creases of the rubber soles. Abby's wasn't that discerning, but that was no excuse for tracking shit in.

The place was mostly empty. A fat woman and a teenage girl working behind the counter, a cook in a white apron working in the back, three kids in little league uniforms, around age ten or so, eating pizza at one of the tables, and the steady ding of the video poker machines in their little side room, hidden away behind a saloon style swinging door. Dave walked up to the counter and studied the menu over the fat woman's head. Her name tag called her Barbara. The teenager hustled off to rub an old wet rag across tables that didn't need it. The little league boys looked up briefly, then went back to eating.

Dave's eyes roved across his options. Different sizes, deep dish or thin crust, and a long list of toppings. His mouth watered at the thought of the hot layers of crust, sauce, and cheese. The fat woman waited, her marshmallowy arms crossed on top of her belly. Dave rubbed one hand across his own stomach.

"I'll have a salad," said Dave.

The woman nodded and rang him up.

"Anything to drink?"

"A regular fountain drink."

"Eight fifty."

Dave pulled his wallet out of his back pocket and handed over a crisp new twenty dollar bill. Dana had pulled it and a couple of others out of the ATM just the day before. She had given two to Dave that morning. The fat woman handed back his change and gave him a number and an empty paper cup. Dave walked over to the fountain drink machine, filled the cup with ice, started to fill the cup with Coke, thought better of it, and switched to Diet Coke instead.

Dave took a seat at a table across the room from the little league boys. They were talking quietly to each other, and every now and again broke out into loud shrill laughter. Two of the boys were Mexicans, they looked like brothers, matching black hair and brown eyes. The third boy had sandy hair and gray eyes. All three wore hats and t-shirts identifying them as the Roseburg Indians. Baseball gloves sat on the table next to them. From the few yammered words that made their way across the room it was obvious they were switching between talking about their latest game and trading what they thought of as dirty jokes.

The sandy haired boy noticed Dave staring. He stared back. Dave felt awkward and broke the gaze, his eyes tracing across the ceiling tiles and down to the flashing lights of the arcade machines in the corner. There were three of them. A racing game with a steering wheel and gear shifter, a claw machine filled with stuffed toys, and a crane machine filled with candy. The racing game was the most interesting to stare at. Sports cars speeding across beaches, snow covered mountains, city highways, and mountain roads. A change machine stood next to the arcade games. Dave took a drink of his pop and grimaced. The teenager brought out his salad and walked away. Dave couldn't help but notice that she was old enough to have some curves. He quickly looked away, feeling like a pervert. The fat woman behind the counter gave him the eye and then walked back into the kitchen.

The salad was bland, the iceberg lettuce limp, more white than green. The tomatoes were pale and watery. The small paper cup worth of ranch was nowhere near enough to make up for the salad's shortcomings. It seemed stupid to Dave to be eating a salad at a pizza place, even a lousy chain one like Abby's, but he had promised Dana that he'd watch his diet. He was tired of the constant comments about his so-called trucker belly. It was just easier to do what she asked. She'd know if he lied. Somehow she always knew.

The two Mexican boys rose and picked up their gloves. A round of goodbyes was exchanged and the two went outside and started walking down the road. The sandy haired boy watched them through the window, sipping on his pop, until they were out of sight. The boy got up and refilled his cup, a mixture of Coke and Sprite, then went back to his table. The teenager came by and picked up the empty pizza tray. The boy sat and played with a discarded straw wrapper, one foot kicking repetitively against the leg of the table. Dave watched the boy from the corner of his eye as he forced down his salad.

The saloon doors to the side room with the video poker machines swung open and an old lady walked through. Her leathery face was covered in deep wrinkles. Her permed hair was a solid shade of brown that could not be its original color. She wore stained black slacks and an old sweatshirt emblazoned with two deer in a forest scene. Her back was slightly hunched, her head constantly peering forward. Two gray eyes locked on the boy through thick glasses. She walked over stiffly and laid a bony hand on his shoulder.

"Your little friends head home?"

The old lady's voice sounded like she spent her time gargling vodka and thumb tacks. The boy kept his eyes locked on the table in front of him.

"Yeah."

"It will just be a little while longer. I've got a streak going."

The old lady reached into her purse, pulled out a twenty dollar bill, and laid it on the table next to the boy. Without another word from either she turned and went back through the saloon style doors. The boy sat quiet for a bit. His eyes focusing first on the table, then outside across the parking lot and down the street. Dave got up and refilled his cup with more Diet Coke. He needed it to help choke down the salad. The boy grabbed the twenty, got up, and walked over to the change machine. He slipped the bill in and the machine spit it back out. He flattened the bill against the top of the machine, rubbing his hand across it, and then tried again. The machine accepted the bill and started spitting out quarters. The boy filled his hat with the quarters and walked over to the racing game.

Each play was a dollar. The boy selected his car, a bright red Ferrari, and selected his course, The Mountain Road. A pixelated woman in a bikini waved the starting flag. The race was on. The course reminded Dave of the portion of his own drive down by Diamond Lake. A curving highway crowded on either side by evergreens broken only by sheer rocky drops. The boy expertly whipped his car around the corners, upshifting and downshifting as needed. The other cars fell behind. It was over in just a few minutes. The same pixelated bikini clad woman waved the checkered flag. The words HIGH SCORE flashed across the screen. The high score screen appeared and the boy turned the wheel this way and that to spell out the initials SRC. All of the scores on the screen were next to the same initials. The boy put in another dollar and picked another course. He won that one too. All of the high scores were under the same initials. The boy played ten times in a row.

Dave finished his salad. The teenager came by and picked up his plate and silverware. Dave sipped on his pop and watched the boy who had moved over to the candy crane machine. He put his head close to the glass, searching across the piles of candy inside. His eyes locked. His hands moved without hesitation. The crane reached out and picked up the chosen morsel. The boy repeated the process seven more times. The candy was put in his hat and he scooted over to the next machine. It was much the same as the candy crane, but cost two dollars. The boy leaned in and picked his target. His hands moved deftly. The claw dropped a stuffed Seattle Seahawks doll into the bottom drawer. The boy retrieved it. Out of money, and his hat full, the boy went back to his table, sitting with his back to Dave. He slowly munched his way through each piece of candy, staring out the window.

Dave's pop cup was empty, but he stayed at his table. The teenager came by the boy's table and picked up all the wrappers. After a bit the old lady came through the swinging doors again. She looked even more folded over. The boy watched her as she approached. Dave couldn't see the expression on the boy's face, but his back straightened and his shoulders rose higher.

"Just going to be a little bit longer. This is one hell of a streak."

The boy nodded and his body slumped back down into his chair. He turned and went back to staring out the window. The old lady stared at the boy's profile.

"You want any more money?"

The boy shook his head no.

"Okay, like I said, just a little bit longer."

The old lady turned and shuffled back into the side room with the video poker machines. The boy stared at the Seahawks stuffed toy in his hat, took it out, turned it in his hand, and then placed it off to the side at the edge of his reach. The boy looked up and noticed Dave staring at him. The boy's gray eyes gave the same defiant look as before. Dave again broke the gaze, feeling embarrassed. Dave got up and started for the door, stopping by the fountain drink machine on his way out. His hand hovered over the Diet Coke button. He looked back at the boy. The boy was staring out the window again. Waiting. Dave shifted his finger over and filled his cup with Coke. He snapped on a plastic to go lid, grabbed a straw, and walked out the door to the waiting truck.

# Five Reasons IKEA Will Ruin Your Relationship

So, you've finally found somebody who is crazy in just the right way to be compatible with you. You've been dating a little while, had a few ups and downs, and now feel secure enough in the relationship to take the big step of moving in together. However, like any young couple, you soon come to realize that a) the hodge podge of furniture the two of you currently own doesn't fill half of your new shared domicile, and b) the stuff you do own looks like it was scavenged from a dumpster behind a Goodwill. It's at this point that one of you comes up with the brilliant idea of making a trip out to IKEA, and hence begins the end of your relationship.

**1) IKEA Is A Damn Maze**

Every grocery store in the country is exactly the same in that the milk is always in the back. Grocery stores do this because every time people go into a grocery store, they're going to need milk and it forces them to walk past everything else, increasing the chance of impulse buys. IKEA has somehow managed to design their stores so that every single item is the milk. It doesn't matter what you want, you're going to have to go through the entire store to get it. Nobody goes to IKEA to just browse. Anyone who has been foolish enough to try is still wandering the store, surviving on meatballs and sleeping each night in the display showing you how you can live in 50 square feet or less. Preparing to go to IKEA is like planning the Invasion of Normandy. You write out lists, make plans, form timetables, and watch it all go to hell the moment you walk by the first Poang chair. "What's this, only $70, we'd have to be crazy not to get it."

Things quickly fall apart from there and you find yourself wandering aimlessly from department to department, suffering from permanent déjà vu as you walk by the same Billy bookcase for the twelfth time. You start to have flashbacks to the hours of your childhood wasted playing Gauntlet. One of you come up with the idea of trying one of the so-called short cut routes, only to find that you've been magically transported back to the beginning of the maze. Somewhere high above from unseen windows a group of Swedish behavioral scientists scratch hurriedly on paper pads as they talk amongst each other excitedly.

In desperation you ask a store employee for directions, only to discover that the entirety of their employee training involved watching that scene from the movie Labyrinth where one guard can only tell the truth and one guard can only lie. Finally, at the moment you're ready to give up, you find one of the items you're actually looking for, somehow magically right next to those same damn Billy bookshelves.

## 2) You'll Be Forced To Realize That Your Significant Other Has Bad Taste

When you're young you have no cares and also no money. The result is your furnishings are less of a representation of your own eclectic tastes, and more a mish mash of whatever you could scavenge whenever your better off family and friends got new furniture. No more though, you're now some kind of moderately successful adult. This is the dawning of a new age. This is your chance to at last show the world how urbane and sophisticated you really are.

Of course your significant other is thinking the same thing, and when they pick up their first Boja table lamp, you'll be forced to realize that their definition of urbane is very different from your own. At this point many of you will be reminding yourselves that relationships are about compromise. That is, until you notice that your significant other apparently wants to decorate your home in a style somewhere between a bad Chinese restaurant in Omaha and your Uncle Barry's shagging pad. You know, Uncle Barry, the one with the sideburns who still wears polyester suits to Thanksgiving.

Forgetting that your significant other is just as frustrated as you are after your two hour trek to reach this point, you casually bring up the fact that you do not really like that style of lamp. Your significant other in response states that they really like the lamp and that it will really tie together the room they have envisioned. With your mind now filled with images of a style motif best described as a rave at a Thai brothel, you calmly declare that there is no way you want that ugly lamp in your home, representing the two of you as a couple. Your significant other takes this as you declaring everything they cherish as total crap and the fight is on.

Fifteen minutes later, both of you are being held back by IKEA employees as you sob like a small child and your loved one apologizes for calling you a fascist megalomaniac with the interior decorating sense of Joseph Stalin. The two of you agree to a lamp that neither one of you like, write the relevant number on your ticket, and head out in search of couches to repeat the process again.

## 3) Boxes Galore

After about your fifth major argument where all communication has broken down to a system of grunts (one for yes and two for no), the two of you agree to collect the items you have chosen and get out of the hellhole that is IKEA as quickly as possible. Hope renewed by a foreseeable exit, you leave the show room section of the store and head into the self-service item collection area. At first you push each other on the oversized cart and it seems like the past few hours may be forgotten, but then your significant other compares the maze of shelves and boxes to the top secret government warehouse in Kingdom of the Crystal Skull and you find yourself looking at them like they're a total stranger who is actively crapping on everything right with the world. Choking down your desire to throttle the stain on humankind you once thought you were in love with, the two of you start searching for the right boxes. A process not helped by the fact that you wrote down all the item numbers in a post argument haze of adrenaline and hate. Of course you make the mistake of handing off the list to your significant other, which then leads to them questioning your ability to write and you questioning their ability to read.

As you start to find the maybe correct boxes, you discover that every single one is awkwardly shaped, and they all weigh a ton, even the one that is supposed to contain cushions. Something you become increasingly aware of as every second box requires the entire cart to be unloaded and reloaded again to keep everything correctly balanced. On the plus side, the beads of sweat covering your face hide the fact that you're crying.

Finally, unable to take anymore, you grab a few more boxes without bothering to check the numbers and make your escape through the checkout line. As soon as you clear the check-out, your last in-store argument takes place when the two of you realize that there is no way you can fit all your purchases into a

Ford Focus, resulting in a reenactment of a year old argument over whether or not you should have gotten the model with the hatchback. Swallowing your pride, you get in another line to pay even more money to have someone else deliver your items to your home while your significant other openly asks strangers whether they'd be interested in trying their hand at contract murder.

## 4) Putting It All Together

As you leave the monster that is the IKEA behind, you finally breathe a sigh of relief, convinced that the worst is behind you, and that the rifts created in the store, while daunting, can be repaired. This of course is utter and complete crap because the greatest challenge still lies ahead. You still have to put all that furniture together.

Imagine doing extremely hard math problems. Now imagine doing extremely hard math problems while your loved one screams suggestions over your shoulder, sobs inconsolably, and questions your basic mental capacity. That hypothetical thought experiment will be one hundred times more enjoyable than putting together your new IKEA furniture.

IKEA made the bold decision of saving money on translating instructions by instead printing them in a complicated language of pictographs involving a man who is always creepily happy with his life of putting together shoddy furniture. The pictograph is a lie. Nobody smiles while putting together IKEA furniture. There are more ways to interpret IKEA instructions than there are ways to interpret Mona Lisa's smile. Does that symbol represent the slightly longer screw or the slightly shorter screw? You can bet your significant other will have a different opinion.

It should come as no surprise that at least one or two parts will be missing from your boxes. Most likely some little screw, or maybe a peg. This will force either you or your significant other to return to the time-suck that is the IKEA to stand around in line while some guy named Doug searches for the part in the back and the woman behind you in line talks loudly on her cell phone about the color of her baby's poops.

The only thing worse than not having all the pieces, is having one too many of something. You finish putting together your couch, look down, and see a lonely lag bolt lying by itself in the plastic bag that once contained a multitude of its brethren. It's probably just an extra bolt, but maybe you screwed up in a way that will make the entire couch collapse at the most inopportune time. Which assumption do you think your significant other will make?

On the plus side, you do get some pretty nifty cheaply made tools to put in your junk drawer and never use again.

## 5) The Nail In The Coffin

Your furniture only half assembled, you and your significant other call it a night, hoping that the light of a new day will bring hope back to your relationship. It's at this point that IKEA deploys its last sinister plot to end your relationship. While visiting the store you of course made the customary stop to enjoy some of the store's delicious so-called Swedish meatballs. You of course did this because it is the only real highlight of going to IKEA. Thus are planted the seeds of your final destruction.

A slowly ticking time bomb sits in your gut, waiting for you to put yourself in the horizontal position before unleashing a torrent of stink particles to assault the delicate nasal cavities of your loved one. On any other day this would just be an inconvenience, but after a day dealing with IKEA and its sadistic ploys, your stench is comparable to you stating that your significant other's mother assisted in the Holocaust. The last bit of civility is gone, and you can bet you'll be spending the night sleeping on a half built Karlstad couch.

The next morning you avoid looking at each other, and without actually ever stating the end of the relationship, you pack your bags and move out. Soon after you acquire yourself a nice studio apartment somewhere, and head out to the IKEA to furnish it, thus increasing quarterly profits for a company that benefits from more people living alone.

# Late Night Text

The last few months have not been the best for me. I've been fighting depression again. I feel like I have isolated myself, walled myself back up. Though I know I have lots of people who care about me, I feel more alone than I have for a while. I find myself filled with doubts, a constant battle to keep them at bay. I find my mind wandering back to a past world that will never exist again.

I feel alone because I don't know anyone like me. It makes me sad. I know that's why when I'm down I think back to her, because in many ways she was like me. For a short period I felt content, and I miss that. Maybe it was the only prolonged period of contentment in my life.

I so rarely feel content. I rarely feel in the here and now. I can't seem to stay in the present, and time keeps slipping by, a never ending march. Everything keeps getting compared to the ideal, and that's not a fair way to judge.

I know I'm different. The way my mind works is different. The quickness, the clarity, the memories never fading, all of it never slowing down. I know it, but I deny it, even to myself. What is the point of saying it out loud? Trying to show off how smart you are only alienates. I'm already poor at social skills and making connections. Why make it any worse?

I never liked the ones who are arrogant. The ones who see themselves as better, some type of elite because their brains work differently. Assholes. I'd rather be with everyone. But I never feel quite there. I don't feel like I'm a part of the whole, rather just a visitor, trying his best to fake customs he doesn't understand in order to fit in.

I feel like I could do anything I set my mind to, but I doubt myself. I feel scared. Scared of being more alone. Sometimes I feel like it doesn't matter what I do. I remind myself that everything each of us do is important, but it makes me feel guilty that I don't do more. It is all so immense. Everything feels so small. At times it makes everything I do feel so pointless compared to the grand scale of it all.

I know there are others like me, but so many of them seem to be broken in some way. Crazy. It scares me. Is that to be my fate, or has it already taken place and I just don't realize it? It makes me feel more alone.

This is getting long. I'm sorry for the random thought late night text. I guess I just needed to say some things out loud. Drag them out of the confines of my head and into the light of day. I'm not good at that, and I know that it makes it worse.

Don't worry. Just releasing. Purging. I'm not sure what to say now. How to finish up. Thank you for making me feel like you want to listen. And thank you for always reminding me what a wonderful place the world is.

# Enema

Ray's dad didn't want to take him, but Ray put up enough of a hassle that he finally did. It had been an easy guilt trip to lay. Ray's dad only got to see him every other weekend during the school year and every other week during the summer. What was the point of it if Ray was just going to sit in the trailer house all day watching television? Ray's grandmother had been an advocate, her other concerns and suspicions easily overwhelmed by her staunch belief in the necessity of a paternal role model.

Ray didn't really want to go with his dad, but he had woken up that morning with a bit of a stomach ache. The cause of the stomach ache was no mystery, an overindulgence in popcorn and candy at the movie his dad had taken him to the night before. His grandmother had noticed right off when she came into the tiny room he shared with her sewing machine. Her dyed brown hair was up in curlers and she was already smoking the first cigarette of the day.

"You feeling okay squirt?"

"Yep. Fit as a fiddle."

Ray's lie had been obvious, but his grandmother only grunted and told him to hurry his ass up for breakfast. The unappetizing pile of oatmeal slopped in his bowl had done nothing to help his situation, but Ray had forced himself to eat every bite. Nothing got by his grandmother. She watched every movement of the spoon, slowly forking runny eggs into her mouth and puffing on her cigarette with its growing witch's tail. No one else paid him any mind. His grandfather hid behind the newspaper and his dad ate his own breakfast, chewing every bite fifteen times and shifting his plate an eighth of a turn after every bite. The full glass of pulp laden orange juice had nearly pushed Ray over the edge. The old lady's eyes narrowed after the glass hit the table.

"You sure you're feeling okay?"

"Yeah. Definitely."

Ray's grandmother was a big believer in the healing powers of a good enema. A little water squirted up one's ass could cure whatever ailed them. Upset stomach. Enema. Constipated. Enema. Head cold. Enema. Sore tooth. Enema. Feeling depressed. Enema. Ray's grandmother had raised three boys to adulthood and not one of them had escaped the miracle of the rubber bag and its long snaking hose she kept in the closet with the towels. Not even Ray's grandfather could avoid the occasional blast of warm water. Ray's grandmother claimed that the old man actually enjoyed them. Ray wasn't sure about that, the old man rarely said anything beyond an affirmative grunt or a negative groan.

Ray's grandmother had easily seen through Ray's lie, but lacked the support to apply her curative. She first attempted to gain the approval of Ray's grandfather.

"Doesn't he look sick Don?"

The old man had said nothing beyond the rustle of the paper as he turned the page. His hearing aids were undoubtedly turned off. Ray's grandfather preferred his solitude and going deaf had been more of a blessing than a curse. Ray's grandmother had next moved on to Ray's dad, a man whose will to resist she had broken long ago.

"Doesn't he look sick Randy?"

Ray's dad had been busily attempting to strain the pulp from his orange juice with his teeth. The old woman's words shocked him out of his own thoughts. He put the glass down and leaned forward to more closely examine his eight year old son, orange pulp hanging from his mustache.

"He looks okay to me. You feeling sick Ray?"

Ray's grandmother didn't give him a chance to answer.

"He looks sick to me."

Ray had known that he didn't have much time. His dad might resist at first, but his grandmother would needle until she got her way. The old woman lit her second cigarette . Ray took the opportunity to divert the conversation.

"Can I go with you today Pop?"

Ray's dad had leaned back in his chair and sucked the pulp out of his mustache.

"I don't know Ray. Not really much for you to do."

The diversion worked. His grandmother's attention was shifted to a more important cause.

"Nonsense Randy. We spent all that money on a lawyer to make sure you got to see the boy. You might as well take him with you."

"It doesn't really seem like the type of thing you take your kid to."

"Nonsense. Having Ray around might even be useful."

Ray's dad had taken a deep breath. Ray's grandfather had returned to the protective wall of the newspaper.

"What do you think Don?"

Everyone waited expectantly. A gnarled old hand missing the pinky finger emerged, tapped the ash off a cigarette into the ashtray, and retreated. Ray's grandmother turned back to Ray's dad.

"There Randy, it's settled."

Ray had been sent back to brush his teeth and get dressed. Ray's grandmother did the breakfast dishes. Ray's dad came back to the bathroom and shaved, exactly three beats against the sink every time he rinsed the razor. Ray's dad spent extra time to make sure he got every whisker and combed and parted his thinning brown hair. When they left the bathroom Ray's dad flicked the lights off, back on, and then off again. The pair put on their coats and headed towards the trailer house door, Ray's grandmother yelling quiz questions to Ray's dad as they went.

"You have the pickup keys?"

"Yes Mom."

"You have your application?"

"Yes Mom."

"Did you remember to take your pill?"

"Yes Mom."

"Don't screw this up. Remember that Eddie stuck his neck out for you on this one."

"I know."

"Be polite, and look them in the eye."

"I know."

"Don't....."

The rest had been cut off by the closing door. It was cold outside. A few blackbirds flew from tree to tree, landing in gnarled branches exposed by the lack of leaves. A breeze carried the sound of televisions, muted conversations, a baby crying, and the creak of loose siding. Sprinkles, Ray's grandmother's bull terrier, ran up onto the porch, growling. Ray shrunk back towards the door. Ray's dad cursed the dog and kicked at it. Sprinkles retreated back under the porch. The dog's white coat was filthy. The yard was mostly mud. The pair went down the porch steps, out the gate, and got into Ray's grandfather's old green rusty Dodge Power Wagon. Both were careful not to step where the mud got too thick.

The pickup doors squealed when they opened them. Ray's dad knocked his fist three times on the dash, pushed on the gas twice, and cranked the engine. The Power Wagon sputtered to life and died. Ray's dad repeated the entire process and cranked the engine again. The Power Wagon roared to life, rumbled a bit, then smoothed out. Ray's dad put on his seatbelt and looked over to make sure Ray had done the same. He put the pickup in reverse, checked his mirrors, craned his head to look behind them, checked his mirrors again, looked behind him again, and backed out.

The trailer park's gravel road climbed the hill, trailer homes on either side. The trailers ran the full gamut of colors, from bright blues to dull creams and tans. Some had manicured gardens and were well maintained. Others were trashed and looked half abandoned. The nicest trailer was at the top of the hill. Mrs. Chin, the park owner's wife, was raking leaves in her yard. She smiled and waved as they moved past. Ray waved back. He had gone with his grandmother the day before to take up the rent check. Mrs. Chin had given him a hard candy wrapped in plastic. Ray's grandmother had taken it as they walked back down the hill and thrown it in the trash when they got home.

The Power Wagon crested the hill and started the looping descent down the other side into Moscow. Moscow Mountain and Paradise Ridge overlooked the town. Ray's dad turned on the radio, but couldn't get any of his preferred stations to come in perfectly so turned it off. The Power Wagon rolled through the university. Past tall brick buildings and the wood chip power plant where Ray's father had used to work. The university was quiet. Saturday morning. Only a few people, some still in costumes from the night before, wandered the sidewalks. The Power Wagon rumbled across the railroad tracks and moved its way through town. Up the highway towards Troy, take a left on White Avenue, past the Eastside Marketplace where they had gone to see the movie. Ray saw his mother's blue car parked in the Safeway parking lot. He kept his mouth shut. His father hummed to himself.

The Power Wagon swung into the Les Schwab parking lot. The square white and red building stood in the middle of an expanse of asphalt. The Power Wagon pulled into an open parking space and the engine sputtered and died. Ray's dad got out and Ray followed. Clean shaven men in pressed shirts with their names on the breast were working on cars parked beneath the roof. Ray and his dad went inside through the glass doors. The lobby smelled of motor oil and vulcanized rubber. Shelves of tires filled half the room. A big man stood behind a tall desk, clicking away on a computer. The chairs were half filled with an assortment of college students, mothers with young children, one cranky looking gentleman, and a few senior citizens, sipping water and reading magazines. A big glass window looked out on the garage floor. Ray's dad walked up to the desk. The big man towered over him. The big man's head was shaved. The patch on his shirt said *Gus*. Ray stayed close to his father.

"Can I help you with something?"

Ray's dad tapped the side of his leg three times.

"I'm here to see Mr. Meacham."

"Okay."

The big man turned and walked down a short hall. He knocked on a door, opened it, and stuck his head into a back office. Faint voices echoed down the hall. The big man closed the door and came back.

"He's on the phone. You can wait over there."

The big man gestured towards the lobby chairs. The phone rang. The big man answered it. Ray and his dad went over to the chairs and sat down. Ray's dad leaned forward and started to alphabetize the magazines on the coffee table. A college aged girl stared until she caught Ray staring back and then went back to reading her own magazine. The minute hand on the clock slowly made its way around. Every now and again the big man would call out a name, someone would get up, pay, and leave. Other people arrived. Ray got bored. He got up and got some water out of the water cooler near the door. He wadded up the paper cup and put it in the garbage. Every time someone left Ray's dad would put their abandoned magazine in the correct order on the table. Ray wandered down the aisles between the shelves of tires, running his hands across the different treads. His dad came and found him and forced him to sit back down.

A fat man came out of the back office. His thick blonde hair was full of styling gel and the blue windbreaker he wore was stretched tightly across his beer belly. The fat man went over to the big man and the big man pointed over at Ray's dad. The fat man walked over. Ray's dad got up, tapped his leg three times, and walked over to meet him. Ray followed.

"You Eddie's friend?"

Ray's dad nodded.

"Yes sir. I'm Randy, and this is my son Ray."

The big man took each of their hands in turn. The fat man had chewed fingernails and fingers the size of hot dogs.

"Let's go back in my office."

Ray's dad nodded.

"Okay. Wait here Ray."

The fat man and Ray's dad went into the back office and closed the door. Ray climbed back into his chair, sitting on his knees and looking over the chair back into the main part of the garage. The clean shaven men were changing tires and working under the hoods of various cars. Ray spotted his dad's friend Eddie's pock marked face. He was taking a tire off its rim. Eddie felt someone watching him and looked up. Ray waved. Eddie waved back, but did not smile. Eddie got back to work. Ray turned around and sat down in his chair. Ray wished he had brought a book. He had a lot of books at his mother's apartment, a Wii too, and a big room of his own that he didn't have to share with a sewing machine, with a real bed instead of just a mattress on the floor.

The big man was picking his nose. He noticed Ray watching, gave him a dirty look, and turned red. Ray's gut gurgled. He thought about using the restroom, but didn't, he didn't want to make trouble. Ray picked up a copy of *National Geographic* from the coffee table. He leafed through it. There was an article on nebula, Roman aqueducts, and the reed dance in Swaziland. The pictures in the reed dance article showed young topless African women carrying tall reeds. Ray held the magazine close, hoping nobody else would notice what he was reading. The back office door opened. Ray's dad and the fat man came out. The pair shook hands. The fat man was laughing. Ray's dad was forcing a smile. The two separated. Ray put the magazine down on the coffee table and got up. The fat man headed back towards his office. Ray's dad motioned for Ray to follow, started walking, paused, and placed the *National Geographic* back in its correct alphabetical place.

They left through the glass door and walked back out to the Power Wagon. Ray's dad tapped on the dash three times, pushed in the gas pedal twice, and cranked the ignition. The Power Wagon started right up. Ray's dad put on his seat belt, made sure Ray was wearing his, put the Power Wagon in gear, checked the mirrors, looked behind them, checked the mirrors again, looked behind them again, and backed out of the parking space. They drove a different way home, heading down Mountain View towards Sixth Street. Ray's belly gurgled again. The Power Wagon came to a halt at a stop sign. A hand lettered sign was taped on the pole.

"Look Ray, a garage sale."

"Dad. I have to use the bathroom."

"Just hold it. It's still early, a lot of the good stuff is probably still there."

"Dad."

"We'll be quick. You know I can't pass by a yard sale."

Ray's dad hit the turn signal. He waited for it to tick three times and then took a right turn. The yard sale was three blocks down the road. Rows of junk covered folding tables lined the sidewalk and front yard. A middle aged woman sat behind a card table on a lawn chair. People milled about, looking for treasure. Ray's dad parked the Power Wagon on the other side of the street facing the wrong way. He turned towards his son.

"You coming?"

Ray shook his head no. There was a growing pain in his belly, rising and falling, a steadily increasing tide of bodily demands. Ray's dad got out of the truck and walked across the street. He stood on the sidewalk for a moment, tapped his leg three times, and moved his way into the crowd. Ray lost track of him amongst the moving heads. Ray didn't feel very well. Every movement in his gut elicited a fearful clench. A sharp pang wound its way through his intestines. The minutes ticked by. The pressure eased, came back, eased again, and came back with a vengeance. Ray opened the pickup door and hustled his way across the street.

Ray found his dad standing at the end of one of the tables. He had found a large box of marbles and was going through them, picking out the blue ones. Already selected ones, in a great variety of bluish shades, were placed in an old jewelry box with a mirror on the lid. Ray's dad was chewing on his bottom lip, completely absorbed with the task. Ray waddled over and pulled on his dad's hand. Ray's dad looked up, startled.

"Dad. We need to go."

"Hold on a sec Ray."

"Dad, we need to go now."

Ray's dad's eyes never left the box, his free hand continued to work its way through the colored orbs. He pulled out a big blue one with a white swirl and put it in the jewelry box.

"I'm almost done here Ray. We'll leave in a little bit."

Ray jerked with all his might, his dad stumbled, caught himself and pulled back. Ray fell for a moment with his father, but managed to regain his footing. The growing pressure in his belly suddenly disappeared. Agonizing relief combined with horror. The stink was terrible. People moved away. Ray's dad looked down at his son, his eyes wide and his mouth open.

"Ray, did you just…?"

Tears were streaming down Ray's cheeks. People were staring. One was pointing and whispering. A younger man was stifling a laugh.

"Please Dad, let's just go."

Ray's dad let himself be hauled by the hand out of the yard sale. Blue marbles fell from his fingers to the ground. Halfway across the street he regained his faculties and the pair hustled to the Power Wagon, getting in on their respective sides. Ray's dad quickly tapped the dash three times, pumped the gas pedal twice, and turned on the engine. The Power Wagon roared to life. Ray's dad put on his seatbelt, checked to make sure Ray was wearing his, put the pickup in gear, checked the mirrors, looked back, checked the mirrors again, looked back, and pulled out into the street. The ride was silent. Ray stared out the window, sitting in his own filth, and cried. Ray's dad unrolled the driver's side window.

The Power Wagon headed out of town, up over the hill, and down the gravel road into the trailer park. The moment the pickup came to a stop Ray got out and ran for the trailer. His grandfather was reading on one end of the couch, his grandmother was darning socks on the other. Only his grandmother looked up when he burst in. Ray rushed back to the bathroom, shut the door, forced off his shoes, and pulled off his soiled pants and underwear. The exposed stench was even worse than in the pickup. He turned on the fan, but it did little to help. Ray cleaned himself as best he could with toilet paper, then sat down as cramps heralded the coming of a second round. The trailer door opened and slammed closed. Ray could just hear the voices over the noise of the fan. His grandmother's forceful tone carried better than his father's mumbling.

"What happened?"

"....sick...... Had..... accident....."

"Poor little squirt."

"Yeah..... damn......"

"Did you get it?"

"No...... not...... would..... know if...... changed."

There was silence from the living room. Ray blew his nose on a piece of toilet paper. His grandmother's voice lowered to a whisper.

"You...... you..... to..... job...... shared custody."

".... know..... Same story... always.... shit. Not..... fault..... know.... wrong....me. Maybe..... lawyer.... help."

"Don't........ money. Maybe.... talk...... her."

"Doubt....... hard enough...... bitch...... first...... around."

"Don't...... way...... mother..... might...... hear."

"Sorry."

Silence. The sound of movement and then running water in the kitchen sink. Ray wiped his ass and flushed the toilet. There was a knock on the bathroom door before his grandmother opened it. She had a cigarette clenched in her teeth. Her eyes looked sad. In her hands she held the rubber bottle full of warm water and the attached rubber hose. Ray involuntarily pulled himself back.

"Sorry to hear you had a rough day squirt. We'll get you feeling better in no time."

The old woman closed the door behind her. Afterwards, she took the filthy clothes and ran a load of laundry. Ray went and laid down in his bed, facing the wall, to sulk. After about half an hour his dad came in and sat down by the mattress, his back pressed up against the wall. Ray's dad tried to put a hand on Ray's shoulder, but Ray pulled away.

"I'm sorry Ray. I don't know what else to say, but I'm sorry. There's something wrong with me. I don't know. I wish I could do better. I really do."

Ray refused to look at his father. He kept his eyes glued to the fake wood paneling of the wall. It was his dad's fault. It was all his damn fault. The two sat in silence. The phone rang. Ray's grandmother answered. She yelled across the trailer.

"Randy. Telephone."

Ray's father got up. He turned off and on the light twice and went out to the living room. Ray didn't move. He could hear his grandmother and father whisper in excited tones and then his father take the telephone.

"Hello….. Yes…... Of course I can start next week…... I need to what?......... No problem, I'm not that attached to it……. Thank you. Thank you very much……. Yes, I'll see you at 6 AM on Monday."

Ray could hear the sound of the telephone hanging up. Ray's dad started whooping and hollering. Ray's grandmother started cheering and laughing hysterically. The trailer shook. It sounded like they were jumping around. Ray didn't leave his bed. He wished he was in his room at his mother's apartment, where he had his own TV, shelves of toys, and never had to get an enema.

# Picnic

"I think we should go on a picnic this Sunday."

The breakfast/dinner table fell silent. For Paul, his little brother Mike, his older sister Julie, and their mother, it was dinner. For the man at the head, the man who worked the night shift down at the potato plant, it was breakfast. Three sets of matching eyes swung from their mother to their father. Paul's father, wearing just boxers and a t-shirt in a failed attempt to escape the heat of the evening, let out a sigh. Paul's mother pressed her attack.

"The weather's supposed to turn. It would be nice to do before the kids go back to school."

Paul's father took another bite of hamburger pattie between two slices of white bread. The buzz of the fan by the open door filled the silence.

"What are you thinking, go up to Hat Rock or something?"

"I was thinking maybe someplace else."

"Where?"

"Ritter Hot Springs."

Paul's father coughed, choking a bit on a bite of food.
"Christ Renee, it's a two hour drive on a windy ass road."
"We used to go all the time when I was a kid."
"I don't see what's wrong with Hat Rock."
"The kids could go swimming."
Three sets of matching eyes filled with excitement.
"They could swim in the Columbia too."
"At least tell me you'll think about it."
Paul's father grunted again. The flow of words stopped,
replaced by the rhythmic sound of mastication. After
breakfast/dinner the kids brushed their teeth and got ready for
bed. Lying in the hot bedroom he shared with his brother, Paul
could hear his father help with the dishes, shave, and get dressed.
Heavy boots moved down the hallway and out onto the porch.
The old '75 Chevy Luv cranked to life and Paul's father headed
out to work. The digital clock on the nightstand glowed
10:30.

It was a half hour drive from the house in Echo to the potato
plant just outside Boardman. Paul's father worked as a line
supervisor on the night shift from 11:00 PM to 7:00 AM. Paul's
father had been working the night shift for as long as Paul could
remember. You got a bonus if you volunteered. They always
ate dinner late so they could eat it as a family. Other than that,
and breakfasts on Sunday, Paul's father was a ghost. Pale
compared to the summer tans of his family. Pudgy from having
to personally sample product every hour. While the children
played in the sunlight, he slept wearing earplugs in a bedroom
with blackout curtains.

For Paul and his siblings, it was never a question of if they
were going to Ritter. Even Julie, the oldest at eleven, had never
seen their mother fail to get her way. Nothing was said the next
morning when the children awoke to find their father having a
couple of beers with their Uncle Rob, actually their father's
cousin, who worked the same shift. Paul's mother leaned

against the kitchen counter in her bathrobe, sipping coffee and watching. She said nothing the next day either, or the day after that.

On Saturday morning the Chevy Luv rattled into the driveway and Paul's father came in with bags under his eyes to greet the weekend. Paul's mother was waiting for him. The children were watching Saturday morning cartoons.

"You going to be up to going to Ritter tomorrow?"

"It's been a long week Renee."

"The kids have been looking forward to it."

Paul's father grunted and dragged himself back to the bedroom. Paul's mother turned up the volume of the television and followed her husband to convince him to change his mind, closing the bedroom door behind her.

Sunday morning they loaded the family sedan, a well driven '85 Toyota Camry, with a picnic basket and swim trunks wrapped in old bath towels. Paul's father looked groggy despite a full pot of coffee in his belly. He pulled his ball cap low over his eyes to shield them from the bright sun and looked down at Paul.

"You're not going to get carsick are you?"

"No sir."

"Okay."

The trip was mostly silent. The radio was tuned to Paul's mother's favorite country station. Paul's father only grumbled occasionally about the stupid premise of a few of the songs and about a couple of dark clouds on the southern horizon. Paul's mother laughed off both. The radio broke up into static as the curving road climbed into the timber. Paul's mother tried to lead her brood in singing a song about a bear in tennis shoes, but only Mike joined her. Julie read a book and Paul tried to until he got carsick, forcing the Camry to pull over. When he started feeling better, Paul entertained himself by picking on his brother and sister, resulting in a serious commotion until his mother turned and with a few loud words put a stop to it. Paul's father stayed quiet, his knuckles white on the wheel, letting loose with the occasional yawn.

The farther south they drove the thicker the dark clouds became. When they reached the turnoff to Ritter the clouds broke loose, unleashing a heavy downpour that gave no signs of letting up. Everybody stayed quiet, the only sound the swishing of the wiper blades. Ritter was a pool behind a fence, a couple of dilapidated buildings, and a few scattered picnic tables. Nobody else was there. Paul's mother looked out at the falling rain.

"No use crying over spilled milk."

She got out of the car, retrieved the picnic basket from the trunk, got back in, and started handing out cheese sandwiches. Paul's father took his sandwich, got out of the car, and sat down at one of the picnic tables. He chewed slowly, the rain soaking his clothes, and his family watching him from the car. Half an hour later he got back in, and they went home.

# Not Bad

Travis' wife Kay insisted on helping him navigate his way down the stairs from the bedroom to the kitchen. Travis gave in, but grumbled the whole way down. He was getting pretty adept with the crutches, and Kay fussing just a few steps below, ready to catch him if he fell, seemed more of a hindrance than a help. It was slow going, but Kay's eyes were full of concern, and as the saying went, happy wife, happy life. They got to the bottom in one piece and Kay made a show of pulling out his chair at the kitchen table, setting a pillow on another chair, and helping him lift his leg up onto the pillow.

Travis leaned his crutches against the side of the table. His right leg was covered in plaster from the bottom of his foot to halfway up his thigh, the top covered by the old pair of red cotton shorts he wore. A worn wool sock covered his bare toes where they stuck out of the cast. A slipper hid his other foot. Travis adjusted his loose bathrobe to better cover his bare leg. The blue plaid flashed sharply against the white of his t-shirt. Kay bent over to help him, but he swatted her hands away. His leg was just broke, he wasn't an invalid. Kay stepped back and went to moving the few breakfast dishes from the sink to the dishwasher. Travis watched her. Rain splattered itself against the window in front of her.

"Are you sure you're going to be alright by yourself?"

"For Christ's sake Kay, I'm a 67 year old man, I can take care of myself."

"I'll be back early this evening. Just don't try to go upstairs."

Travis rolled his eyes at his wife's back.

"I'll try not to play with matches or anything."

Kay turned around and gave him the look. Travis averted his eyes to the plaster on his cast. It had been enough of a fight just to get her to let him come downstairs. The thought of spending another day cooped up in their bed watching television was enough to make his teeth clench. Daytime television was the worst. He couldn't understand how people could let their minds rot to the point where it could be called entertainment. The only show he liked was the Price Is Right. Every now and again he did find something racy, that wasn't half bad, but the rest was just trash. Kay had not wanted him to come downstairs. She had wanted him to stay in bed. Travis had put up a fit. A fit like a damn six year old. It had been embarrassing, but here he was, downstairs.

"What time is it?"

Travis glanced up at the clock on the wall.

"7:30."

"Shit. I have to get going."

Kay finished up the dishes and went to running about like a chicken with its head cut off. Grabbing one thing, forgetting another, going back for it. Jacket. Purse. Check her purse. Grab her keys off the hook. Check her purse again. Pull out her wallet. Open her wallet. Close it. Put it back. A steady stream of orders flowed from her as she moved around the room.

"If you need anything just call my cell or give the Johnson's a call. Just make yourself a sandwich for lunch, there's plenty of stuff in the fridge. Don't forget to take your pain meds. I'll be back this evening, probably around six or so."

"You already said that."

Kay stopped her spastic movements.

"What?"

"You already said you were coming back this evening. I know."

Kay stared at him a bit, her thoughts obviously elsewhere. Travis waited patiently.

"I wish I didn't have to go."

"It's okay."

"It's just that I'm in charge of the Cattlemen's fundraiser this year."

"I'll be fine."

"I know. It's just...."

"Just nothing. Now get going, you're going to be late."

"Are you sure?"

"Yes. Now get. Without you there they'll probably serve chicken at the banquet again this year."

Kay smiled and brushed a bit of dyed brown hair out of her eyes. She leaned over, gave Travis a peck, turned, and headed out the door. Travis breathed a sigh of relief. He could hear Kay walking down the walk. Footsteps came the other way. Hellos back and forth. A man's voice. Muted conversation. Goodbyes. Kay's retreating steps. Heavier footsteps headed towards the door. A knock.

"Come in."

Morris opened the door and came in. The skinny man stood in the doorway eying the older heavier man in the chair and biting his lip. He was wearing cowboy boots, blue jeans, t-shirt, Carhartt vest, and a Charlotte Hornets ball cap. Travis motioned for him to come the rest of the way in.

"Hurry up and close the door. You'll let all the damn heat out."

Morris moved into the kitchen and shut the door.

"Sorry. Just thought I'd better come by and check-in before we got started today."

"Taking that group of cows up to the Northrup pasture?"

"Yeah."

"Who do you have helping you?"

"Mad Dog and Roger Johnson."

"Okay. You watch that Johnson. Jackass ain't much of a horseman."

"I will."

"Have you already checked the water up in Northrup?"

"Yeah, when I took up salt yesterday. Everything looked good."

"Good. Which bulls you taking up?"

"Numbers 12, 26, and 27."

"27? I thought we were sending 15 up there?"

"No, 15 came up lame. Been fighting too much. Kay told me to trade him out for 27."

"She did, did she."

"Yeah."

"Okay, she would know. Fucking 15. He bad enough we'll have to send him down the road?"

"Don't know. The vet's coming tomorrow."

"Okay."

The two men stood quietly. Travis with his mouth set in a hard line. Morris fidgeting. Travis enjoyed making Morris feel uncomfortable. It was good to remind the young buck who was still the boss. He motioned towards the half-full coffee pot.

"You want coffee or anything?"

"No thanks. I better get going."

"All right then."

"See you tomorrow."

"See you tomorrow."

Morris turned and headed back out the door. As he pulled the door closed a brown and black mutt forced its way inside. Morris cursed and stuck his head back in the door.

"Damn it Brewster. You want him outside?"

The dog ran up and put its head in Travis' lap. Travis pat the dog on its wet head and lovingly scratched behind his ears.

"No, it's okay. Just don't tell Kay."

"Okay. See you later."

"See you later."

Morris pulled back his head and closed the door. The dog shook the water off of its coat. Travis laughed.

"You lucky bastard. You want to hang out with me today?"

The dog looked up at him, panting, and then curled up underneath the table.

"This will be our little secret."

The dog didn't answer. It was too busy licking its paws. Travis looked out the window over the sink. All he could see was gray sky and the waving branches of the elm out in the yard. It was still raining. Number 15. Fuck. That was a $5,000 bull. If he was lame he was good for nothing but hamburger. Travis picked the Western Stockman up off the table. He thumbed through the newspaper to the back where the prices were. Slaughter bulls were going for about $90 per hundredweight. Number 15 probably weighed around 1700 pounds. Travis did the math in his head. $1,530. Not bad. Not great, but not bad. Travis chewed on the end of his mustache. Not much he could do about it until the vet looked him over. No use worrying over what you can't control.

Travis flipped through the Western Stockman and started reading. He read the personals first. There were usually only about four or five. They were always his favorite. Then through the classifieds. See who was selling out, who was hanging on. Getting harder every year. He'd need to get a new tractor by winter for the hay chopper. Nothing good caught his eye. Then the news articles. He snorted as he read.

"Hey Brewster, listen to this."

The dog raised its head.

"Some viro group called the Western Forest Alliance is suing the feds to get cattle kicked off 300,000 acres of the Malheur National Forest. They claim the cattle are causing irreparable damage to the sensitive forest biome and riparian areas."

Travis laid the paper on his lap and looked back out the window. Such things were getting more common. Some non-profit with more zeal than sense sues the government. The government settles to avoid a lengthy lawsuit. The rancher who never even had a voice through the whole process gets the shaft. No more grazing on national forest lands. No more summer pasture. No more staying in business. The facts didn't matter. It all depended on the lawyers. Travis didn't have any grazing permits in the Malheur National Forest, but he had some in the Umatilla.

"Can you believe this shit Brewster? Hell, any rancher worth a shit knows he's raising grass, not cattle. We have to go back every year. Why the hell would we cut our own throats? Makes no damn sense."

The dog whined and put its head back down on its paws.

"Assholes."

Travis let out a disgusted sigh and put the paper back down on the table. The clock said 9:30 AM. Time for the Price Is Right. Travis put his leg down, hoisted himself up, grabbed his crutches, and hobbled out to the living room. He carefully lowered himself down into his easy chair. Safely settled, he pulled the lever into recline mode. Travis lifted the remote and clicked on the TV. Power, guide, scroll. Go through the crap. Find the local channels. Go past them. Go back. Click on the right one. Travis put down the remote and settled back in the recliner. Brewster trotted in, circled, and lay down in front of the fireplace. There was no fire. Travis laughed to himself and went back to watching the show. He found trying to guess the price of the various items strangely enjoyable. Outside, the rain started coming down harder. A dog scratched at the kitchen door and whined. Brewster raised up and looked back towards the kitchen. Travis did not avert his eyes from the TV.

"That pup can stay out there. Serves him right."

Brewster curled his head back towards his tail. Sixty-seven years. Sixty-seven years riding the range without a single damn accident. Never spilled from a horse. Never a bone broken. All undone in a single day. The horse had been one of the better ones. A good steady six year old that had never been that excitable. Travis couldn't blame the horse. It wasn't really the pups fault either. Pups got excited, that's all there was to it. Just stupid bad luck. It was easy to think that now. It hadn't been so easy when the horse had started bucking and then went down. Thank god his boot had come off. Thank god he hadn't been dragged. It could have been worse. It was supposed to have been an easy day. Just go out on his own and find some strays. Some easy day. Three hours dragging himself through the dirt until Morris had found him. Kay was a worrier. Sometimes it wasn't a bad thing.

"Hell, lucky no wolves came along. Mad Dog claims he's seen some over on the Platt place."

Brewster didn't say anything. Just one more thing. One more worry that the people up in Portland didn't have to have. Damn viros. Living in a fairy land. Everything is simple and easy when you don't have to pay the costs. Sons of bitches. The faces on the TV droned on. Brewster started barking. Travis jerked awake. Brewster had his paws up on the window sill, barking at birds out in the trees. It wasn't raining anymore.

"Shut up."

Brewster kept barking.

"I said shut up god damn it."

Brewster jumped down and retreated into the kitchen. Travis winced. Christ his leg hurt. What time was it? The clock on the VCR said 12:32. Damn it. He should've remembered to take his damn pill. Travis popped the recliner back up, grabbed his crutches, and hobbled back into the kitchen. The pill bottle sat next to the sink. He opened it and shook a pill out into his hand. He turned on the water, bent over and filled his mouth, stood back up, popped in the pill, and swallowed it all down. Brewster was laying under the kitchen table, his head between his paws, looking ashamed. Travis looked down at the dog.

"Oh, ya big baby. I'm sorry I yelled at yeah."

The dog's tail beat the floor.

"You ready for lunch?"

The dog's tail beat the floor again.

"I've got something special."

Travis moved across the kitchen and through the door into the mudroom. Washer, dryer, chest freezer, upright freezer, coats, boots, and other random junk. Once upon a time it had been a garage. The garage door had long since been replaced by a solid wall. Travis opened up the upright and reached into the back, behind the ice cream sandwiches and Schwan's microwave dinners, and pulled out a small green package from its hiding place. He tucked the box under his chin, closed the upright, and made his way back into the kitchen. Brewster watched him come back in. Travis hurried as fast as he could. The box was cold. Travis dumped the box down on the counter. The label was bright green with swirling white letters. *Moonshine Farms Veggie Burgers*. Brewster whined.

"What? I'm just curious."

The dog whined again.

"Oh, enough. Don't go telling Kay. I'd never hear the end of it. Had to get Morris' wife to get these for me."

Travis opened the package and deposited two frozen patties onto the counter. Both were a light brownish in color, specked with green and orange. Travis picked one up, smelled it, and put it back onto the counter. He reached down and picked up the box, looking for the directions. It was all a blur. He held it further out but it did no good. He had three pairs of reading glasses. One was upstairs by the bed, one was in the living room, and one was god knows where.

"Fuck it."

Travis put the box back down on the counter. He pulled a frying pan from the cupboard and put it on the stove. He turned on the burner and put the two patties in the pan. Brewster watched with interest. The patties started sizzling. The smell was a little off. Travis got out a spatula and checked the bottom of the patties. How the hell was he supposed to know when they were ready to flip? Travis glanced back at the box on the counter. He picked it up and buried it down deep in the trash can under the sink, shuffling the garbage so it was close to the bottom. He thought about taking it out to the burning barrel and lighting it on fire. That would guarantee Kay would never know. It was muddy outside. It would probably be alright.

Travis looked at the bottom of the patties again. They were turning brown. Probably good enough. He flipped the patties. There was little to no grease. No sizzle. Travis got two small plates out of the cupboard and put them on the counter next to the stove. He checked the bottom of the patties and put one on each plate. The two patties steamed. Travis turned off the stove. He took one plate and put it on the floor. He got a fork out of the drawer. Brewster got up, stretched, and ambled forward. The dog sniffed at the patty, licked at it, and then turned and lay back down underneath the kitchen table. Travis laughed.

"That good huh?"

Travis used the edge of his fork to break off a chunk. The inside was the same color as the outside. He stabbed the chunk and put it into his mouth. Travis looked out the kitchen window at the elm tree and the corrals and hills beyond the yard. How was Morris doing? Was he getting the cows moved all right? Probably. Travis chewed. It was a different taste, that was for sure. Travis swallowed. He looked down at the dog.

"Not bad."

# Time To Move

Fuck it's cold out here. God I wish I was in bed. No, better not to think about it. Nothing you can do. Best to think about something else. Everything's packed up. All the boxes are in the truck. Are we forgetting anything? No. The damn house is empty. What about the garage? No, been through it three times now. We've got everything. Nothing more to worry about. Get up, eat some granola bars, hit the road. Two thousand miles. Two thousand and forty-six to be exact. Could probably make it in two days. Probably take three. Margie has never been one for long drives. Hell, probably take four with how many times she'll have to stop to pee. Ought to have her pee in a Gatorade bottle like the truckers. Ha, yeah right.

I wonder if Portland will be nice? You hear good things. It seemed pretty nice when I flew over to buy the house. Probably not as nice as Manitowoc. Different office, going to be the new guy again. Great. Just like high school. Fucking high school. Larry Donovan giving me swirlys. Kids think they have it tough. Christ. I still flinch when I hear a toilet flush. Fuck. Not this shit again. I'm an adult. I got a family and a career. Not in high school any more. Don't dwell on the past. Always focus on the future. Who told me that? Doesn't sound like something the old man would say. Probably some inspirational poster or something. Sounds like that kind of crap. God it's going to be a long drive tomorrow.

I better remember to pack this lawn chair in the morning. Hate to have to go buy a new twenty dollar lawn chair. Did the curtains just move? Probably her peeking out. Yeah, that's right honey. I'm still out here. Just go to sleep or back to balling your eyes out, whichever as long as you stay in your room. God, never seen such a fuss. Girl has the rest of her life ahead of her. She's only sixteen. There will be plenty of boys. Cripes, there's a thought. Plenty of boys. Just what I need to worry about. Looks just like her mother. It would have been a hell of a lot easier if she looked like me. I'm not so bad looking. I've aged well. Better than some. Ha, doesn't mean I'd make a good looking woman though. Damn, what time is it? Twelve fifteen. Christ it's cold. Should have brought a warmer jacket.

I hope the house sells soon. Things have been going fairly well. It will probably sell fairly quick. It's a pretty nice house. Could be nicer. Wish it was two stories instead of one. This would probably be a lot easier if it was two. Ha, yeah sure. Like you never shimmied down a drain pipe before. God, lucky I never broke my neck. What was I thinking? Never did much. Mostly just wandered around. Some other things too. Now there's a memory. What was her name? Christi. That sounds right. Damn, that girl would let you do anything, and I mean anything. Town bicycle. Better a shared bike than no bike at all. Christ. What a dumb ass I was. Lucky I didn't catch a disease. Always wore a condom.

I wonder if they wore a condom? No, better not to think about it. Some things a man just shouldn't think about. Margie said she found a wrapper, but that doesn't mean anything. Lisa is a smart girl, but that pecker head. Oldest trick in the book. Feels better without one. Pecker head. With a family like his, you'd think he'd know better. My daughter. My little girl. My Squirt. Wait a minute. Shit. What a terrible nickname. Squirt. Been calling her that since she was little. Never really thought about it before. Kind of gross when you do. Squirt. Ha. I'll have to tell Margie that one. She'll probably find it funny. Maybe not. Have to catch her in the right mood. Probably won't be tomorrow.

I wonder how Margie is doing. Can't be too fun in the hallway. Probably better than here. At least she's warm. Damn. How are we going to do this? Neither one of us is going to get a lick of sleep. Fuck. Just got to make it a couple hundred miles down the road. Then we can sleep. Don't have to be in the office for a week. What's an extra day? Ought to go right now. Wake up the family, load up the last of the stuff, and hit the road. Nah, let Harry sleep. Harry has been pretty good about all this. Not a peep. Let him sleep. Ha. That rhymes. Clever. Good kid Harry. Did right with that one. Of course we used to say that about Lisa, before she went all wild child. God damn teenagers. All the hormones. Just makes you nuts. Nothing to be done. We all have to go through it. I did. Margie did. Harry will have to. Just a fact of life.

I'm being pretty harsh. She's not a bad kid. Hell, she stayed in the house. We told her not to leave the house, and by god, she stayed in the house. Sneaky little shit. I'm glad Margie was the one that walked in on it. God, some things you just can't unsee. Funny how it's only fathers and daughters. Margie could probably walk in on Harry and it would be no big deal. Like the time Mom walked in on me cranking it. Weird. It was probably weird for her too. I don't know. Too much dick and not enough brains I guess. Probably because I can remember how I was at that age. Fuck. I don't know. This is getting a little too deep for this late.

Pretty moon tonight. Looks like it will be full in a couple days. Keeps things bright. Good. Easier to see things when it's bright. Nice stars. At least those will be the same in Portland. Probably we'll never see them. They say it rains there a lot. Everyone was making jokes about it when I visited the Portland branch last week. They seemed like a good bunch. Probably be all right to work with. I don't know about that secretary. God, she's been there for a while. What a bitter old bitch. Always be nice to the secretaries. Makes your life easier. Got to make sure not to stare at her mole. That's going to be tough. Damn thing looks like an old Junior Mint stuck to the side of her neck. Ought to have that thing cut off. Maybe she has. Those things grow back sometimes. Nothing you can do. I'm lucky this transfer came up. Perfect timing. Still, I'm going to miss Manitowoc.

Car driving by. Pontiac. Green. Yeah, I see you. Keep driving. I'll break off your side mirror again. Fucking Jacob Jenner. Every half hour. Little bugger. Go bother someone else. I'm not going to bed. She ain't sneaking out. Not on my watch. No sneaking in here either. Go home and jerk it. Take a cold shower. I don't care. Christ, of all the boys at her school, fucking Jacob Jenner. What about that Davis kid, the football player, he seemed nice. That was probably the problem. Jenner though. Why did it have to be a Jenner? There he goes. Little shit is probably scared of me. Thought I broke my damn hand. Over reacted. Shouldn't have done that. Didn't help any. Just made things worse. Kids have to revolt, no two ways about it. Guaranteed they'll do the opposite. Every fucking time. Little shit. Parking right outside the house. Gutsy little turd. Lack of respect. Yes sir. Got to put the fear of god in these kids.

She's probably stewing in there. Well stew away darling. Think all the terrible thoughts you want about me. Part of being a dad. Better this way than the other. God, can you imagine. Sixteen. Got her whole life ahead of her. Christ. There's plenty of girls at that school. Couldn't that damn kid pick a girl who doesn't have a future? Who's that friend of Lisa's? Staci? Is that right? Dumb as a box of rocks? Wouldn't wish it on anybody, but that girl, at least that girl doesn't have a future. She'll be lucky if she ever leaves Manitowoc. Probably end up working at the gas station or something. That's probably not fair. They're all pretty dumb at that age, but some don't ever come out of it either. If Jacob Jenner wants to get his damn dick wet, why not Staci?

Getting myself all worked up again. Got to calm down. God. I could've broke his arm. Never seen a kid run like that. Must have scared the shit out of him. Didn't even take his shoes. Threw them in the trash. Lisa probably dug one out to keep. Girls get weird about things like that. Sentimental. A stinky shoe. Jesus. There was a condom wrapper. It's not too late. Lucky. That's what we are. Damn lucky. Was it the first time? Lisa told Margie it was. Hopefully she's telling the truth. Two months. Two months is a long time. Is that right? Yeah, two months since I broke the side mirror. Lots of shit can happen in two months. We told her to stay away from him. Why couldn't she just stay away from him? Yeah right. Like herding cats. Anybody else. It wouldn't matter if it was anybody else. Kids do what kids do. No way around it. Pretty much anybody else would be fine.

Harry now. Don't have to worry about Harry. That kids into Star Trek. Ain't no way that kids getting laid before college. Even if he did. Different worries. Not the same. Okay, maybe a little bit the same. It would be just as bad if it was Harry. Maybe a little different. I don't know. Fuck. It would be the same. Just feels different. That's a little fucked up. What you going to do? Just feels different. Not logical. Christ. A daughter. I grew up with just brothers. What business do I have raising a daughter? How did Mom feel when Ricky knocked up Tammy? Sure, that was in college, first year, but still. Sure as hell made her tighten up the leash on the rest of us, that was for damn sure. Started going to church regular again. Billy's a good enough kid I guess. Not his fault how he started out. Still. Things could have been a hell of a lot easier. So long football scholarship. So long degree. Hello working at the plant making woodworking machines. I don't know. I guess they're doing okay, but it could have been better. Ricky was the smartest of the three of us. He could have gone a lot farther.

Fuck it's cold. Another car. I swear if it's that damn kid again I'm going to go out there and give him what for. No. Someone else. Probably a drunk. Only drunks out at this hour. And horny teens. Shit, to be that age again. Well, maybe not. Fucking Jacob Jenner. What are the odds? Random chance. Attraction. What a fucked up game. Anyone else, he couldn't set his eyes on anyone else, and Lisa, she couldn't have gone all goo goo over a different one? Shit. Never thought I'd be leaving Manitowoc. Was pretty sure I was going to die here. What ya going to do? Nothing, that's what. Nothing you can do. Just do the best you can with what you got. Who knows, Portland will probably be nice. God only knows what things are going to be like in Portland.

One more night. Just have to make one more night. Caught her trying to sneak out last night. Little shit. Not going to risk it again. Not when we're so damn close. Am I overreacting? Margie thinks so. Sure, she won't say it out loud, but I can tell. Twenty years I've been married to that woman. I can tell her moods. Just let it blow over. That's what she thinks. Let things run their course. Great idea. I'm sure that's what the parents of those other three girls said too. Don't worry about it. She's a smart girl. These things never last. Then what? Wham bam thank you man. A new grandkid in their arms in less than a year. No thanks. Not me. Not my daughter. Better to uproot everything and move. No convincing kids at that age. The more you push the more they push back. No god damn sense at that age. I don't care how smart you are.

Jenner. Why did it have to be a fucking Jenner? That family must have super sperm or something. How old was the second oldest Jenner boy when he knocked up that girl? Seventeen? What about the third one? Barely out of high school. The fourth? Seventeen too. Hell, except for Jacob, only the oldest one doesn't have kids, and I'm pretty sure he's gay. Christ, you think their parents would lock them up or something. Maybe they're just numb to it. Little swimmers must just punch their way right through the condoms. Fertile sons of bitches. Must be a family thing. All those boys are just like their dad. Ward was just like that in high school. Horny bastard. Stick his dick in anything he could get his hands on. Look what it got him. How old were we when he knocked up Dawn? I was eighteen. She was in my class. He was a year older. Christ. His parents were the same way. Generations. Fucking generations. What a legacy. What time is it? One AM. Six. We'll get up at six. Five more hours to go.

# Sister Sarah Silver

The electronic chime of his cell phone snaps Dave out of dreamland. An entire world collapses in on itself, popping like a soap bubble. The countless denizens go without a scream. The landscape folds and is gone. All destroyed in an instant by an auditory signal designed to grab one's attention. Nothing left but a few stray feelings of the lone survivor, which try in vain to claw their way into memory before drifting away on the never ending winds of time. For a moment, stuck between worlds, Dave follows the signal to the existence of his bedroom. At first Dave thinks it's his alarm. Time to get up. Time to shower. Time to start another day. It's still dark out. This time of year there's light in the windows when it's time to get up. A gray glow which creeps across the wall.

It's not the alarm. It's the ringer. Telephone function. His hand gropes through the darkness towards the insistent device, lit by the small screen on the front, showing the number and the time. Four in the morning. A number he doesn't recognize. A smart man would ignore it. A smart man would go back to bed.

Dave has to know. He cannot stand a mystery. His hands grab the phone, unhook it from the cord connecting it to the wall, and flips it open.

"Hello?"

Dave's voice is groggy. Garbled. Rough. The voice on the other end is feminine. Pleasant. Almost chipper. Not the voice one expects to hear in the wee hours of the morning. There are three types of voices for 4:00 AM. Drunk, scared, and needy. The one on the other end of the connection doesn't make sense.

"Hello. This is Sister Sarah Silver from the Longview Mission. I was just calling you to let you know that we have your daughter?"

Dave's brain dumps its clutch. The motor dies and the psyche desperately cranks the ignition, trying to get things going again. Unreal. Dream world. No. The dream had been something else. Something about being on a hike. Something like that. Not this. Blindsided. T-boned.

"What?"

The word is drawn out. Buying time. Allowing for the hard restart.

"This is Sarah Silver from the Longview Mission. We have your daughter here."

The sounds work their way through his ears and to his brain. Electrical impulses working their way along neural networks. Input. Compute. Response.

"I don't have a daughter."

Silence on the other end. Breathing. Another thought train knocked off the rails. Practiced speech now pointless.

"Is this 208-310-1238?"

Each number stated separately. Things are moving quicker now. The boat is sailing far from the Land of Nod.

"Yes, but I don't have a daughter."

Or at least one that I know of. The terrible old joke goes unsaid. Bad timing. Poor form.

"Terribly sorry."

The line goes dead. Dave closes his flip phone, plugs it back in, and lays it back on the nightstand. Cool air across his shoulders. The covers pull back up tight. Warm embrace. Daughter. Funny. What the fuck? Weird. Just weird. Older. Ten years older. Red frizzy hair. Aged but still good looking. Glasses. She wore glasses, but she took them off. She took it all off. She told him to wait while she got ready. Her form through the half open bathroom door. Completely naked. Brushing her teeth. Trimmed red fuzz between her legs. Should he take his clothes off? Would that be weird? The shoes. At least take off the shoes. Driving behind her. Following her car. She swerves. Hits the curb. Nearly takes out a mailbox. Her on top of him. Rubbing. Grinding. Children's toys scattered around the living room. No worries, he's at her mother's. Whatever. None of his business. Condom. He should have worn a condom. She's a stewardess. No, they prefer flight attendant. Private planes going out of the smaller Hillsboro airport. Not PDX. Nike. Intel. Just a moment. Just a look. Animalistic. His dick in her mouth. The startling sudden jab of a finger up his butt. Go again in the morning. Bend her down. Go behind. I didn't expect you to be this good. Screaming. Moaning. Come in me. Come in me damn it. High heat. Obeyed commands. Reassurance. I'll drop by the pharmacy on my way to work, grab a morning after. Apartment. Just a generic apartment building. She goes her way. He goes his. He never saw her again.

Dave lays in his bed with his eyes closed, but he cannot sleep. Thoughts race their way through his head, a perpetual motor that can't slow down. How long ago has it been? Six years? Five? A little girl with red frizzy hair. Running and smiling. Her first loose tooth. Something unexpected. Not bad. Just unforeseen. It fits with the rest of life. Surprise after surprise. Never the steps one expects. It wouldn't be bad.

Progeny. Continuance. Little one. Do you have a smile for Daddy? No one ever seems disappointed.

Ridiculous. Stupid train of thought. Fantasy. Weird. Just strange. What the hell? Dave lays quietly under his blanket. He stretches out his limbs to the four corners of the queen sized bed. The spaces underneath the blanket away from his core are cold as ice. The first gray tendrils of sunlight hit high on the wall above. What was her name? What was the woman's name?

# Shit

Chin Lao belched and scratched his belly. The TV had a John Wayne movie on. The phone on the counter rang. Lao frowned. His wife was out. The easy chair was comfortable. The phone rang again. Maybe he could ignore it. Probably nothing important. The phone rang again. Damn it. It might be important. He was the landlord. Probably some asshole bitching about nothing. The phone rang for a fifth time. Lao muted the TV, unreclined the chair, and got up.

"Hello?"

The voice on the other side was angry.

"Is this Mr. Chin?"

"Yeah, this is Mr. Chin. Who's this?"

"This is Dusty."

Dusty. Number 11. Younger guy always wearing Wrangler jeans and pearl snap shirts. Lao licked his lips and thought about having a cigarette. No. His wife only allowed him three a day.

"Yeah, what you want?"

"There's shit in my house."

"Yeah?"

"I mean literally shit. It's coming up out of the toilet."

"Just a clogged toilet. Deal with it yourself."

"No, you fucking deal with it."

"It's not my problem. Eat more fiber."

Lao looked out the window over the kitchen sink. Two rows of trailers descended the hill in a line on either side of the road. All on his property. All using his hookups. He could see Dusty's crappy pink trailer, second down from the bottom on the same side as his. The cowboy kid wasn't done complaining.

"I've been gone all week. Went home for Christmas."

"So?"

"This isn't my fucking shit."

"You lock your door when you were gone? Maybe it was some kids."

The kids in the trailer park were like some kind of wild tribe. They roamed around, going where they pleased, getting into anything not locked up. Cost of running business. Nothing you could do. They never went into Lao's trailer. Lao was always home. Lao had a gun he kept in a drawer. No bullets. Just a gun. Sometimes reputation was enough.

"Listen chinky, you're just not listening. The shit is coming up out of the fucking toilet."

"Hey, you can't say that. It's racist."

"Fuck you. I have three inches of shit on my floor."

"No, fuck you. Fuck you cowboy. You apologize?"

"I'm not going to fucking apologize. I have fucking shag carpet."

Lao took a deep breath and let it out. He reached into a drawer and pulled out a Ziploc bag with two cigarettes left in it. His wife had promised to give him something special if he only smoked one that day. She meant a blowjob, but she was too refined to say it. Fuck. Damn it.

"Okay. Okay. I'll come down tomorrow."

"Fuck that. My house is full of shit. You come down tonight."

"I'll not come down tonight. I'll come down tomorrow."

"If you don't come down tonight then I'll come up there."

"You threatening me?"

"I'm not fucking threatening you."

"Fuck you. I'll call the police. I have a gun."

"Go ahead and call the police. They can document what a shithole you're running. Take away your license. There ain't nobody that is going to take your side on this one. You hear me. I'll go down to the courthouse in the morning. File a complaint. Get inspectors out here."

Lao growled deep in his throat. He ripped open the Ziploc bag, took out a cigarette, lit it, and inhaled as deeply as he could. Damn it tasted good.

"Okay. Okay. Calm down. I'll come down right now."

"You better."

"Just calm down. I'll be down in a minute."

Lao hung up the phone. Grumbling to himself he slipped on his coat and a pair of rubber boots. The snow was constantly melting during the day and freezing up at night. The road was nothing but mud, six inches deep in some places. It was getting dark out. Lao pulled a small flashlight out of a drawer and put it in his pocket. He opened the front door, paused, walked back in, got a pipe snake from his toolbox, and walked out the door. John Wayne was pointing his gun at a desperado. Lao was going to miss the best part.

The evening air was cold, but the last bits of the sunset were spectacular. Lao stopped for a minute to stare at it. Always important to appreciate each day. The ash of the cigarette in his mouth dropped off and burnt his hand. Lao cursed and the cigarette dropped into the mud. Lao cursed again. This time in Chinese. He rubbed his hand, squished the cigarette into the mud under his boot, and started squishing his way down the hill.

Twelve trailers on one side. Twelve trailers on the other. All paying rent. All a pain in his ass. Mrs. Carnie, Number 7, peaked through her curtains as Lao walked past. Nosey cunt. Always watching. Had to know everything. Lao kept going, taking small steps to make sure he didn't slip in the mud. Halfway down sat a blue trailer. Number 6. It was empty. Lao knew he shouldn't really complain about Dusty. Dusty was a racist redneck, but usually no problem. College student. Part time. Worked out at some farm. Always paid his fees on time. No complaints from the neighbors.

Number 6 was always a problem. The police were always coming around, busting Number 6 for selling crack. The people in Number 6 would get hauled off to jail. New people would move in. They'd pay rent. The police would show up. The new tenants would go to jail. It was a never ending cycle. It didn't make a lot of sense. A lot of the people didn't even know each other. The trailer was owned by some guy in town. Nice guy. Always paid the lot fees on time. Maybe there was a whole shit ton of crack in Number 6, hidden away somewhere. Maybe the vents. People would be coming by and knocking on the door anyway, looking for crack, might as well sell it. Nice turnkey business. It was none of Lao's business. If you wanted to run a trailer park, you couldn't be too nosey.

Dusty was waiting outside his trailer next to his flatbed pickup. He was wearing an old Carhartt coat and his flat top cowboy hat was pushed back on his head. Chewing tobacco leaked out of either side of his mouth. He had a round cherub face and glasses. His normally smiling mouth was set in a hard line.

"Took you long enough."

"Yeah. Yeah. I'm here. Show me what the problem is."

Dusty gestured towards the trailer.

"Go see for yourself."

The pink single wide trailer was about the smallest one they made. Maybe only ten feet wide. Portions of the pink tin siding were starting to hang loose. Other parts were clumsily nailed back in place. Three to five nails per spot, half or more bent over. A badly made covered deck ran down one side, built of rough cut scrap wood. A big lock hasp was screwed to the door. An open padlock hung off it. The deck next to the door was wet and covered in chunks of something that had once been food. Lao pulled on the door, it wasn't latched, a bungee cord held it closed. The smell hit him. A stink wave that forced its way into the outside world, up his nostrils, down his throat. Lao retched and added to the wet spot by the door. Dusty hadn't been kidding. The entire floor of the trailer was covered in three inches of shit. Lao let the door swing back shut and stood bent over, his hands on his knees, gasping for fresh air. Dusty watched from over by his pickup.

"Well?"

"Well what?"

"You going to figure out what's going on?"

Lao glared at Dusty. Dusty glared back. Asshole. Lao took his handkerchief out of his pocket and held it over his nose and mouth. He took a few deep breaths, opened the door, and walked in. The trailer was a bit of a shithole. Old easy chair and couch. TV with rabbit ears. Little table with two chairs. One of the old fridges with the rounded top and big metal latches that locked it shut. A velvet painting of a nude woman hung above the table. The place smelled even worse inside. The heater had been set at a low level, but was still on. There must have been shit in the vents, slowly baking. Lao walked through the tiny kitchen, past a set of bunk beds built into the wall, piled high with random junk, and into the bathroom.

The shit was definitely coming from the toilet. A big box of Q-tips sat on top of the tank lid. Shit was piled high up over the top of the rim. Brown stains streaked down the outer sides. Lao couldn't hold his breath anymore. He turned and moved quickly towards the door. In the kitchen he almost slipped, but caught himself on the counter. Out the door. Onto the porch. The wet spot next to the door got bigger again. Lao stood back up straight, breathing heavy. Dusty was texting on his phone. Lao walked out into the deepest spot of mud he could find and started scraping his boots on the ground furiously. Dusty looked up and smirked.

"Pretty bad, ain't it?"

"Yeah, pretty bad."

"So what's going on?"

"Clog in the sewer line. Everyone's shit is coming up in your house."

"Fuck."

"Yeah."

Lao stopped scraping his feet. His boots still felt dirty. He blasted a snot rocket out of each nostril. He couldn't get the smell out of his nose.

"You been flushing Q-tips?"

"What?"

"You been flushing Q-tips. Maybe tampons. You know. Swell up. Clog the pipe."

"Why the fuck would I be flushing tampons?"

"None of my business. You probably bring women around here."

"Are you fucking serious?"

"Just trying to figure out what happened."

"Fuck you."

"No, fuck you redneck."

"I haven't been flushing any god damn Q-tips or tampons."

"You have a big box in the bathroom. You have really dirty ears?"

"Fuck you."

"Okay. Okay. Whatever. Might be someone further up."

"Damn straight it might be someone further up."

Lao raised his hands. Dusty looked mad. He looked like he was mad enough to hit somebody.

"Okay. Okay. I make some calls. Get someone to fix the pipe. Get someone to clean the carpets."

"Damn right you will."

"Probably won't be till tomorrow. Too late to get anyone today."

"So what am I supposed to do?"

"Don't know. Your business. Go stay at some lady friend's house. Flush Q-tips down her toilet."

"Fuck you."

Lao waved his hand dismissively.

"Whatever."

"You're going to pay for a hotel or something."

"Not my problem."

"Not your problem?"

"Not responsible to find you some place else to live. Read your lot contract."

"Fuck you."

"Go live someplace nicer if you don't want to deal with this kind of shit."

Lao turned and started working his way back up the hill. A big glob of mud flew through the air and hit the back of his coat. He ignored it. Lao heard Dusty open and slam shut his pickup door. The diesel engine roared to life. The pickup thundered up the road, spitting mud to either side, plastering trailers and parked cars. Lao couldn't blame him. He'd be mad too, but then again, Lao never flushed Q-tips down the toilet. Too bad. Normally Dusty was no trouble. Lao brushed some mud off his face. Mrs. Carnie, staring out of her window in Number 7, watched him go past.

At his house Lao scraped his boots off. He couldn't tell if he was cleaning off shit or just adding mud. Fuck it. Lao took off his boots and left them on the ground outside. He walked into the house, put his coat back on its hook, and took the last cigarette out of the Ziploc bag. Lao sat down in his easy chair and lit the cigarette. He unmuted the TV. The John Wayne movie was over. Fuck. It had been his favorite one. A car pulled up next to the house. Rapid footsteps outside. The door opened, his wife came inside with an armload of groceries. She saw the smoke rising from the cigarette. She stopped in the doorway. Her eyes narrowed. She started screaming in Chinese.

Lao sat in his chair, watching his wife. Her face was bright red. She moved about the kitchen, putting away the groceries. Never once did her mouth stop moving. She came into the living room and snatched the cigarette from his mouth. She threw it in the sink and ran water over it. Still she yammered on, almost too quick to follow. Lao took a deep breath and got up, his movement so violent that the easy chair rocked back and hit the wall. He moved into the kitchen. His wife shrank back in the corner against the stove. Lao brushed past her, went to the bathroom, and shut the door. He turned on the sink and ran cold water over his face. He looked at himself in the mirror. He was breathing heavy. Lao looked at the shut bathroom door. He could hear his wife moving around. Lao looked at the toilet. Pristine shining white porcelain. Lao reached over, flushed the toilet, and laughed.

# Blind Man's Bluff

A group of cows in a field flashed by on the right hand side windows of the long cheese wagon. The big black heads rose up from their grazing, watched the bus slide by in the last of the evening sun, and went back to their dinners. Nate's loud voice broke over the raucous murmuring.

"Those are some pretty fine looking cows Norm!"

High school laughter filled the confined space. Paul laughed along with them. Norm, the bus driver, kept his eyes forward, not even bothering to glance back in the big mirror over his seat. The six coaches said nothing. They kept their faces in iron masks, only the slight twitch at the corner of Coach Hobart's mouth giving away her internal chuckle. Cattle rustling seemed like something out of an old western, but it still happened in the modern era. Cattle still graze out in wide open spaces. Drive out with a trailer, set up a couple panels, entice them with some feed, and haul them off to market. Brand slips aren't that hard to forge. A man who's served his time has to work, but such a memorable crime isn't likely to be forgotten. Nate let out his best impression of a bovine, a surprisingly accurate low.

"Moooo. Holy shit! I think there's something in the cargo hold!"

The laughter came again. Coach Johnson turned around in his seat, his big hairy hands gripping the vinyl, the dim outside light reflecting off the bare spots of his head shining through his combover.

"Watch your god damn language Wilkins."

Coach Johnson turned back around. Nate gave a mock salute to the back of his head. Paul went back to playing Boo-Ray, laying cards on top of eight withered dollar bills on a backpack sitting in the aisle. Paul's seatmate, Tony the booger eater, kept pushing closer, trying to watch over Paul's shoulder. It was distracting. Vince kept winning all the tricks. Paul didn't have much trump, but it was easier to blame Tony. On the way home from the last away game, Tony had been caught picking his nose in the darkness. Nobody was sure what he had been doing with the boogers. Now despite being varsity, nobody wanted to sit with him. It was a bit of a golden opportunity for Paul. Sure he had to sit next to the gross son of a bitch, but he was sitting further back in the bus than any other freshman, not counting the girls of course.

Paul was only mid-way back, but it was farther than he had ever dreamed. The mysterious world of the rear of the bus was in view, far from the commanding silence of the coaches. Varsity. Juniors and seniors. Filthy jokes and overblown laughter. Snuff spit in soda cans. Couples sitting next to each other, hands clasped or resting on each other's thighs. The occasional quick kiss. Sam Johnson, Coach Johnson's son, was sitting next to Margaret McCoy with a blanket over their laps. Her shoulder, visible over the back of the seat in front of them, kept twitching. Sam reached up to grab her boob, she slapped his hand playfully away. Two guys were playing the flinching game, punching the arm of the one who winced, calling each other gay. Fully blossomed girls rolled their eyes, talking about sex, boys, each other, and what the hell they were going to do once they got the hell out and went to college.

Vince won another trick. Amy Tan, his seatmate, pushed herself closer to get a better view, pressing her thin lithe body tight against his. Paul did his best to keep his eyes locked on his cards. Amy was the only other freshman sitting so far back. She earned it though. Only a freshman, but already on the varsity basketball team. She didn't need to sit next to Vince to be so far back, she just preferred to. Tony was a distraction. Amy was interference. How could somebody concentrate with Amy so damn close? Paul could smell the scent of her shampoo wafting from her coal black hair. Her long supple fingers toyed with an errant lock. Vince won the last trick. He scooped up the small pile of money, grinning like an idiot.

Coach Hobart leaned forward, tapped Norm on the shoulder, and pointed towards a freeway exit. Norm flicked on the blinker, geared down, and eased the yellow monster off Interstate 84. The green sign said Exit 182, Hermiston, Lexington. Just off the exit sat a small truck stop. A couple of gas pumps, a convenience store with an A&W connected to it, and a cheap run down motel. An irrigation pivot sat unmoving in a yellowed field across the road. The smokestacks of the potato waste plant, with their blinking lights, sat a mile away. The bus ground to a halt next to an orange plastic construction fence held up by thin white fiberglass poles. Norm shut off the engine and levered open the door. Coach Johnson rose up and stood in the aisle.

"Listen up. You have half an hour for dinner. You don't get your asses back on the bus by then, we're leaving you."

Coach Johnson sat back down. Fifty high schoolers got off the bus, dressed up like respectable ladies and gentlemen. The boys all wore ties and button down shirts tucked into pressed jeans or khakis. The girls all wore dresses with high necklines and hems that touched the ground if they got down on their knees. One girl had failed the test that morning. Coach Hobart had sent her home. It was a slow file off. One of the older kids pushed Paul from behind. He made his way past the coaches and stepped off the bus. The air was cold and stank of potato waste. He was wearing black Wranglers, brown cowboy boots, a blue and white mesh belt, a blue button down shirt, and a black tie covered with miniature red hot sauce bottles. The tie had never been untied all season. Amy was wearing a white dress with blue polka dots and Vince's jacket.

The A&W was mostly empty, just two Mexicans eating at a booth. Later, back on the bus, several of the girls would claim that the two men had been staring at their tits and asses. The girls would act disgusted, but make sure everybody knew that they had tits and asses worth looking at. To Paul, the two men looked as though they would have rather the mob never entered the quiet A&W. The workers behind the counter were cleaning the grill. They weren't ready for such a crowd. With sighs and tired eyes they sprang back into action, taking orders, preparing food, and working their way through the mass as fast as they could. The coaches didn't come inside. Coach LeFleur, the girls JV coach, went into the convenience store, bought some pre-made sandwiches and pop, and took them back onto the bus. Norm took a nap in his seat.

Paul, his tray holding burger and fries, looked for a place to sit. His eyes ran across the booths and tables. There was a spot open next to Amy Tan. She was sipping a root beer float. Paul made his way towards the open seat, but stopped before getting there. Vince hadn't sat down yet. If he took the seat there would be trouble. Breach of protocol. Retaliation acceptable. Paul paused, unsure. From a booth, several of his friends waved for him to come over, calling his name. Paul went and took an empty seat at another table between Sam and Tony. The table was full of juniors and seniors. The seats all around Tony were empty, a protective barrier for his peers, a perfect opening for a freshman trying to impress.

Sam and the other varsity players were discussing game highlights. Paul pretended to listen, eying Amy at the next table over, hoping that she'd look up and see him sitting with such a prestigious group. Paul tried to act casual, as though it was where he belonged. Tony's zit covered cheeks loosened and tightened as he chewed his food. Sam sat with his back to Paul, laughing at something one of the other varsity players had said. Paul's heart beat heavy in his chest. He prayed that Amy would look up and see him before any of the other table's occupants noticed his presence. Amy's lips wrapped her float's straw in a perfect circle, her cheeks pulled in. Watching her made Paul feel dirty. Thoughts he'd never say out loud reverberated through his head.

Vince and Nate walked into the A&W. The majority of the players went silent. Nate was gripping Vince's arm firmly just above the elbow. Vince was wearing a big pair of aviator sunglasses, his head cocked slightly back and to the right, as though he was trying better to hear something. In his hand was one of the thin white fiberglass poles that had been holding up the construction fence outside. They moved as a unit. Nate dragging Vince gently by the arm. Vince taking careful steps and skittering the bottom of the stick back and forth across the floor in front of him. An evil grin spread across Nate's face. He turned his head back and forth to make sure everyone could see it. He pulled Vince forward, bashing him into a cardboard display. A snicker erupted somewhere behind Paul, but was quickly stifled. Vince reared back.

"What was that?"

"Just a display. You have to be careful."

"Sorry, always tough in a new place."

"No worries."

"Which way to the counter?"

Nate gave a tug on Vince's arm.

"Over here."

"Thanks."

Nate prodded Vince to the counter. He left him facing 45 degrees in the wrong direction. The woman behind the register stared at the two, her eyes suspicious, but too tired to really care. She was a short woman in her late forties. Round and weathered. She opened her mouth for a moment to say something, then closed it to reconsider. The kid probably wasn't blind. It seemed like bullshit, but what if it wasn't? What was she going to do? Call out a possibly blind kid in front of everybody? It was a no-win situation. Nate smiled cheerfully at her. The woman raised her eyebrows and let them fall. Her voice sounded like she ate lit cigarettes, filters and all.

"What can I get you?"

Vince jumped and reoriented himself towards the woman's voice. He nervously moved his free hand forward, groping through the darkness until it made contact with the counter. He was a good actor. Paul wouldn't have been surprised if his eyes were closed to create a better illusion. Vince's body stiffened.

"I'm not sure. What is there?"

The woman let out an audible sigh. Nate somehow made his saccharin smile sweeter, and without waiting for a response, launched into a detailed description of the menu. Numbers, prices, meals, combos, sides, and drinks. He described all of the pictures to a minutia, weaving a vivid tapestry of the optical world with his words. The whole thing took about five minutes. Some of the players were visibly shaking, their hands clamped tight around hissing mouths. The woman behind the counter was obviously not happy. She clicked the pink press on nails of one hand against the counter. Her face told the tale, a silent hope that the grill would catch on fire, or some equally chaotic event would end her misery. Vince stood, thinking, running his options through his mind.

"What was #2 again?"

Nate launched back into the appropriate portion of his dialogue, filling in further details. The placement order of the burger, cheese, tomato, and lettuce. An estimate of the number of sesame seeds on the bun. An essay on the pros and cons of ordering a large rather than a regular. Vince went back to thinking. The woman behind the counter rolled her eyes, both arms stiff on the counter as though trying to hold it down. Nate shrugged apologetically. Vince kept his face impassive and unaware.

"I'll have the #4."

The woman let out a long breath and tapped in the order.

"Eight fifty."

Vince pulled his wallet out of his back pocket. It was canvas with velcro. Paul's was black leather, a recent gift from his Uncle Teddy. Vince opened his wallet, and handed it over to Nate.

"Can you give her the money?"

Nate took Vince's wallet.

"Sure, no problem."

Nate took out a ten dollar bill and handed it to the woman. She handed him back a dollar fifty. Nate put the money in his pocket, gave the woman an exaggerated wink, pulled forty dollars out of the wallet, put it in his pocket as well, and then handed the wallet back to Vince. The woman's eyes went wide, then narrowed. The muscles around her mouth tightened. Nate winked at her again. A loud guffaw echoed across the silent dining area. Vince held his wallet in his hand.

"Thanks for helping me out. Let me buy your dinner too?"

"No need."

"Please, I insist."

"Okay, fine."

Nate spent a moment studying the menu as though he had never considered what he was going to eat. He ordered a #2. Vince passed back over his wallet. Nate took out another ten. He again pocketed the change and another ten for good measure. The woman behind the counter stared down at her register, refusing to look at either of the teenagers. Her face was beat red. Nate gave Vince back his wallet. Vince returned it to his back pocket.

"Thanks man, you're a good friend."

Nate gave Vince a friendly slap on the back and turned him around to go find a seat. The fiberglass stick skittered back and forth. Nate sat Vince down in the booth with Paul's freshman friends. Nate walked back to the counter to pick up the tray with its two sets of burgers and fries. All eyes followed him, even those of the Mexicans. Nate moved across the dining area, sat down at a table as far from Vince as possible, and proceeded to eat both burgers. Laughter exploded like a bomb. Hands pounded tables. Vince swung his head left and right, his voice filled with mock confusion.

"Nate? What's going on? Where's the food?"

The laughter doubled. The woman behind the counter, so mad that her body was vibrating, stalked off out of view behind the grill. Paul didn't really think it was all that funny, but everyone else did, so Paul laughed along with them, just as raucous as all the rest. Paul wished he could be as funny as Nate and Vince. Everybody loved Nate and Vince. Maybe if he was just as cool she would notice him. Sam Johnson shook Paul's shoulders with merriment as though they were old friends. Paul looked at Amy to see if she noticed. She hadn't. Amy wasn't laughing. She was staring down at her float, disgust written across her face.

# The End

A couple beers sloshed in his belly. It wasn't that late. She wasn't that far away. He should really take care of it. He called twice on his cell phone. She didn't pick up either time, it just went straight to voicemail. Her phone never went straight to voicemail. In the two years of their acquaintance her phone had never been turned off. Green light. Time to go. The car lurched forward, another salmon in the stream. It wasn't true. There were a few times her phone had been shut off. Usually when she was mad at him. Usually when she wanted attention, wanted him to react. Red light. Stop. He was close. He might as well just take care of it. He pulled back up his phone and typed out a text message. The T9 interface was slow. He needed to get a new phone. The old flip phone could be a pain in the ass. Green light. Go. He kept half an eye on the road and half an eye on the phone to finish his text. He should really be more careful. Buzzed driving is drunk driving. That was the slogan. His finger hit send.

*Coming by to pick up my 100.*

He put the phone down between his legs. His legs hurt. The run had been a good one. Across the new Tilikum bridge, up the waterfront, across the Steele, and then back. It had felt good to stretch his legs. Get a little sweat going. Have a couple beers. A little one on one time with a friend. Good day. It had been a good day. Time to stretch out a bit. Time to break away from the old routines. Time to spread his wings and all that crap.

She had called him yesterday. He had been having post-game beers with a group of people, most of which he didn't know. A message on Facebook. A friend had needed an extra player for futsal. The team was short. He hadn't played soccer in probably three years, and even then he wasn't much good. He had volunteered to fill in. Might as well. Something new. It had been good. Run back and forth. Work up a sweat. Flail around and try to figure out what to do. Meet some new people he'd never met before. A couple of attractive women. All had boyfriends. Oh well. Sit and sip a beer. Listen to the conversation. His phone had buzzed in his pocket. He had gotten up and walked to a quiet corner to answer it.

"Hello."

"Hey."

"What's up?"

"I have something here that's yours."

"Yeah, what is it?"

"You remember when you gave me some cash for dinner last night at trivia?"

"Yeah."

"I was looking through it, and one of the bills was a hundred dollar bill."

"Oh, I was wondering what happened to that. I just noticed it was gone today, and I couldn't remember whether or not I had spent it."

"Well, it's here."

"Okay."

"I don't really want to be carrying it around. I can just leave it at the house if you want to swing by some time and get it."

"Okay. Thanks for letting me know."

"Yeah."

"It was nice of you to call to let me know."

"Yeah."

"Not that I'd expect you to do any different. I mean. Crap. Sorry. Thanks. We'll get it figured out sometime this week."

"Okay."

"I've got to get going. I'm in the middle of a futsal match."

"Oh. Yeah, I better let you go."

"Thanks again. We'll get it figured out later this week."

"Bye."

"Bye."

The tall red and yellow sign of the Ethiopian restaurant came into view on the side of her building. Her apartment was on the second floor, right next to the sign. It looked like her light was on, but it was hard to tell. He took a left turn onto a side street alongside the building. He had to drive down two blocks to find a parking space. Probably a concert at the Wonder Ballroom. Parking in her neighborhood was always a bitch when there was a concert at the Wonder Ballroom. He got out and slipped on his rain jacket over his running clothes. It wasn't raining. Just chilly. He walked down the dark street, humming quietly to himself. It would be good to see her. Good to see how she was doing. He hoped she was okay. It was harder for her than him. It was always harder on her. He didn't see her car along the street. Maybe she wasn't home. Part of him felt glad. Part felt sad. Part wondered if he should just turn around and go home. No matter. He had a key.

He rounded the corner. No lights in her apartment windows. Maybe she was already in bed. She'd been tired lately. Work had been hell. Lots of sixteen hour days. Maybe she had turned in early. The front door of the building was propped slightly open. The deadbolt was closed, but not latched into the other door. He pulled open the door and went inside. He started up the flight of stairs. Up to the first landing. Up to the second landing. Up to the second floor. How many times had he climbed these stairs before? It had to be in the hundreds. Sometimes bouncy. Sometimes dour. More than a few times trying to hide an erection.

Down the hall to the apartment at the end. He knocked once and waited. The cat mewed plaintively inside. No dog. No scrambling little body. No harsh high-pitched barks. If she had the dog with her she was likely not going to come home any time soon. Maybe she'd gone on a run. She sometimes took the dog with her when she ran. There was a run out in Beaverton. If she'd gone to that she wouldn't be home until late. He knocked again and waited. The cat mewed again in response. He unlocked the door and went inside.

The apartment was dark. The black cat ran up and rubbed against his leg. He bent down to pet it and leaned back against the door. It was the same position he had been in two nights before. Tears had filled his eyes and she, standing opposite, had draped herself over him so the back of his head had rested just below her breasts. He could feel her tears soaking into the back of his shirt.

"I love you more than I've ever loved anyone before."

"What do you want me to do? I wish I felt the same way, but I don't. I'm tired of hurting you. I don't want to hurt you anymore."

"I don't know what to do either. I don't know what to do without you. I don't know what to do."

"I'm sorry. I hate hurting you. I hate hurting you so much. I don't want to hurt you anymore."

Clinging desperately. Touch. The healing power of touch. Looking for refuge in the source of pain. He shook his head, stepped into the apartment and switched on the light. It was a small apartment. Living room, tiny kitchen, bedroom, bathroom. He looked on the table by the door. Nothing. He looked on the coffee table by the couch. Nothing. No hundred dollar bill. He stared at the couch. Sweaty. Naked. Thrusting. No. Best not to think of such things. There were more recent memories on the couch. The two of them sitting on either side. Her eyes sad and angry. Their voices steadily rising.

"I can't believe you did that."

"I wish I hadn't done it. I'm sorry."

"You can't even remember her name. That's what really bothers me."

"I regretted it before I even started."

"Why did you do it then? Why did you do it?"

"I don't know. I guess because I could."

"You threw it all away, just because you could."

"It's not like you ever told me I couldn't."

"Fuck you. I shouldn't have to tell you."

"Bullshit. We both know what this is."

"I was so scared that this was going to happen. I was so worried all weekend."

"Why didn't you say something then?"

"I shouldn't have to say something."

"It's not like we're in a relationship. It's not like this is any different than the other times."

"It is different."

"Why didn't you say something?"

"Because I had no right to. We're not in a relationship. But now it's over. It has to be over."

"Part of me is glad I did it."

"Get out of my house."

"Part of me is glad. For the first time in my life I knew I didn't want to go back to how I used to be. From the moment I started I didn't want to be there."

"Did you at least use a condom?"

"Of course I did. I'm not an idiot."

"You never did with me."

"Why don't we talk about the real problem?"

"We are."

"Bullshit. You know what it is. You just won't say it out loud."

"No I don't."

"Bullshit."

"What is it then? What is it that I'm supposed to know?"

"The problem is you want me to feel the same about you as you feel about me and I want you to feel the same about me as I feel about you. You want me to love you, and I want you to be okay with just being friends."

That's when the tears had started falling. She had sat there, tears dripping down her cheeks, turning her head and hiding her face with her hand. He had not wanted to make her cry, but it needed to be said. The same problem as all the times before, raising its ugly head, demanding attention. It couldn't be ignored. He had been tired of hurting her. Tired of being stuck in limbo. Just tired. Just plain old tired.

He looked in the bedroom, but didn't turn on the light. Nothing on the nightstand. A large pile of dirty clothes lay next to the dresser. The bed was neatly made. The bed was always neatly made. Two nights ago he had lain beneath the covers, the small dog laying in between them. Her hand rested on his side. His hand rested on her belly. They had made broken small talk, short periods of time where they pretended nothing had happened, that nothing had changed. She had drifted off to sleep. He had lain in bed and stared up at the ceiling.

He turned around and walked back through the living room to the bathroom. He lifted the toilet seat and took a piss. The bathroom stunk of kitty litter and cat urine. He pressed the handle and watched the yellow water go down. His eyes did one more check before he switched off all the lights. What was he doing here? The cat mewed again. His hand rested on the doorknob.

"If you walk out that door then it's over. No more. It's done."

She had put his spare keys in his hand. He had put hers down on the table. He should have left right then and there. It would have been better for her if he did. A sharp pain. Time to heal. He was just dragging it out. He hadn't left. He had stood there. Unsure. What was he doing? Was he doing the right thing? No one had ever loved him as much as she had. No one had ever treated him better. In her presence he was the sun. What was he throwing away? Why? Just because he didn't feel a pull that he might never feel again. A strong emotional discharge pushing him against all logic. A fear. A fear that he would resent her. He cared about her. She had stood there in front of him. Crying. Upset. He hated to see her hurt. He hated to see her in pain. Part of him had wanted to wrap his arms around her. To protect her. To tell her everything was going to be okay. He had started to cry.

"I don't know what to do."

"I don't want to lose you."

"I don't want to hurt you anymore."

"Don't go. Please don't go. Just stay tonight."

"I should go. We're just kicking a can down the road."

"Just stay tonight."

He opened the door, checked to make sure it was locked, and closed it behind him. Down the familiar hallway. Down the stairs with the two landings. Out the building door, still propped open on its deadbolt. He paused on the sidewalk, dug his phone out of his pocket, and slowly tapped out a text.

*Came by your house. Nobody home. Will try another time.*

Where was she? He started back up the sidewalk. A car moved down the street. His eyes watched it go past. Not hers. If she was out at the run she wouldn't be back until later. It made the most sense. If she had gone out anywhere else she wouldn't have taken the dog. It would have greeted him at the door. Jumping into the air. Tail wagging. He got back into his car, started it up, and headed back towards home. Something didn't feel right. His gut felt like it was slowly twisting. His whole body began to shake. Tiny vibrations from his core that worked their way to the tips of his extremities. A violent storm that passed over his body, raged for over a minute, and then passed as though it had never happened. Red light stop. Green light go. He sat in his car, the radio off, the lights of the city moving past, thinking.

His car rounded the final corner and moved down his street. The headlights moved across the familiar shadowy shapes of lawns, houses, and shrubbery. Hidden worlds partially opened by illuminated windows. Picturesque scenes rolling past. Brief views into other universes. A car sat in front of his house. An older model. Dark faded paint. Her car. The knot in his gut pulled tighter. He pulled into his driveway. The porch light was on. All of the other lights were off. He considered pulling back out and driving away. His limbs began to vibrate again. Better to face whatever it was. These types of talks with her always lasted a long time. It was going to be a late night. He turned off the engine and got out of his car.

Up to the front door. Weeds crowded the sidewalk. They needed to be taken care of. Maybe next week. His key slipped into the lock. High pitched barking. The door opened. Her dog stood on the back of the couch, hackles raised. He turned on the living room light. The room was empty. Just the dog. The dog jumped off the back of the couch and ran up to him, whimpering. He leaned over and patted the dog, then stood back up. The house was silent.

"Hello? Is anyone here?"

No answer. What the hell? A strange need to turn around and run back out the door. He moved forward, turning on lights as he went. Dining room. Kitchen. Bedroom. Office. All empty. The dog jumped back onto the couch and watched him intently as he moved. The door to the bathroom was closed. Light shined from underneath. He softly knocked.

"Hello?"

Nothing. Just silence. His hand went to the doorknob. He stopped and listened. Still nothing. His entire body tingled. The knob turned. The door opened. His knees buckled. He tumbled to the floor. She lay in the tub. Her eyes closed. Her mouth partially opened. His breath was loud and ragged in his ears. She didn't move. Her sleeves were pulled up. Long gashes covered her forearms. Rivulets wound their way past her legs to the drain. The red was bright against the chipped white porcelain. Almost black in comparison.

He crawled out of the bathroom and shut the door. The dog pranced over and licked his hand. He pet the dog. His body shook violently. Why? Why? Why? The storm passed. The dog licked his hand again and then walked back into the living room. He sat and stared at the retreating form. Call someone. He should probably call someone. He dug his phone out of his pocket, found a name, and hit send. A few rings. Voicemail. He hung up the phone. He found another name, and hit send. A few rings. Voicemail. He hung up the phone. Police. He should probably call the police. Should he call 911 or the non-emergency number? Was this really an emergency? There was nothing anyone could do. Nothing at all. The phone fell from his fingers and landed on the floor. What was he supposed to do? The dog barked from the living room.

He needed to pee. He pushed himself up to his feet and walked back into the living room, through the dining room to the kitchen. He unlocked the back door and went outside onto the patio. Another wave of shaking overtook his body and he nearly fell to the ground again. The moment passed. He peed on the rosemary bush next to the patio. He put his dick away and went back into the house. He shut the back door behind him and locked it. The dog stood in the dining room doorway. It barked and then let out a whine. A bag of dog food sat on the kitchen counter. He pulled a small dish out of the cupboard, put some dog food on it, and put it on the kitchen floor. The dog trotted up and started to eat. His eyes filled with tears and he collapsed again. He lay on the floor balling. The dog watched him for a bit, and then trotted over and licked the tears off his face. He got up and went looking for his phone. He needed to call the police. He needed to talk to somebody.

The light turned green. The car behind his honked its horn, snapping him back into reality. What the fuck? What the fuck was that? He put his car in gear and moved forward. What the fuck? What the fuck was wrong with him? She was just on a run. Nothing to worry about. Jesus Christ. His car rounded the final corner and moved down its street. His eyes searched the street ahead for any sign. Red reflectors in the distance. A car two houses down. The street in front of his house was empty. The house was dark except for the porch light. He pulled into his driveway and shut off his car. His palms were sweaty. He rubbed them dry on his shorts. He got out of the car and moved up the walk to the front door. His key went into the lock. He paused. Silence. He opened the door and moved inside. All quiet.

"Hello?"

No answer. Nothing. He moved through the house and turned on all the lights. Crazy. He was just acting crazy. What the fuck was wrong with him? He took a couple of deep breaths and let them out. The house was empty. He was alone. All alone. He made dinner and ate it while watching Netflix. He took off his clothes, masturbated, brushed his teeth, and climbed into bed. He lay in the dark, staring at the phone, sitting on the nightstand, hooked to its charger. The phone stayed quiet.

# Blotches

Two days until they zap my eyes. Pew. Pew. Two days until high powered lasers shave and reshape the lens of each ocular organ into what they tell me is the preference for normal. Twenty-twenty vision. A forgotten standard of personal view from a forgotten age of uninhibited emotion and unending curiosity. Two more days until clarity.

I awaken the way I always do, to a world of colorful blobs punctuated by light and dark. An impressionist's vision. A view just slightly out of focus. Nothing is really anything when I wake up in the morning. I'm cut off from the world. Apart. Severed. Separated by my faulty lens' inability to correctly converge the light flowing in from the outside world. I move this way through the beginning of my day. Bedroom. Bathroom. Pee in toilet. Flush it down. Go to the kitchen. Eat. Bathroom again. Shower. Get ready for work. I know what is around me, but it is more an exercise in memory and faith than anything truly tangible. The world lacks details. It is nothing but blotches.

I put my glasses on and the world springs into clarity. The pool of white that is the bathtub next to me resolves itself into basin and tile, splotched pink and black with grime. I emerge into the world around me. I can remember the first time that it happened. I was ten. A story like all the others. No one noticing until I could no longer read the blackboard. An appointment. A man in a bolo tie telling me to read off letters of shrinking sizes. The whole world as described, suddenly thrust into existence. The birds, no longer dots, winging their way through the air. The trees, once green splotches, turned to individual leaves fluttering in chaotic frenzy. It was as if I was seeing another world, viewing it through a magic mirror.

I've never enjoyed wearing glasses. I'm only doing it now because I can't wear my contacts just before the surgery, not that I really enjoyed them either. Dust, rain, and smudges. All conspiring to muddy the water through which I swim. They told me with my sensitive eyes I would never be able to wear contacts. They did not bargain on the stubbornness of a frustrated boy who spent most of his life outdoors. Three hours I sat in that office. Putting them in and taking them out. Proving I was capable, until finally, with a huff of surrender and a last volley of doubt, the man with the bolo tie let me have my victory. It was an upgrade from the glasses, and now the final step is here.

Will I miss it? I don't know. I've lived in the world of blotches for so long that it's hard to imagine any other. It's hard to imagine climbing through the magic mirror to live permanently in the world on the other side. I guess, there is a certain aesthetic to wearing glasses. I've never really taken advantage of it, but zapping my eyes definitely removes the possibility. I'll be damned if I ever become one of those people who wears fake glasses just to complete a look. I've never thought about it until I'm on the cusp of losing it, but there is something comforting in my morning ritual. Something nice about having time between coming awake and having to face the full brunt of the world in lurid detail. Now it's going to be gone, and I don't know how to feel. The beauty of the world is in the details, but so are the ugly bits. Is it going to change me? How much of who I am is tied to this physical part? How much is my view of the world changed by the corrective lenses that I will soon cast aside? I don't know, but I'm willing to bet I'll probably clean my shower more often.

# The Nine Lives Of Mr. Snuggles

The woman behind the front desk snapped her gum at Linda's entrance, but didn't look up from the phone in her hand. Linda didn't bother to say hello, a habit long since abandoned. The woman behind the desk, for her part, had never even put in the effort. To be fair, Linda came like clockwork every week. Wednesday 4 PM. Her visits locked in as part of both womens' routines, but it still bothered her. The two women were close to the same age, both in their mid-fifties, so Linda held the woman to the same standards in which she held herself. Good money paid for the place, not Linda's money, but perfectly good money nonetheless. The least they could do was greet visitors.

The decoration of the nursing home's lobby was spartan and mostly bare, but the walls were freshly painted and the nooks and crannies were kept well dusted. A large decorative piece of hammered brass hung on one wall, interconnecting swirls. A vase of fresh flowers sat on a shelf, daisies, bright yellow eyes fringed by white petals. Minus the less than attentive door keeper, it gave the sense that it was not a bad place, but also not one with too many frills.

The woman behind the desk snapped her gum again. Linda walked through the lobby and entered the maze of memorized hallways which led to Tatie Martha's room. The hallway carpet was thin, clean, and durable. The whole place stank of chemical cleaners, medication, and a slight undertone of urine. The first two rooms she passed were the sitting room and the dining room, french doors pulled open. The decoration closely resembled that of a mid-line hotel. The head nurse, her name was Boggs, was leaning over and helping an old man with a puzzle. The old man breathed through a tube in his nostrils and he sat as a building with its top floors slowly collapsing into those below. A floating red balloon was tied to his chair. Nurse Boggs, seeing Linda walk by, rose and moved to follow.

"Mrs. Dubois?"

Linda stopped and turned. The head nurse was a large woman. Not fat, just bulky. Big arms and shoulders pressing against the confines of her scrubs. Perfectly formed for lifting and carrying. Despite her bulk she was light on her feet. Gliding across the ugly carpet in her bright red crocs.

"Yes?"

"Mrs. Dubois. I assume you are on your way to visit your aunt."

"Yes."

Linda wanted to state that there certainly wasn't anyone else she had any interest in visiting, but did not. Nurse Boggs was a humorless woman.

"Good. I wanted to catch you before you saw her. Mr. Snuggles died last night."

Linda bit her lower lip. Mr. Snuggles was Tatie Martha's cat, or apparently, had been her cat. A big elderly Maine coon who had spent most of his time lying in the bathroom sink, meowing at anyone who entered until they gave in and ran the water on him. Mr. Snuggles had been the compromise when it had come time to move Tatie Martha into the nursing home. It had been an expensive compromise, but in Linda's mind, well worth it.

"When did he die?"

The head nurse's face betrayed no emotion.

"We found him this morning when she was at breakfast and we were cleaning the room. He was dead on the bed."

"I see."

"He was an old cat."

"Yes, I know."

"She doesn't know that he's dead yet."

The two women stared at each other for a moment. Nurse Boggs stank of cigarettes and canned air freshener.

"Beg pardon?"

"Your aunt, she doesn't know that Mr. Snuggles is dead."

Linda squeezed at a tight spot on her shoulder.

"Why haven't you told her?"

"Union contract says we don't have to tell her. We already deal with enough without delivering your bad news on top of it."

"I see."

"She won't quit asking about that cat."

"I'll take care of it."

"Okay then."

Linda turned and started down the hall. Nurse Boggs' voice carried after her.

"Mrs. Dubois?"

Linda turned back.

"Yes."

"What would you like us to do with it?"

"Do with what?"

"The cat?"

Linda twisted the wedding ring on her finger. She gave herself a moment before she spoke.

"The dead cat?"

"Yes. Mr. Snuggles."

"You want to know what to do with a dead cat?"

"Yes."

"It's dead. Just throw it in the dumpster."

"Okay. Just checking. People often do all sorts of weird things with their pets. Get them cremated, pressed into diamonds, all sorts of crazy things. I have a cousin who does that kind of work. Eighty bucks just for yours, forty if it gets done with a bunch and you're okay with just getting an equivalent amount of ash."

"A bunch, like a bunch of pets all at once?"

"Yes, whatever gets brought in that day."

"Just throw it in the trash." "Okay, just checking, she really loved that cat."

"Yes, I know."

"I'll leave you to it then."

The head nurse turned and stalked back to helping the old man with his puzzle. Linda turned and headed further into the maze. Tatie Martha's room was on the end of the west hall. Most of the doors were closed, names neatly written on each. The door three up from Tatie Martha's was open. A dresser had been shoved across the opening, blocking the bottom two thirds. A distinguished gray haired gentleman stood behind the dresser in freshly ironed pajamas, the creases perfectly straight and razor sharp, a broom held at the ready.

"Halt, who goes there?"

Linda moved herself towards the far side of the hall and sidled past.

"Just me, Mr. Martin, Linda Dubois."

The old man blinked his milky eyes and squinted.

"Of course, Mrs. Dubois. Be careful out there. The last patrol hasn't reported in yet."

"I will Mr. Martin."

Mr. Martin relaxed and put the broom on his shoulder, standing more erect than many younger men. Linda moved past down to the end of the hall. Tatie Martha's name tag was written in a flowing cursive with flowers made of tissue taped to either side. Linda knocked on the door.

"It's open."

The voice was gravelly and sounded similar to someone speaking with a large marshmallow in their mouth. Linda opened the door. The apartment was not large. A small sitting area with a loveseat and chair facing a TV. A tiny kitchenette with a two burner stove top and a mini-fridge. An open doorway leading back to the bedroom and bathroom. A large painting, dark with age and grime, hung on one wall. A telephone and a few personal knick knacks sat on two end tables. Tatie Martha sat in the chair, watching the TV. At Linda and Roger's wedding she had been spry and thin, wine glass in hand, dancing with the younger men, laughing at their reddening faces as she whispered in their ears. That had been thirty years ago. The woman sitting in the chair was gaunt and decidedly crone-like. Skin hanging off of bones. Gray half combed hair hanging down to her shoulders. Tatie Martha wasn't wearing a shirt.

"Linda, how good to see you."

Linda hurriedly closed the door behind her.

"Tatie, you're topless."

The old woman looked down at herself and then went back to watching the TV.

"They put wires in my shirt."

"Tatie, what are you talking about?"

"The wires. The wires in my shirt. You know, so they know when I get out of bed."

"Tatie, that was only in the hospital."

Tatie Martha had toppled over in the hallway a month ago, which had earned her a stay in the hospital for a couple of days. Tatie Martha, a widow for over forty years, had never been one to ask for help. Though unsteady on her feet, she had balked at the doctor's orders to have a nurse help her use the restroom. The result had been a gown wired with electronics to tell the doctors when she moved. Tatie Martha had not been pleased.

"Are you sure dear?"

"Yes, Tatie, just in the hospital."

Linda went into the bedroom and got a shirt out of the closet. She took it back into the main room and showed Tatie Martha the back and front.

"See, no wires."

"Show me the back again."

Tatie Martha leaned in close and studied the shirt carefully, then demanded to see the front again and studied it as well. Finally satisfied, she allowed Linda to help her put the shirt on, but insisted on buttoning it herself. Settled, Tatie Martha turned off the TV and got unsteadily to her feet.

"Damn idiot box. Suck the life out of you if you let it."

Linda kept her mouth shut. Tatie Martha had never been much of a reader, and aside from social activities put on by the home, Linda doubted she did much but watch the TV. Tatie Martha gesticulated with her bony hand.

"Do you want some tea dear?"

"Thank you. I can get it."

"Nonsense. Nonsense."

Tatie Martha gestured for Linda to sit down and shuffled her way slowly to the counter of the kitchenette. Linda sat on the edge of the loveseat, her limbs as tense as a spooked deer, ready to spring up at a moment's notice. The old woman put a kettle of water on one of the electric burners and pulled a box of teabags out of the cupboard.

"How is Roger dear?"

Tatie Martha always asked about Roger. Tatie Martha adored Roger, or at least she adored the younger version of him that had gotten stuck into her head. Roger used to come by to visit every now and again, sometimes with Linda, and sometimes by himself, but then had stopped nine months ago. He had come alone and found himself talking to a woman, who though answering every question, was obviously very confused. When he had gone to use the toilet Tatie Martha had called the nurse to report that there was a strange man in her bathroom. Roger had quit coming after that. When Linda bothered him about it, he had said he really didn't see the point. Tatie Martha never forgot Linda, though to be fair, it might have been more of a function of repetitiveness rather than any kind of special bond.

"Roger is fine Tatie, he sends his love. He's quite busy."

"That boy, always up to something. If I was him, I wouldn't work so hard if I had a wife like you at home."

Linda didn't answer, she just sat, twisting her wedding ring on her finger. The ring felt too big. Linda found herself repeatedly checking to make sure it didn't fall off. Tatie Martha hummed to herself as the kettle began to boil. She steeped the tea and poured it into two cups she pulled from the cupboard.

"That idiot box. I'll tell you, the things I see on it, and to think that Philip Foss once called me uncouth. There's nothing I ever did half of what you see on that thing."

Linda smiled politely. She had no idea who Philip Foss was.

"Milk dear?"

"Thank you."

Tatie Martha shuffled back over with a tea saucer firmly clenched in each hand. With each step hot tea slopped out onto the saucers. Linda rose and took the saucers, and then handed one back when the old woman had gotten herself settled. Tatie Martha had left the burner on, but Linda ignored it. They were made to automatically shut off after fifteen minutes. A prudent safety precaution given the number of meals burnt to a crisp in the waning days of Tatie Martha living in her own house. The two sat quietly and sipped their tea.

"So how are things going Tatie?"

"Oh as fine as can be expected. I'm very old you know."

"Yes Tatie, nearly ninety."

"The nurses tell me they'll have a big party. Quite a milestone. You'll have to come of course."

"Of course I'll be there."

"Probably the usual. You know, cake, ice cream. You have to give people here something to look forward to, something to live for, otherwise they'll just up and die you know. Of course we'll have to get a party hat for Mr. Snuggles."

Linda looked down at her tea. Tatie Martha did not seem to notice.

"He'll look so handsome, a big cat like him in a party hat. We'll have to get lots of pictures."

Tatie Martha finished her tea and put the saucer on the side table.

"I'm not sure where the big brute is right now. He was still asleep on my bed when I went to breakfast, but he was gone by the time I got back."

The old woman gave a lecherous wink.

"Probably out carousing. He's still fairly roguish for such an old cat."

Linda took a deep breath and let it out. Her hands were shaking so she balled them into fists and willed them unsuccessfully to stop.

"Tatie?"

"Yes dear?"

"I have to tell you something."

"What is it dear?"

"Mr. Snuggles is dead. He passed away last night."

"What?"

"The nurses found him dead on your bed this morning when they came in to clean the room."

The old woman turned away and stared at the blank TV screen. Her jaw worked back and forth and a muscle in her cheek twitched. A couple tears fell, and then the old woman balled like a child. She curled over herself as best as her arthritic joints would let her, held her knees, and balled. Wet eyes. Snotty nose. The works. Linda had never seen anything like it before.

"Mr. Snuggles…..my dear little kitty…..Mr. Snuggles."

Linda laid her hand on Tatie Martha's back. She got kleenexes so the old woman could blow her nose. The old woman didn't stop crying. Not for a moment. Not even when the nurses came to take her for dinner at 5:30 PM. Tatie Martha tried to compose herself, but she just kept sobbing. The nurses were insistent that she go eat. Nurse Boggs had Tatie Martha in her strong grip.

"There, there dear. We'll get a little food in you. It will help you feel better."

Linda thought about trying to stop them, but after watching Tatie Martha cry for an hour, she was out of ideas. Linda had never seen Tatie Martha show so much emotion about anything. The door shut and the room fell into silence. Linda washed and dried the teacups in the small sink, put them away, and drove home. Roger wasn't home. A message on her phone told her that he had to work late. Linda had two glasses of wine at dinner instead of the usual one.

The flowers in the lobby needed water. When Linda came into the nursing home she tried to mention as much to the woman at the front desk. The woman at least had the grace to take her eyes off her phone for a minute, but it was only to look at the vase and then stare at Linda until she walked away. The old man in the sitting area was still working on his puzzle, wheezing through the hissing hose in his nose. Linda took a step far enough in to try and see what the puzzle was. Most of the outside was complete and about a third of the interior. Something with hot air balloons. Every movement by the old man was sure and careful. He eyed the pieces until he saw what he wanted, then picked one up and put it in its place. He never lifted a piece unless he knew where it was supposed to go.

The hallway down to Tatie Martha's room was quiet. Mr. Martin's door was open as it always was. The dresser was gone. Farther in, a barricade had been built using various chairs and end tables. The center of the barricade was an old overstuffed flower print couch with the seats facing inward. Mr. Martin was crouched on the cushions, his broom pointed over the top of the back of the couch. His normally immaculate pajamas were badly out of order, and Linda could see the whites all around his pupils. Linda glanced in the room, hesitated, and started to go by.

"Get down you damn fool!"

The yell made Linda jump. She scurried down the hall, her heart racing, to get herself out of the way. At Tatie Martha's door she paused to compose and prepare herself. It had been a week. Surely things were okay by now. Linda knocked.

"It's open."

Linda opened the door. The old woman was sitting in her chair watching television.

"Linda, how good to see you."

"How are you doing Tatie?"

"Very good, thank you for asking. Please, sit down."

Tatie Martha motioned for Linda to sit down on the loveseat. Linda did so gratefully, pulling her skirt to keep it from getting rumpled. Tatie Martha turned off the TV.

"This idiot box. What a waste of time. You wouldn't believe the things you see on it. Some of the things would turn even old Philip Foss's face red, I'll tell you that much."

Linda smiled.

"How is Roger dear?"

Linda's fists involuntarily clenched her skirt. When she noticed she nervously smoothed it with her hands. Tatie Martha didn't seem to notice.

"He's fine. He wanted to be here, but he had to work."

"Oh that scamp. He's always working too hard. What's the point of working if one isn't going to enjoy life."

"Yes."

"Would you like some tea dear?"

"I can get it."

"Nonsense, you stay right there."

They chatted about the weather while Tatie Martha made the tea. Linda tried not to watch her too closely. If Tatie Martha noticed Linda watching her too closely, waiting for her to burn herself, she got very cranky. Linda mostly watched from the corner of her eye and occasionally looked out the window. There was a nice middle aged elm in view. The leaf covered branches swayed in the breeze. Tatie Martha shuffled back with the cups and saucers. Linda got up to help her. The two women sat down to enjoy their tea.

"Well Tatie, you seem better this week."

"Thank you dear. Better than what?"

"Than how I left you last week. You know, when I told you about Mr. Snuggles."

Tatie Martha put her cup and saucer down on the end table and pulled a blanket onto her waist. At the mention of Mr. Snuggles her attention, normally scattered, coalesced onto Linda.

"What about Mr. Snuggles?"

Linda felt a pit deep in her stomach. Her mouth moved of its own volition.

"When we talked about how Mr. Snuggles had died."

"Mr. Snuggles is dead?"

The voice sounded small, almost childlike. Someone speaking from a much farther distance away. Linda reached forward and put her hand on the old woman's blanket covered knee.

"Tatie, he died last week."

"Why didn't anyone tell me?"

"I did tell you."

"Oh god."

Tatie Martha collapsed into sobs, her head as close to her knees as she could get it, her back wracked by heavy phlegmy blubbering. The crying was every bit as bad as last time. The old woman drowning in a sea of escaping emotion. Tatie Martha wouldn't stop crying. Linda did her best to comfort her, but it did little and soon collapsed into handing over kleenexes and studying the large painting hanging on the wall. It was of a shepherd trying to force his flock into a small shed in the middle of a severe snowstorm. One hand held his hat, the other a crook outstretched to force the last of the sheep in. It looked warm inside the shed. The frame was finely made, dark and polished, with swirls and sweeps.

Tatie Martha cried until the nurses came to take her for dinner at 5:30 PM. The nurses insisted she go eat. She was still weeping when Nurse Boggs lifted her with her big hands, cooing as they moved her along while the shepherd with his crook watched.

"There, there dear. We'll get a little food in you. It will help you feel better."

Linda gave the head nurse a dirty look for not warning her. Nurse Boggs ignored it. The door closed and the room fell into silence. Linda washed and dried the teacups in the small sink, put them away, and drove home. Roger wasn't home again. There was another message that he would have to work late. Linda ate dinner, drank two glasses of wine, thought about a

third, and compromised with a half. She then had a quick
frustrated cry and went to bed.


The flowers in the lobby were visibly drooping. Nurse
Boggs was waiting for Linda when she came inside. The head
nurse's big arms were crossed in front of her. Slabs of flesh,
tense and obviously agitated. She was holding a piece of paper
in her hand which she held out the moment Linda walked in the
door.

"Mrs. Dubois, we need to talk."

Linda took the piece of paper. It appeared to be a flier with
handwritten flowing cursive letters. A photograph of a large old
gray Maine coon had been pasted in the center beneath the
words, *Missing Cat*. Linda heard a slight snort behind her. She
turned her head and looked at the woman behind the front desk.
The woman didn't look up from her phone, but Linda could
almost swear that she saw a ghost of a smile on her lips.

"Mrs. Dubois?"

Linda returned her focus to the bulky woman before her.

"Yes?"

"This is something we need to take care of."

"It's just a poster."

"She's put several up throughout the center."

Linda looked at the poster again. It was kind of funny.
Almost like something a child would make. She smiled to
herself. Nurse Boggs wasn't smiling.

"Mrs. Dubois, things like this can upset the patients. This is
a situation we need you to take care of."

"I don't know what you want me to do. I've already told her
twice."

"She is your aunt. We need you to take care of this. If we
try and take them down she gets very upset."

Mr. Martin marched by the lobby door. His pajamas were
parade ground pressed and his broomstick was placed perfectly

on his shoulder. The old man's slippers flopped with every step. Seeing Nurse Boggs, Mr. Martin did an about face, came to attention, and shot the head nurse a perfunctory salute.

"Still no sign of the missing cat ma'am, but we'll keep up the search."

Nurse Boggs glowered. Another quiet snort came from the woman behind the front desk. Mr. Martin stayed at attention, waiting for his return salute, but after a few heartbeats gave up, made a quarter turn, and marched off down the hallway. Nurse Boggs leaned in close to Linda, her jaw clenched, her breath reeking of menthols.

"Just take care of it."

Nurse Boggs turned and stalked after Mr. Martin. Linda carefully folded the flier and put it in her purse. There were more. One in the sitting room where the old man with the hose in his nose did his puzzle, one in the dining room, and one on Tatie Martha's door. Tatie Martha must have run out of good pictures of Mr. Snuggles. The flier on her door did not include a photograph, but rather a rough sketch of the big cat, which Linda had to admit didn't look half bad. In the lobby it had been a little funny, outside Tatie Martha's door it wasn't funny at all. Linda took a deep breath and let it out. She took a second. No time like the present. Linda knocked on the door.

"It's open."

Linda opened the door. Tatie Martha was sitting in her chair, scribbling on a piece of paper on top of a hardback book on her lap. The television was turned off. Linda closed the door and the old woman looked up.

"Linda, how nice to see you."

"Hello Tatie."

"How's Roger dear?"

"He's good Tatie."

Linda sat down on the loveseat. The old woman went back to working on her poster. It was another flier with a hand drawn picture of a large Maine coon. Linda's hands wouldn't quit shaking, so she latched them onto her knees. It couldn't wait. Tatie Martha had to know.

"Tatie, the nurse wanted me to talk to you about the posters."

Tatie Martha's face went cross.

"Does that witch still want me to take them down? Mr. Snuggles is missing. I'm quite worried."

"Tatie…"

"That woman is colder than Philip Foss's wife."

"Tatie. Mr. Snuggles is dead."

"What? When?"

"Two weeks ago."

Linda would have probably been better off waiting. The implosion was every bit as impressive as the two times before, only now it had the added impressiveness of longevity to its magnificence. The clock read 4:15 PM when Linda broke the news. Over the next hour and fifteen minutes the storm failed to subside even a little. Linda couldn't fathom where Tatie Martha got the energy. She was a perpetual motion machine of anguish and despair. Linda sat through it as best she could. The shepherd in the painting stared down at her from his perch on the wall. His hand clenching his hat to his head to keep it from blowing off in the gail, the other guiding his frightened flock. Linda held onto the edge of the loveseat with one hand, and with the other held out kleenexes.

Tatie Martha's blubbering rose and fell, bringing and dashing hopes of it subsiding with deft swell swoops. The pile of dirty kleenexes grew into a mountain. At 5:30 relief finally came. Nurse Boggs and another nurse entered and carried the still weeping old woman out to dinner. Linda sat for about fifteen minutes, basking in the silence, and then left. The fliers were all gone. Linda caught sight of Tatie Martha in the dining hall, sitting at the end of one table, silently sobbing into her soup.

Mr. Martin sat next to her, chattering away and happily slurping up the contents of his own bowl.

There was no message that night, but Linda knew Roger wasn't going to be home at a reasonable hour. She made herself dinner and ate it alone in front of the TV. The three glasses of wine felt like a necessity.

The flowers were in desperate need of water. Several of them were noticeably hanging over the side of the vase, their bright yellow faces staring at the ground. Many of the white petals were curling back. The woman behind the front desk didn't give them any notice. Linda went into the dining room and came back with a glass of water. She stared at the woman as she poured the water into the vase. The woman behind the front desk looked up for a moment, slipped a lock of hair behind her ear, and went back to staring at her phone. Linda took the glass back to the dining room. Her throat hurt, so she drank some water and then stood with her hands clenching white knuckled to the edge of the sink. Stupid bitch. Why the hell was a woman like that allowed to work in a place like this?

Nurse Boggs came into the dining room. The scuffle of her bright red crocs on the ugly carpet the only thing giving her away.

"Afternoon Mrs. Dubois."

Linda's entire body tensed up. She slowly willed all of her muscles to release, and then turned towards the hulking form of the head nurse.

"Afternoon Nurse Boggs."

"Mrs. Dubois, I just thought I'd better tell you that we are still experiencing our little problem with your aunt."

"The cat still."

"Yes, Mrs. Dubois. Mr. Snuggles."

Linda stared down at the head nurse's crocs, the woman's white socks shining brightly from the holes in the foam resin. Linda took a deep breath and let it out.

"Thank you for letting me know."

Nurse Boggs turned and walked out of the dining room. Linda's jaw tightened and she shook her fists with frustration. Stupid bitch. Stupid good for nothing bitch. She couldn't do it anymore. She couldn't keep telling Tatie Martha about the damn dead cat. She just couldn't. Not today. Not this week. If the old woman didn't want to remember, then so be it. Linda could just play along. Linda took a few more deep breaths to calm herself down, and then headed down the hall.

Mr. Martin's door was closed. It was the first time Linda could ever remember the door being closed. As she moved past a shadow flickered on the carpet, almost as if someone was laying on the floor, trying to stare through the crack underneath the door. Crazy ass old man. Linda stood in front of Tatie Martha's door, clenched and unclenched her hands, put a smile on her face, and knocked.

"It's open."

It was the same as it was every week. Tatie Martha sitting in her chair, flicking off the TV as soon as Linda entered. The same complaints about the stupid idiot box. The same niceties in the exact same tone. A frozen world of deja vu.

"How is Roger doing?"

"He's still amongst the living."

"Are you coming down with something? You sound a little hoarse."

"No, I'm fine. Just strained my voice."

Tatie Martha made the tea. Her slow unsteady movements raising the hairs on the back of Linda's neck with every shuffling step. The two sat and chatted, Linda letting the older woman direct the conversation.

"It will be my ninetieth birthday soon. They tell me I'm going to have a big party."

"I know Tatie. I'm looking forward to it."

"They'll have cake and ice cream. Everyone will be there, even Mr. Snuggles. We'll have to put him in a party hat. He'll look so handsome."

"Yes Tatie. We'll have to make sure to get some pictures."

"That old scamp is somewhere carousing. I haven't seen him all day. The nurses tell me he's off entertaining some of the other residents. Isn't that sweet of him?"

"Yes Tatie."

Linda kept her smile plastered on her face. She took the tea cups and washed and dried them while Tatie Martha waxed about her favorite subject.

"That Mr. Snuggles, such a strange cat. Did I ever tell you Linda how I never had a cat before, but when he showed up begging for scraps, I just couldn't turn him away."

"Yes Tatie."

"Such a strange cat. He used to always hop in the shower with me. Can you believe it? Have you ever heard of a cat who likes water Linda? Of course I shut the bathroom door so he can't do it now. The last thing a woman at my age needs is a fall in the tub, but sometimes I run the shower just for him. Can you believe it?"

"Yes Tatie."

"Do you remember when he got that piece of tape on his side? I swear, he was walking around just like Mr. Philip Foss at the company Christmas party."

"Yes Tatie."

On and on it went. Linda found it difficult to look at Tatie Martha. She looked up at the painting on the wall. The shepherd seemed to be staring down at her with disapproval. She could almost see him shaking his head. Linda kept her eyes on her knees, or the arm of Tatie Martha's chair.

"Dear, are you alright?"

"Yes, I'm just tired."

"Are you sure you're not coming down with something? You sound so hoarse."

"Yes Tatie. I'm sure."

The clock ticked over towards 5:30. Tatie Martha looked up at it and smiled.

"Look at the time. It's almost time for dinner. This has been such a lovely visit."

"Yes Tatie, I better leave you to your dinner."

"It was so good to see you."

"I'll see you next week."

"Of course, hopefully you'll be able to see Mr. Snuggles then."

Linda rose. The shepherd glowered down at her. She moved to the door, paused, took a deep breath, and turned around.

"Tatie, there's something I need to tell you."

"What is it dear?"

"It's about Mr. Snuggles."

"What about Mr. Snuggles?"

The jagged words caught in Linda's already roughened throat. She swallowed them back down, and tried again.

"Well, you see....."

"Yes dear?"

"Mr. Snuggles is dead. He died a couple of weeks ago."

It was like a bomb going off. Tatie Martha's eyes grew wide, the tears began to fall, and then the inevitable collapse. The nurses opened the door right as it began, a youngish nurse followed by Nurse Boggs. The youngish nurse froze in horror at the spectacle before her. Nurse Boggs tried to push the youngish nurse forward, but was thrown back by an anguished sob. The pair retreated into the hall and Linda hastily followed. Nurse Boggs had the youngish nurse by the arm and was hissing orders into her ear.

"Get the sedatives."

Nurse Boggs gave the youngish nurse a healthy shove down the hallway and then turned towards Linda, her features ablaze with irritation. Linda, her face crimson and tears pouring down her face, rushed past in full flight. As she moved by the sitting room the old man with the hose in his nose raised his head and watched her go by. The woman behind the front desk didn't even look up. Out the door. To the car. Linda drove as if possessed. The car came to a halt ten blocks away and Linda laid her head onto the steering wheel and cried until a friendly policeman knocked on the window to make sure she was okay.

When Linda got home Roger was sitting on the couch watching television. He watched her come in with hangdog eyes. Linda went into the kitchen without a word and ate leftovers by herself.

The bright yellow centers had faded and the white petals were streaked with brown. Linda marched through the lobby without looking left or right. She had made her decision in the car. She wasn't going to tell Tatie Martha about Mr. Snuggles. What was the point? If she was constantly going to forget, why did Linda have to keep putting her through the pain week after week? It wasn't fair to either of them. She strode past the sitting room where the head nurse was helping the old man with the hose in his nose with his puzzle. It was a new one now. It looked like a Monet painting. Nurse Boggs straightened her back as Linda strode past.

"Mrs. Dubois?"

Linda didn't stop.

"Not now."

The head nurse hung back, a look of surprise on her face. The old man with the hose in his nose watched Linda stride past the open French doors, and then went back to his puzzle. Mr. Martin's door was open, but there was no sign of the old man.

Linda stopped and listened, wary of an unexpected surprise. One heartbeat. Two. Silence. Linda walked past and knocked on Tatie Martha's door.

"It's open."

Tatie Martha in her chair. Comments about the idiot box. Off-hand reference about Philip Foss, this one involving how no one on TV was ever dressed up and how Philip Foss was always immaculately dressed in a fine suit and vest with a perfectly knotted bow tie.

"How's Roger?"

"Fine."

"Still working hard?"

"Probably."

"Oh, that nephew of mine. All work and no play makes Jack a dull boy."

An offer for tea which Linda of course accepted. The old woman performing her usual shuffle, each step choreographed perfectly to the week before. Linda watched from the loveseat. The shepherd in the painting seemed to be glaring down at her. Linda glared back. When Tatie Martha returned with the tea Linda smiled at her. The old woman smiled back, showing the slowly wearing away teeth of the elderly.

"I'm going to have my ninetieth birthday soon."

"Yes Tatie."

"It will be so exciting. I'm going to try to get Mr. Snuggles in a birthday hat."

"Yes Tatie."

"Do you think he'll wear one?"

"Probably."

"He's such a funny cat."

The conversation drifted gently down the stream of thoughts. Linda could feel the shepherd in the painting staring lightning bolts down on her. Linda ignored him. She smiled. She laughed demurely. She did everything she was supposed to do.

"Linda dear, do you remember when Roger got me that laser pointer?"

"Yes Tatie."

"Oh what fun we had using it to play with Mr. Snuggles. The little scamp just couldn't figure it out. Darting from one end of the room to the other. I don't think I've laughed that hard in years."

It had been years since Roger had brought the laser pointer. The clock made its way around with a beat that seemed to slow the farther along it went. 5:00. 5:15. 5:25. Tatie Martha noted the position of the hands and gave a smile.

"Oh look at the time. This has been such a wonderful visit. I hardly want it to end."

"It will be dinner soon Tatie."

"Oh yes, of course. Even an old bag of bones like me needs to eat."

The two women rose. Tatie Martha in a slow and shaky ascent. Linda easier, but with a weight on her shoulders. She could almost hear the shepherd in the painting screaming at her.

"Give me a hug dear before you leave."

Linda embraced the old woman. She smelled of dust and Bengay. They released and Tatie Martha walked Linda to the door.

"Yes, such a nice visit. I look forward to next week."

Linda opened the door. Mr. Martin was outside. He was part way through a pirouette to march back up the hall when he saw the two women. He came to attention and gave a smart salute. When his hand fell his mouth opened.

"Good to see you out and about ma'am. I was very sorry to hear about the death of your cat a couple weeks ago."

Collapse. Screams. Tears. The nurses came rushing down the hall. Linda didn't even try to stay and comfort the old woman. She couldn't do it anymore. She just couldn't. That son of a bitch. Fucking Mr. Martin. That big mouth son of a bitch. She had been so close. It had been such a nice visit. Linda moved down the hall at a rapid pace. She kept her eyes pointed at her feet. She refused to look anyone in the eyes. Past the nurses and past the sitting room. The old man with the hose in his nose watched her go, shaking his head with disapproval. Through the lobby and out the door. To her car. Driving home. Straight home. Escaping. Running away. That stupid senile son of a bitch.

Roger wasn't home when she got there. Linda didn't bother with dinner. She sat in the kitchen and drank glass after glass until the wine bottle was empty. At midnight she heard his car in the drive. The sound of his key in the front door. She tipped the last of her glass down her gullet, and thus focused, headed forward to intercept his entrance.

The petals were falling. Half were already gone. Stiffened and curled they lay in a sickly white halo around the vase. Linda was late coming in. She had waited in her car around the corner until she saw Nurse Boggs come out the side door for her smoke. The big woman held the cigarette with a surprising daintiness for her size. A bear with a baby bird in its paw. The woman behind the front desk ignored her as she always did, though Linda could have sworn that she felt the woman's eyes following her once her back was turned. They all watched her. The man with the hose in his nose. The nurses going about their business. Even Mr. Martin, sitting sedately on his couch, watching a fly buzz around his room. Linda ignored them all. She just couldn't take it anymore. She just couldn't handle it. If nobody liked how she was handling the situation, then they could deal with it. The hell with them. Linda knocked on Tatie Martha's door.

"It's open."

It was a perfect copy of the week before. The scene unchanged. Everything in its place. Tatie Martha knew her lines by heart. Idiot box. Some random comment about Philip Foss.

Who the hell was Philip Foss? The polite offer for tea. An offer to help declined. The same moments in the same order.

"How's Roger?"

"He's okay I guess."

The shepherd glared from his perch up on the wall. Linda ignored him, same as all the others. Tatie Martha brought back the tea and they sat and talked. For a moment, Linda held out the hope that the news had finally stuck, that Tatie Martha's memory, wearing away with every cycle, like an overplayed cassette tape, had finally managed to retain this single kernel of knowledge. The hope was in vain. The old woman started in about her birthday. Her ninetieth birthday. It was a natural progression from there. Linda knew every part by heart. Mr. Snuggles would look good in a birthday hat. They would have to get some pictures. Where was Mr. Snuggles now? Probably just out carousing. You know how he is. Such a lively cat. He'll probably be pawing at the door any moment now, wanting to get let back in. Linda's hands began to shake so badly that she had to put her cup and saucer down on the end table and clutch her knees. She was tired. She was just so fucking tired.

"Such a funny cat. You know dear, he was always hopping in the shower with me. Mr. Snuggles just loves the water. I of course had to put a stop to it though. The nurses were worried that he'd trip me up and I'd fall. Plus, you know, my modesty."

The old woman gave an exaggerated wink.

"Yes Tatie."

The image of Mr. Snuggles laying in the sink drifted up before Linda's eyes. The cat's giant gray body filling the space completely, meowing for her to turn the water on when she went to use the bathroom. How many times had she lifted the bulk from the sink? How many times had she acquiesced? Mr. Snuggles would roll his eyes, put his head back, and purr with ecstasy as the cold flow touched down, his entire body buzzing with contentment. If you lifted him out he would yowl loudly in complaint, sometimes even batting a hand with his paw, claws closed, just to show that he could. It had just been easier to give in. Easier to go along with the demands of the feline who commanded Tatie Martha's heart. What was the right thing to do? What was the right thing to say? Tatie Martha wouldn't shut up about the damn cat. Mr. Snuggles was the center of her tiny world. Linda settled her hands and changed the subject.

"Mr. Martin seemed subdued today. Is he on leave?"

"Mr. Martin? Oh yes. I think they sedated him. They had quite a brawl today. The nurses pushed past his barricade and he hit a couple with his broom. They felt the need to disarm him, so I guess the war is over."

Tatie Martha leaned close conspiratorially.

"You know dear, just between you and me, I don't think he was ever even in the military. Some people's minds are just cracked."

The discussion floated from topic to topic. With every lull Linda filled the void. The weather. The news. The foibles of various relatives both alive and dead. Anything to keep Tatie Martha from her favorite subject. The time ticked by and the clock said 5:30. They made their goodbyes, Tatie Martha insisting on rising up to give her a bony hug. Linda cradled the back of the old woman's head the way one would cradle a child's. They broke away. Linda waited by the door for a second, listening to make sure nobody was there, and then left. She walked proudly down the hall. Any eyes that dared raise up to look at her, she stared down until they looked away. Mr. Martin, the nurses, the man with the hose in his nose, and even a cross looking Nurse Boggs. Only the woman behind the desk avoided Linda's challenging gaze, never once lifting her eyes from her phone as Linda strode past and out the door.

Roger was home when she got there. The two did not speak. He ate his dinner out in front of the TV and Linda ate hers in the kitchen. She didn't drink any wine that night. She didn't need it. Water was just fine. Cold and clear. She could see Mr. Snuggles in the sink when she filled the glass. Linda left her dirty dishes in the sink. If it bothered Roger, then he could wash them himself. She went upstairs and went to bed. She listened to the sounds of Roger making himself comfortable on the couch. It would be difficult, his back wasn't as good as it used to be. Linda didn't care. She drifted off to sleep with a deep sense of satisfaction.

The phone rang. The jangling bells echoed across the house. The first ring woke her up. The second snapped her towards reality. She lunged for the receiver, throwing herself across the covers. The bedroom phone was on Roger's side of the bed.

"Hello?"

"Hello, Mrs. Dubois?"

"Who is this?"

"I'm calling about your aunt Mrs. Dubois."

Linda's heart rate spiked. Nurse Boggs.

"Is she all right? Has something happened?"

"Her health is fine Mrs. Dubois."

The head nurse's voice was a throaty growl. Linda glanced at the digital clock on the nightstand. 3:35 AM.

"What is it then?"

"It's about the cat Mrs. Dubois. She won't quit asking about it. She's convinced that he's missing and she's worked herself up into a frenzy about it."

"Then tell her the damn cat is dead."

"We are not here to do your dirty work for you Mrs. Dubois. It's in our contract."

"God damn it."

"Mrs. Dubois, if she doesn't calm down we're going to have to sedate her. She's disturbing all the other residents."

Linda took a deep breath in and let it out. She curled her knees to her chest and massaged her temples with her free hand.

"Let me talk to her."

"I'll transfer you to her room."

The phone clicked and then clicked again. A beeping tone indicated that it was ringing. Someone picked up the phone and said something that Linda couldn't hear. Tatie Martha's cranky voice sounded on the other end.

"Who is it? Hello?"

"Tatie Martha?"

"Oh Linda, thank goodness you called. These damn nurses. Mr. Snuggles is missing and these damn nurses won't do a thing about it."

"Tatie."

"I keep trying to tell them that he never stays out this late, but they just won't do anything about it."

"Tatie."

"How am I supposed to sleep without him curled up next to me? How am I supposed to sleep knowing he's out there scared?

"Tatie."

"What is it dear?"

"Mr. Snuggles is dead. He died six weeks ago."

Linda hung up the phone and unplugged it from the wall. If it rang downstairs it would be Roger's problem. Linda laid back down, her body curled up in the fetal position. The couch squeaked downstairs. She could hear the steady nasally rasp of Roger's gentle snoring, each blast blowing away the last of the self-satisfaction that she had felt earlier. Linda waited for sleep to come. When it failed to, she settled on a good cry instead.


There were no more winking yellow faces. The stems were turning brown. Only a few petals still hung on to life, white just on the tips. Linda arrived at 4:00, but she sat in her car until 4:30 when she finally gathered enough energy to rise and walk through the doors of the center. The woman behind the front desk didn't watch her as she walked by. Nurse Boggs did not appear. Even the old man with the hose in his nose was missing, his latest puzzle, a group of ducks on a pond, left unfinished. Mr. Martin's door was still closed. All was quiet. Just the hum of air through the vents and Linda's footsteps on the carpet. She felt small standing before Tatie Martha's door. The viewpoint of an unwilling child, forced to go forward by the prodding hand of an unseen adult. Linda was tired. It felt like she hadn't slept in days. Her eyes were puffy. She nervously twisted the ring on her finger. Circle after circle. Never ending. Sisyphus and his stone. A part of her hoped, but deep inside she knew she hoped in vain. She raised up her hand and knocked.

"It's open."

Tatie Martha sat in her chair watching television. She smiled as Linda entered, for a moment forgetting to keep her lips tight to hide her worn out teeth. The old woman flipped off the TV.

"Linda dear, how good to see you. You wouldn't believe some of the things on this idiot box today."

Linda forced a smile back.

"How's Roger dear."

"Busy Tatie. Always busy."

"Silly boy. Even Philip Foss knew how to relax."

Linda released her hand from the wheel and let the ruts in the road take her where they would. Tatie Martha rose unsteadily and made the tea. Linda watched her while she worked. Tatie Martha had once had the most beautiful hands that Linda had ever seen. White and unmarked. Long supple fingers. They had fluttered about her, twin butterflies, when she spoke, highlighting and emphasizing every nuance and turn of phrase. Tatie Martha's hands were old now. Swollen knuckles and creased joints. Dry skin, almost translucent. They didn't flutter anymore when Tatie Martha spoke. She held them tight, unwilling to let them take wing. Unwilling to show the added wobble and tremble. It was only in the making of tea that they were unleashed. The flight was no longer smooth, nor quick flitting about as before, but they were still beautiful. One could still see the old life buried beneath the ruined exterior, dancing to the melody of her voice.

Linda could see those hands as they were. She could see those hands giving her an envelope stuffed with five hundred dollars. Tatie Martha had given Roger and Linda two hundred for their wedding, but had given the five hundred just to Martha, in secret. The hands had held out the envelope and the eyes had given a sly wink as the painted red lips whispered in her ear. *Things are always better when they aren't an obligation. A woman has to watch out for herself in this world, even with a good one.* It was a lot of money back then. Tatie Martha had always taken care of herself. Even when her husband was still alive.

Linda could see the hands opening the front door and wrapping her and Roger in a warm embrace before crimson lips kissed both of Linda's cheeks and laughter filled her ear. Tatie Martha's Christmas parties were still talked about within certain circles. A congregation of family, friends, acquaintances, business associates, and a few who had wandered in on their own, attracted by the joy permeating from the house. Tatie Martha would walk amongst her guests as though a goddess, a drink in one hand, dressed in fashions more out of style every year, but never seeming quite out of place. Tatie Martha sitting on the davenport that had been her mother's under the painting of the shepherd that had been her father's, laughing gaily through wine stained teeth, playing Indian poker with her cousin, her garbageman, a local accountant of some note, and a stranger named Ron. The hands had danced as they gestured for Linda to join the fun.

Linda could see through tear filled eyes the hands slicing the air with sharp authoritative cuts as Tatie Martha called Roger's mother a shit filled cunt after the latter dared to publicly call Linda a bitch in front of Roger's entire family. Roger's mother had never been warm to Linda. She had never believed that the woman who had married her son was ever good enough for him. Learning that the couple had absolutely no plans to ever have children had been the last straw in a long battle of a thousand cuts. Of course Roger had no interest in children, but his mother only saw it as further proof of the vile influence that his bride had over him. Roger's family had shrank back in awe of the monster that had been unleashed. Shocked into terrified silence by the assault of vocabulary that would have been called scandalous if it had not been so magnificent in its breadth and scope. Linda could still feel one of the hands resting protectively on her shoulder as Tatie Martha spit and snarled with the other. The outburst split the family, and things were not smoothed over until Tatie Martha agreed to give up her mother's davenport. They had been beautiful hands.

Tatie Martha smiled and brought back over the tea. Linda rose and helped her as she always did. The old woman resisted, but gladly gave up one of the saucers. They sat and talked as they always did, Linda letting Tatie Martha control the conversation. It went as Linda knew it would, down the well carved stream bed. Mention of the upcoming ninetieth birthday party. Tatie Martha wanted red balloons. Her favorite color was red. Tales of the exploits of Mr. Snuggles. Questions of where the big cat might be. Linda felt tears in our eyes. The shepherd in the painting stared down at her. She knew her role in this macabre play. She knew her lines.

"Tatie, I have to tell you something."

"What is it dear?"

The explosion was just as bad as it always was. Linda braced herself, leaned into the wind, and stayed. She stayed through the howls, the blubbering chokes, and the snot and tears. She held the old woman and cried with her. Salty tears flowing down their faces and intermixing in puddles of anguish. She brought kleenexes and water for them both. She stayed when the nurses came to take Tatie Martha to dinner, and though Nurse Boggs insisted that the old woman needed to eat, needed to stick to her routine, Linda refused to let them take her. Linda stayed until they were both wrung out and there were no more tears left in either.

It was 7:35. Tatie Martha was tired. Linda helped the old woman change into her nightgown and to get into bed. Tatie Martha fell asleep almost immediately. Linda used the bathroom and blew her nose. She stared at herself in the bathroom mirror, puffy eyed with gray hair around her temples. Linda took a deep breath and walked out of the bathroom. Tatie Martha slept peacefully. The portrait of her late husband sat on the nightstand. Linda had never met the man. He had been long dead when she married Roger, and was rarely spoken of. Roger had described him as quiet and prone to nervous spells. The man in the black and white portrait was lightly boned, but sharply dressed with perfectly parted hair and a thin mustache gracing his upper lip which was curled partway in a bemused smile. He did not look nervous. The eyes were kind and the portrait was set so they could lovingly watch the old woman sleep. Linda bit her lip and twisted the ring on her finger in circles. She could feel tears welling up in her eyes again. Linda turned out the lights and left.

Nobody was about in the nursing home. The halls were all quiet. The woman at the front desk was still in her place, but noticed Linda no more than the dying flowers as she headed out the door. Linda got into her car. 7:50 PM. She had promised that she would give him until 9:00. Linda drove to a hotel bar, and though she had never done it before in her life, had a drink in a bar alone.

*　　*　　*

The flowers were dead. Completely and irrevocably dead. No color of life remained. No bright yellow, no white, and no green. Just brown. Nothing left but a fragile husk of what once had been. Linda strode in and passed the woman at the front desk as quickly as she could. Linda had been crying in the car. It had started the moment she had turned off the ignition. She knew she looked a mess. Nurse Boggs was helping the man with the hose in his nose with his puzzle. The head nurse looked up as Linda strode by the sitting room's doorway. The head nurse made no move to intercept her. She just watched Linda move by. Mr. Martin's door was open. The old man sat sideways on his couch, staring at the birds flitting through the branches of the elm. His shoulders were slumped and only the slow movement of his eyes gave any clue of the man still within. Linda stopped and watched him for a second. Mr. Martin didn't notice. What attention he had was reserved for the birds. Linda moved past and knocked on Tatie Martha's door.

"It's open."

It was as it always was, a moment frozen in time, no longer a part of the world of the living.

"Linda, how good to see you. Please sit down. Just let me flip off this idiot box."

Linda did as she was told. Her knees felt weak.

"How is Roger dear?"

Linda felt her shoulders involuntarily rise. The diamond ring on her finger twinkled in the sunlight from the window.

"Okay I guess."

"That's good. Tea dear?"

"Sure."

Tatie Martha rose to make the tea. The shepherd on the wall stared down at her, still battling the storm to save his flock from freezing. The old woman hummed some forgotten tune as she worked. Linda grasped for things to say, but found nothing in her cluttered mind. Searching. Seeking. Her eyes trailed across

Tatie Martha's tiny world until they fell upon the elm tree outside the window.

"Mr. Martin seems unusually quiet."

Tatie Martha stopped humming.

"What's that dear?"

"I said Mr. Martin seems unusually quiet."

Tatie Martha glanced at Linda for a moment, then went back to making the tea.

"Oh, they've got him doped to the gills with sedatives, poor man, he was making too much of a nuisance of himself."

"It seems strange not seeing him marching around."

"Yes."

The branches of the elm tree swayed lightly in the breeze, knocking a few leaves off to go twirling to the ground. The tree was a mismatch of green, red, and gold. The sunlight from the window felt warm on her hand. The kettle whistled and Tatie Martha poured the tea. The old woman was shuffling her way over when Linda began to cry. At first it was only a couple of tears, but a few drops quickly turned into a torrent, and then the full force of the storm unleashed with wracking sobs.

"Linda dear, what's the matter?"

Linda couldn't answer. Her entire being vibrated with the release. Guilt and shame swirling with all the rest. Tatie Martha put the two cups of tea on the end table, sat down on the loveseat next to Linda, and put a skinny frail arm over the younger woman's shoulder.

"There, there dear. There, there."

"Oh Tatie……"

Linda's words fell back with gulps of air moistened by snot and sinus drip. Tatie Martha held on, making comforting sounds in a quiet voice.

"It's okay. It's okay."

"Oh Tatie, he's leaving me."

"Who's leaving you dear?"

"Roger…. Roger's been having an affair with a woman half my age. He's moved out. We're getting a divorce."

"That stupid son of a bitch."

The sharp declaration rang through the room, shocking all else into silence. Linda sucked back the snot in her nose and wiped her still flowing eyes.

"What?"

"Roger dear. Stupid son of a bitch."

"But Tatie….."

"Look at you my dear. Look at who you are. Half your age, bah, any man who leaves you is an idiot. A damn fool."

"But Tatie, he's your nephew."

"So what? I can't think my nephew is a fool? Listen to me dear. This has nothing to do with you. It has everything to do with him."

Linda began to tear up again, but Tatie Martha grabbed her face and kept it from falling down.

"None of that now dear."

"But why Tatie? Why?"

"Because he's getting older. Because he's scared. Because he thinks he'll find the fountain of youth between that hussy's legs. He's weak Linda. We all have our weaknesses. Me, you, Mr. Philip Foss, everyone. Hell, my husband, god bless his soul, loved to drink, he never raised his hand or his voice a day in his life, but the man didn't care about anything he couldn't pour inside him, including me. Mr. Martin wishes he had lived his life as someone else, a war hero instead of some boring old plumber. We all have our weaknesses."

"What's my weakness?"

"You're a lovely woman Linda, just such a lovely woman."

Linda curled herself into Tatie Martha's embrace. The old woman's shoulder smelled of Bengay and cat hair. One old arm rubbed Linda's back, while the other cradled the back of her head. Tatie Martha affectionately whispered in her ear.

"He's just a stupid son of a bitch dear. It's all going to be all right. You're a lovely woman. Such a lovely woman to visit an old woman like me every week in heaven's waiting room. He's just a stupid son of a bitch."

Tatie Martha stroked Linda's hair until she cried herself out. Linda leaned back from the embrace and turned away to wipe her eyes.

"Would a nip of brandy help dear? I have a bit hidden away where the nurses can't find it."

Linda smiled a bit despite herself.

"No thank you. I'm sorry about all this."

"Sorry for what dear, for not being Superwoman?"

Linda smiled again and blew her nose in a kleenex from her pocket. She had brought extra. Tatie Martha gave an encouraging smile and put a gnarled hand on Linda's knee.

"I'm just sorry that Mr. Snuggle isn't here. Giving him a good stroke always helps me feel better."

Linda blew her nose again. The tissue ripped between her nervous fingers.

"Oh Tatie, there's something I have to tell you."

"What is it dear?"

"It's Mr. Snuggles Tatie. He died."

The old woman looked past Linda and out the window at the tree swaying in the breeze. Her eyes teared up and Linda braced herself. A few tears rolled down the old woman's cheeks, but nothing else came.

"Tatie, are you okay?"

Tatie Martha's eyes refocused. She brushed a tear from her cheek. Her hand gave Linda's a gentle shake.

"I'll be all right dear. Let's just worry about you right now."

The tea had gone cold. While Linda cleaned herself up in the bathroom, Tatie Martha made more. The two women drank and talked about nothing. At times both seemed to drift away, but they always found their way back to each other. When 5:30

rolled around Tatie Martha went to dinner and Linda went home. The house was quiet. Linda cried a little when she climbed into bed, but Tatie Martha's voice floated in her head. Stupid son of a bitch. Such a lovely woman.

The flowers were gone. The vase, the fallen petals, everything. No evidence remained that they had ever existed. Linda walked through the front door, resigned to her fate. It had been a hectic week. The divorce was proceeding as well as could be expected. Roger wasn't putting up a fight. Maybe he felt guilty, or maybe he just wanted to move on with his life. He was living with his younger woman. What would be the right word? Mistress? That didn't feel right. If Roger was no longer married, then it was no longer an affair. Girlfriend? Bitch felt like the best choice, though to be fair, Linda had never met the woman. It didn't really matter. Nothing could turn back the clock. Nothing could make the world the way it once was.

Linda had been dreading coming to visit all week. She knew what was going to happen. It had been the next morning when Nurse Boggs had called.

"Mrs. Dubois?"

"Yes?"

"This is Nurse Boggs, Mrs. Dubois, I'm calling concerning your aunt."

"Is she okay?"

"She had a breakdown last night, Mrs. Dubois, during dinner."

"Mr. Snuggles?"

"Yes, Mrs. Dubois, Mr. Snuggles."

"She seemed alright when I left."

"I don't know what to tell you Mrs. Dubois, but she became quite upset at dinner. The other residents were quite disturbed. We had to sedate her."

"You had to sedate her?"

"Mrs. Dubois, this is starting to become quite the problem. It's possible that maybe this center isn't the right place for your aunt."

Linda hadn't known how to answer. It wasn't really her problem. It was Roger and his sisters who handled Tatie Martha's finances, not her. She was a nobody now, not even family. Just the last of the faithful, keeping vigil as the old woman floated towards the edge of her sanity. Linda didn't know what to do. The ghost of Mr. Snuggles refused to leave. Like the divorce, there was nothing that could be done. Some things were just the way they were going to be.

One of the overhead lights in the lobby was close to burning out. The fluorescent bulb buzzed and flickered. The woman behind the front desk sat as she always did, head down, eyes locked on her phone. Bitch. How was a person like that allowed to work in such a place? The queen of a crumbling world, without a care in the world. Linda walked over to the desk and put her closed fists down on its dusty top.

"Excuse me?"

The woman glanced up, then went back to her phone.

"Excuse me?"

The words were louder and more drawn out. The woman behind the front desk took a deep breath, let it out, and put her phone down.

"What?"

"There's no flowers."

The woman behind the front desk shifted to look behind Linda at the empty spot where the flowers had been. She studied the spot for a few seconds and then re-focused back on Linda.

"Yep."

"Don't you see that as a problem?"

The woman behind the front desk chewed on a thumbnail and spit a chunk onto the floor.

"No one's mentioned it but you."

The woman behind the front desk, with her eyebrows raised, waited. Linda, with her best attempt at piercing eyes, stared back, but broke first. With a huff, she shifted her gaze to the ground and took a step back.

"I'm sorry. I've had a tough week, but that's no reason to take it out on you."

The woman behind the front desk bit off another chunk of fingernail and spit it on the floor. Linda felt uncomfortable. She started to turn to head down the hall.

"Your aunt's the one with the cat right? Mr. Noodles?"

"Mr. Snuggles. He's dead though."

"No shit."

The two women stared at each other for a moment. The woman behind the front desk reached down to open a drawer.

"I've got something for you."

The woman opened the drawer and pulled out a wooden box, stained the color of cherry wood, with a brass clasp and hinges. She held it out and gestured for Linda to take it. Linda stepped forward and took the box in her hands. She could feel a weight inside. Engraved black letters adorned the lid. Mr. Snuggles.

"What is this?"

"What does it look like?"

Linda popped open the latch. Inside sat a ziploc bag full of ash.

"We had a similar problem with my Dad when my Mom died. Had a hell of a time getting it to stick in his head."

"Where did you get the ash?"

The woman behind the front desk gave a hint of a smile.

"Fireplace. Don't worry, I picked all the burnt wood chunks out."

Linda ran her finger across the plastic of the bag and closed the lid. The woman behind the front desk was already back on her phone.

"Will this work?"

The woman didn't even bother to glance up.

"You got any other ideas?"

Linda turned and walked down the hall. The man with the hose in his nose was in the sitting room, still working on the duck puzzle. The old man stared at the pieces before him, found the one he wanted, and put it in its place. He felt Linda watching him, and turned his head and watched her back as she strode past.

Mr. Martin's door was open, but there was no Mr. Martin to be seen. A younger nurse and Nurse Boggs were packing things in boxes. The couch was already gone.

"Where's Mr. Martin?"

Nurse Boggs looked up, but gave the second nurse the eye when she stopped working as well. The second nurse bent back to the task.

"He died three days ago. Nobody bothered to get his stuff, so we're packing it up so we can move a new resident in. Damn wait list must be half a mile long."

"He seemed to be in such good shape."

The head nurse shrugged.

"That's the way it goes."

Nurse Boggs went back to work. Linda moved on down the hall to Tatie Martha's door. She held the box so tightly that the edges bit creases into her hands. She took a breath in, let it out, and knocked.

"It's open."

The old woman reacted as she always did. She screamed. She howled. She doubled herself over as best she could, clutching the cherrywood colored box in her once beautiful hands. Linda did the best she could, bringing kleenexes, rubbing the old woman's back, and saying the expected empathetic words. The shepherd stared down from his painting, and Linda stared back for a while. The shepherd did not seem to mind. His attention was too focused on getting his flock in out of the storm.

The nurses came to take Tatie Martha to dinner, but Linda wouldn't let them. Nurse Boggs let it go without a fight.

Linda stayed with Tatie Martha, waiting for the tempest to subside. Linda thought of Roger on their wedding day. How safe she had felt in his arms. How handsome he had looked in his tuxedo, smiling down at her as though she was the only woman in the world. She thought of Tatie Martha at the reception, lithe and vibrant, a glass of wine in her hand, insisting that all the young men dance with her, and laughing at their reddening faces as she whispered lewd comments into their ears. Tears spilled down Linda's cheeks. The two women wept together, both mourning the lives that they could never get back, a world that could never be inhabited again.

Linda stayed with Tatie Martha until she cried herself out. Exhausted, the old woman let Linda help her get ready for bed, and fell asleep before her head even hit the pillow. Linda covered the aged form with a blanket, placed the cherrywood box full of fireplace ashes on the end table next to Tatie Martha's chair, and let herself out. Everything was dark and empty. When Linda got home, she poured herself a glass of wine, drank half, but dumped the remainder down the drain. Linda put on a jacket, went out to the backyard, sat in a lawn chair, and stared up at the stars for half the night.

Linda walked into the lobby with a vase of tulips and a package wrapped in tissue paper. With a smile on her lips she deposited the vase on the empty shelf and turned towards the woman sitting behind the front desk.

"Good morning."

The woman gave a neutral grunt in response.

"I brought some fresh flowers."

The woman glanced up for a moment, and then returned her attention to her phone.

"What do you want, a medal or something?"

Linda nervously twisted the spot on her finger where her ring had once been.

"I didn't get a chance to say thank you last week."

The woman behind the front desk looked up again, gave a half smile and a nod, and went back to ignoring the world around her. Linda smiled again, turned, and walked down the hall. The man with the hose in his nose was in his usual place. He was still working on the ducks which were proving more difficult than normal. Nurse Boggs' bulk leaned on the table next to him. The head nurse reached out, picked up a piece, and put it in its correct place. The old man smiled and gave the head nurse's hand a congratulatory squeeze. Nurse Boggs smiled back. What had once been Mr. Martins' door was closed. A new name was already written on it. Janice Boyer. Linda moved past without a second glance. She did not hesitate to knock on Tatie Martha's door.

"It's open."

The room looked as it always looked. Tatie Martha sat in her chair watching the TV, which she switched off the moment Linda entered.

"Linda, how good to see you."

"It's good to see you too Tatie. I've brought something for you."

"For me? My birthday isn't for a few more weeks."

"Just an early present."

"Oh, you shouldn't have."

Linda pressed the package into Tatie Martha's arthritic hands and sat down on the loveseat. The old woman smiling, gave the gift a gentle shake near her ear, licked her lips, and gently pulled open the tissue paper to reveal the framed picture hidden underneath. Tatie Martha let out a small squeal of delight.

"Oh, Mr. Snuggles. It's wonderful. Simply wonderful."

"I thought you'd like it Tatie."

The old woman held the picture close to get a good look at it, and then put it back on her lap. The two women's eyes tracked across the room to the cherrywood colored box on the end table.

"He was such a funny cat Linda. Just such a funny cat."

"Yes Tatie, he was a good cat."

A few tears fell down Tatie Martha's cheeks, but were quickly wiped away.

"Would you like some tea dear?"

"Yes, thank you, but I can get it."

Linda made to rise, but Tatie Martha waved her back.

"Nonsense. I might be old, but I can still make a cup of tea."

The old woman shuffled over to the counter. Linda picked up the framed picture from where Tatie Martha had left it on her chair. It was a fine picture. The last photograph taken of Mr. Snuggles. The big gray Maine coon with a red party hat on his head. Linda stood and started looking around for a good place to put it. An idea popped in her head and she moved into the bedroom.

"Tatie, would you like me to put it on the nightstand?"

"What's that dear?"

"Would you like me to put the photo of Mr. Snuggles next to the portrait of your husband?"

"That's not my husband dear."

Linda returned to the doorway. The kettle was starting to whistle. Tatie Martha pulled it off. The old woman was smiling to herself.

"You know, most people would say it isn't proper, but when you get as old as me, worrying about such things just doesn't seem as important."

Tatie Martha poured the tea into the cups and shuffled her way back towards her chair.

"Who is it Tatie?"

The old woman put the tea cups down on the end table, settled herself into her chair, picked up her cup, took a drink, and gave out a sound of satisfaction. Linda walked over, sat down on the loveseat, and took a sip from her own cup of tea. The old woman studied the painting on the wall, her eyes tracing across the shepherd in the storm. For a moment she seemed cast adrift, floating between one time and another with no anchor to hold her back. Tatie Martha smiled and looked back at Linda.

"How is Roger dear?"

Linda paused, unsure.

"Roger is fine Tatie, he sends his love. He's quite busy."

Tatie Martha took another drink of tea.

"That boy, always up to something. If I was him, I wouldn't work so hard if I had a wife like you at home."

# Previously Published Works

**Decent People**
First published in *The Molotov Cocktail*, Fall 2015

**Picnic**
First published in *Tin House Online Flash Fridays*, Winter 2018

**The Closet**
First published in *Clackamas Literary Review*, Volume 24,
Spring 2020

**The Nine Lives Of Mr. Snuggles**
First published in *Eunoia Review*, Mid-June 2020

# Dates Written

| | |
|---|---|
| Decent People | August 2015 |
| Scio Girls | December 2015 |
| Strays | April 2016 |
| My Favorite Christmas Memory | December 2015 |
| Vikki Mulroney Is Missing | October 2015 |
| Late Bloomer | January 2016 |
| I'm Bored, Let's Make Everyone Really… | August 2015 |
| Snowball | July 2015 |
| The Closet | November 2015 |
| Tipping The Scales | February 2016 |
| The Best Movie Review | February 2016 |
| Passing Of The Old Guard | January 2015 |
| Tuesday | May 2015 |
| Skills | May 2015 |
| Five Reasons IKEA Will Ruin Your… | October 2015 |
| Late Night Text | March 2016 |
| Enema | January 2016 |
| Picnic | September 2016 |
| Not Bad | December 2015 |
| Time To Move | May 2016 |
| Sister Sarah Silver | March 2016 |
| Shit | September 2015 |
| Blind Man's Bluff | March 2016 |
| The End | September 2015 |
| Blotches | October 2016 |
| The Nine Lives Of Mr. Snuggles | August 2016 |

# Also Written By The Author

## *The Uncanny Valley*

We all know a Paul. A person who seems to see stuff that isn't there. The type the polite call quirky and the blunt call nuts. Conspiracies? He's got a few. He's got his finger on how the world really works. He knows what kind of shit is coming down the pipe. Flee across the West Texas desert to Mexico? Makes sense to him. Feel like you're being watched? You bet your ass someone is watching. Best turn off your cellphone. Troubles? Of course, that's just part of life. Doubts? No time for doubts. Shit is getting real. Get in, buckle up, crack open a beer. The only real question is, how far down the rabbit hole are you willing to follow?

## *An Unsated Thirst*

They say that an author's first stories are their most raw. Here is a collection of S.W. Campbell's first short stories and writings. Combining both published and unpublished works, An Unsated Thirst explores victory and defeat, triumph and shame, and an unflinching view of our naked selves. How one views such stories is dependent upon the mood of the reader. Whether we are at our highs or at our lows. However, it is hard for any of us to claim that such stories are ones that we cannot identify with. Contained within these pages are parts of our lives which we try to forget, though they are an important part of what makes us whole. Such stories should be embraced, accepted within ourselves so we can better accept them with others.

## *Papaya*

When a devastating hurricane hits the Caribbean island of Domenique, its inhabitants are forced into a singular struggle to survive and rebuild. Isolated in their midst is Ted, a Peace Corps volunteer who fled the ashes of his former life only to find himself labeled an outsider. Infatuated by the enigmatic wife of his only friend, Ted thrusts himself into a world beyond his comprehension. As obsession turns to desperation, tensions grow and Ted is forced to decide exactly how far he will go to rebuild amidst the muddy ruins.

## *Stumptown*

There are places where people say things are better. Where the downtowns do not empty after dark and people dare to dream beyond their means. Quirky utopias where the sins of the past are washed away by gentle rains and we all go forward arm in arm together into the brightening sunshine. Distant locations flocked to by young pilgrims, unencumbered by the deeply driven roots of age, where everything will be different. Combining both published and unpublished work, Stumptown is a collection of stories about ordinary people, navigating their personal anxieties and drama in a time when uncertainties were still tucked away and not allowed to distort the sense of hope in the air. It is a soliloquy to naivete, and the belief that a better world is a place rather than an idea.

## The People's Republic of 47th & Long

Perhaps the world would be a better place if we thought of ourselves less as good people, and more as lousy people who manage to do good things. My friend Leopold was always a dreamer. The pandemic and our reactions to it left us broken and divided. Most of us just wanted to feel safe again, but others dreamt of something better. Leopold was one of these. Though I think he likely joined the People's Republic of 47th and Long purely out of geographic convenience, I know once part of it, he fully shared in its egalitarian vision. All I have are his letters. Sometimes I wish I had burned them, but I didn't, so now here they are. Maybe you can find a use for them. Perhaps they can help remind you who we truly are. The good, the bad, and most importantly, the indifferent.

## The Man In The Sodden Cap

The Man In The Sodden Cap is a collection of twenty-six short stories written during a period of emotional unleashing, a madcap rush to get words to the page. As with any such period of unrelenting literary expulsion, the results are a mix of emotional, personal, poignant, and inane. For many authors, these are the types of stories that often get kept in a drawer somewhere, not shared with anyone. But what use are stories if they are not shared? Individually these are good stories, but taken all together they tell the tale of heartbreak and remorse, and the need to move on. In this context, The Man In A Sodden Cap is in many ways a sequel to S.W. Campbell's first short story collection, An Unsated Thirst, a continuation and fitting conclusion to that earlier work.

### *Senseless Sensibilities*

It is the human condition to try and find meaning in this life, to make sense of the chaos and randomness around us. At times this need overwhelms common sense, building layers of cognitive dissonance until we are left running our lives based upon senseless sensibilities. Contained within these pages are thirty-six short stories which explore the ability of people to adapt and survive the world around them. Stories which provide insight into slices of existence, and which highlight the strange ridiculousness of everyday life. Whether it's an old man adapting his hobbies to his aging body, a commodities trader who finds himself to be the commodity, or a lonely man fulfilling two needs in a single cross-country trip, each shows the resilience and mental flexibility shared by us all.

More information can be found at:

www.shawnwcampbell.com

# About The Author

S.W. Campbell was born in Eastern Oregon in 1983 after a harrowing drive through a fog. He currently resides in Portland, Oregon where he works as an economist and lives with a lovely house plant named Morton. He has had many short stories published in various literary reviews, some of which appear in this work, and has also self-published several books. His work can be found at www.shawnwcampbell.com.

www.ingramcontent.com/pod-product-compliance
Lightning Source LLC
Chambersburg PA
CBHW060625260626
47161CB00008B/2805

* 9 7 9 8 9 8 7 0 2 8 7 6 6 *